For Tammy —

Secret Harbor
Fair Winds!

ANDREA K.
AWARD-WINNING AUTHOR
STEIN

Andrea K. Stein

SECRET HARBOR

Published by Muirgen™ Publishing, LLC

Print ISBN – 978-0-9909566-3-1
Ebook ISBN – 978-0-9909566-2-4

Cover Design and Interior format by The Killion Group
http://thekilliongroupinc.com

DEDICATION

For Patsy and John, shining examples of the
best "Happily Ever After" I know

ACKNOWLEDGEMENTS

Superheroes: Editor Judy Brunswick & Final Beta Reader Harriet Hamilton

Rocky Mountain Fiction Writers critique partners – Aaron, Dianne, Harriet, Jan, and Jennifer

Working Hero Cover Model:
A big thank-you to Drew, a Colorado ski patroller who specializes in snow safety (avalanche mitigation). His special interest is the Kees Brenninkmeyer Foundation that financially assists alpine guides, patrollers, or instructors who require surgery to continue their careers. Two percent of all sales of this book will go toward this cause.

CHAPTER ONE

1759
Guadeloupe Archipelago

Sand oozed between Marie Galante's toes along her path to the cove. She'd trod this trail every day since she was a child. But this time, her dead husband haunted her thoughts — the man who died with an apology on his lips, the man who needed forgiveness for more than infidelities, the man who lost her home in a game of cards.

Gnarled limbs of dwarf trees snatched at her thin muslin shift. Cross gusts of wind flattened the gauzy nightdress against her calves and billowed the garment above her knees.

In spite of the clear pink and turquoise dawn, despair swallowed her like fog rolling over the island from the sea. She'd endured hurt and loneliness during more than twenty years of marriage, but the final betrayal still shocked her to the core.

She reached a secluded crescent of sand sheltered by the headland and peeled the gown over her head. When she tucked the shift under a bush and dove into the waves, she left the hurt behind. Pure pleasure swept over her with the saltwater.

Resurfacing beyond the drop-off, Marie circled her arms to tread water. The morning sunlight revealed gold striped fish and coral several fathoms into the depths below. The prism of the cool, blue-green water distorted her pale arms and legs. She hung suspended for a moment to gauge the pull of the tide before swimming out beyond the point.

With each powerful stroke, she sliced through the water, pushing herself as far away as possible from the painful truth of her marriage.

After her husband fell dead at her feet of a seizure the week before, she'd assumed his last words, "I'm sorry, Marie," referred to his unfaithfulness.

Their *avocat* had delivered the bad news. She must harvest the cane and pay off *Monsieur* Galante's gambling debt. If not, her plantation would belong to her neighbor, Antoine Courbet, the wealthy, ruthless planter.

Marie alone could save their home for her children. If she failed, she would have to beg her sister to take them in when her sons returned from school in France.

⊱✕⊰

Jean Blanchard raised a spyglass to his eye and squinted at a creature swimming out from the headland. A dolphin? No, couldn't be. Not the right shape. Wait. The animal rolled a bit, and the unmistakable curve of a breast broke above the surface. His breath hitched for a moment. Why would a woman swim that far from shore?

He reluctantly shifted his line of sight to a crowd of workers gathered in front of the main house on the island. Jean lowered the glass for a moment to rub absently at the stubble of beard on his jaw. *Mon dieu*, but the hair on his face grew quickly. Was it only the night before he had taken a razor to the stubborn growth?

When he raised the glass again, the number of workers had increased to surround the faded rose-colored, two-story house. All of the white shutters swung open to the morning breeze, with the sun glinting off the red-tiled roof. The well-kept planter's home sat atop a bluff overhanging the ocean below. He couldn't resist swinging the spyglass back toward the headland where the mysterious woman had appeared. No sign of her now.

Jean gently turned the wheel with one hand to maneuver his ship into a shallow cove on the leeward side of the island. He wove his way through a narrow cut in the reef by eyeing the hand signals of one of his men. The smuggler lay flat on the bow and pointed toward the depths revealed in the morning sun. Jean gave the order to strike the mainsail and let the ship's momentum head them into the wind.

"This will do. Throw out the lead line and wait for five fathoms before you drop anchor," he said. A quick and easy run. How hard could it be to overwhelm a few plantation workers and take the island's old healer? He ignored the lump of guilt lodged in the middle of his chest. His men were dying. He had no choice.

"I'm not sure we should make this woman come with us." His first mate, Francois, frowned and took the glass from him. "One of her people could go to the garrison at Guadeloupe and alert the English."

"By the time the soldiers get here, we'll have her back."

"If only I were as confident as you." Francois moved away from the wheel and muttered under his breath.

"Wait," Jean called.

The man pivoted mid-stride and gave him an insolent look.

"Once the anchor is secure, have all the men join us here. I don't want anything to go wrong. This should be a simple attack – we can be in and out of here with the healer in a few hours if everyone heeds my words," Jean said.

"Whatever you say, Captain." His first mate nodded and stepped toward the men at the capstan. When they released the anchor, the heavy links clattered and unwound into the depths.

Jean turned back to the wheel and threaded a bright coin through the fingers of his free hand. He would trust Francois with his life, and often did, but lately something in his second-in-command's manner and tone of voice caused little ripples of unease to skitter along his spine.

That familiar niggling had kept him alive over the years. Francois was not the first crewman to challenge him, nor would he be the last. He laughed out loud and tucked the coin inside his shirt.

A few minutes later, Jean surveyed his crew gathered in front of him. Misfits one and all, but they were loyal. They had sailed half the night with him from their smuggling outpost on the rocky north coast of Dominica.

"Men – we're here this morning just to find the healer and bring her back to our island." He paused to make sure he had their full attention. "Francois will issue pistols, but no shots will be fired." He gave the circle of crewmen a steady, dark stare until heads bobbed in assent and grumbling ceased.

The damned illness had decimated his crew, and he was determined to discover the cause of the mysterious ailment disabling them one by one, no matter the cost.

"Any of you could be next to fall victim to this scourge." He swept his view around the circle while his mate handed out the store of weapons from locked chests. "We need this old woman to come along without force. No one is to be injured, and no looting."

A few more mumbled complaints followed his last orders, but when Jean gave the command to lower the shore boat, his men followed him over the side.

⁂

Yancey rubbed the sleep from his eyes and stretched. A lazy fly inched across the palm leaves on the ceiling of the sleep nook in his grandmother's cabin.

He jumped from his pallet and stood on tiptoe to splash water onto his face from a cracked basin on a table in the corner. The boy tossed on pants worn thin at the knees and an oversized shirt inherited from one of the older boys on the plantation.

His *Grand-mere* called through the open door of the tiny stone cottage, and he ran toward the sound of her voice. She grasped his arm and pulled him along to the communal wood-fire oven.

"You must put something in your stomach, *mon petit*." She speared a roasted plantain from the coals and wrapped it in leaves. "You run too fast and eat too little." She laid a work-weathered hand on his head and smoothed his hair before tucking the food into his hand.

"*Oui, Grand-mere*." He tried to squirm away from her, but she gathered him into her arms for a close embrace.

"Let us join the others." A warm smile belied the stern tone of her voice. She waggled a finger at him and led the way up the sand-covered path to Galante House.

⁂

The scene at the plantation house was grim. Jean's men had forced all the workers into a tight circle, but no one would talk to him. He had been unable to make them reveal the whereabouts of the healer, even after the offer of a reward.

He understood their reluctance. Jean surveyed his men and observed what the frightened islanders saw. They were heavily armed and battle-scarred. Bathing was an infrequent occurrence, and there were few clean-shaven faces among them.

After a long silence, a fierce old grandmother stepped forward. "We know nothing of any healer," she said, the expression on her face defying him to contradict her. "You are mistaken. Leave us and go invade another island."

Jean did not miss the brief look of censure she passed to the others. Maybe she was the one he sought. He hoped not. A sour harpy was the last thing he needed on board his ship.

Jean slipped a coin through his fingers faster and faster until it disappeared. He pantomimed a search for the lost disc and then showed his empty hands. While his audience was at rapt attention, he darted toward the small boy who clung to the disagreeable old biddy, scooped him up, and produced the missing coin from behind the child's ear. Wide-eyed, the boy seemed torn between delight and wariness while Jean walked with him into a copse of scrubby trees.

"Yancey," the old woman cried in a strangled voice and rushed toward Jean. Francois stepped forward blocking her way.

Jean hoisted the boy onto his shoulders and slipped through the trees. "Now, my fine young man, you know where the healer is, don't you?"

The boy tightened his hold around Jean's neck.

"All right, then. If you take me to her, the coin is yours to keep."

"Will you show me how to make it disappear?"

"Of course," Jean assured him, struggling not to smile.

Yancey slithered to the ground and took off through the underbrush toward the beach on the headland. Jean followed close behind and prayed the healer he sought would not prove as stubborn as the rest of the islanders.

"There she is." The boy stopped and pointed toward the surf rolling into the small cove. "Now, can I have the coin?"

When Jean flipped the shiny piece to the boy, Yancey rounded and ran back up the hill, leaving him to gape at a sea creature emerging from the waves. Perhaps the legends of mermaids and sirens were true.

When she caught sight of him, she jerked her arms across her breasts before moving her hands lower. This was no sea goddess, but a flesh-and-blood woman. The glare she sent made him grateful she was not armed, a fact he could easily determine from her complete lack of clothing.

Her creamy skin gleamed with a heated flush from the sun, sand, and anger. She stalked toward him, her eyes full of hatred. He doubted Calypso first greeted Ulysses this way, but he could understand how curves such as these in one's arms would obliterate any desire to return home.

A weakness attacked his arms and hands and then spread to his legs and knees. His fingers ached to touch her, but instead, he unbuttoned his shirt. Shrugging the light cotton covering from his shoulders, he extended the offering toward her.

Without warning, the mermaid straightened and abandoned her modest stance, dripping dark ribbons of hair over her shoulders and down her full, firm breasts. She came close enough to poke him hard in his chest and pluck the shirt from him only to toss it to the sand.

He stumbled and took an awkward step back. Ignoring his conscience, he stared hard, letting his gaze sweep downward from the sweet flare of her hips to the shapely legs below.

"You... you're not the old healer?" Jean's tongue and power of speech failed him.

"I am Marie Galante. This is my land. Why are you here?"

"I must find the old woman who can cure my men." He threw out his arms in supplication.

"There is no healer here," she said with a low growl. "Leave before I have you thrown off the island."

"But I can pay, and pay very well," Jean said. "I am Jean Blanchard from Dominica." His words sounded like babbling even to him. Somehow, he had to mollify this fierce she-devil.

Could she be the one he sought? Why was she not a frail old crone?

"Jean Blanchard? The smuggler?" Her laugh mocked him. "You are wanted by both the English and the French. You must be a fool to risk coming here."

He struggled to gather his thoughts. Thoughts made more difficult by the full, soft bow of her lips and warm, brown eyes. The delicate brows above resembled the wings of the exotic birds swooping through the trees at the edge of the beach. The stubborn set of her mouth and jutting chin, however, didn't bode well for his mission.

Head held high, as if pride were all she had left with which to bargain, she brushed past him and strode toward the crumpled shift she'd secured under a rock. When she grabbed for the nightdress, he was quicker.

CHAPTER TWO

The increased height of the sun in the sky made Jean uneasy, but he planted his boots wide on the hot sand of the pebbled beach. He had to win this battle of wills with the healer.

Wadding the flimsy material of Marie's shift into a ball behind his back, he felt his earlier weakness and shock retreat. His body tensed, and he grasped her arm hard.

"Are you mad? There are scores of my people waiting for me over that rise. They will beat you within an inch of your miserable life," Marie said, and swatted at him with her free hand.

Her fingers were warm and moist where they clutched at his.

"You make this too hard. All I want is your help." He held the shift farther from her grasp.

"I would die before going with a monster like you." Although revulsion was still evident on her face, her voice quavered and lost intensity.

"I am not an ogre, and you will come with me." When he pulled her close and produced the shift, she tried to push him away, batting at his hands. He slipped the thin covering over her head and could swear her stiff stance softened a bit.

Just when he thought the healer was warming to him, she bit his lower lip. When he jerked back, she leaned into him, pushing against his chest with curled fists. While he waved his arms in the air to keep from toppling onto the sand, she lifted onto tiptoes and delivered a stinging slap to his face.

Reeling from the attack, Jean dabbed at the blood trickling from his lip and rubbed his cheek where she'd struck him. The pain was not nearly so bad as the thought that she hated him. She didn't even know him. He cleared his mind, slowed his breathing, and deliberately chose a path of conciliation. This was no time for wounded pride. He needed the healer.

"I'm sorry," he said, and sucked on his throbbing lip. "I had no idea you would be so beautiful, so stubborn." After a moment's pause, he added, "Unfortunately, I have no choice but to take you with me. My men's lives depend on your healing skills."

Marie smoothed her hands down the thin, sea-soaked nightdress before straightening to full height. "No, I am not going. You cannot force me."

Jean clamped his hand over Marie's wrist, but she jerked out of his hold and ran. He pounded up the hill close behind, his boots slowing him down. He sank into the soft sand, struggling to keep up.

She turned once and flashed him an impish smile, a smile he was sure was meant to sap his better senses. What little he had left.

When the chase wore on, he tired of the game. This annoying hellcat was nothing like the biddable healer he'd expected to find. Jean clenched his jaw and ran faster.

And why did she have to be naked when they first met? Even now, the thin muslin of her shift left little to the imagination. He could not keep his eyes off the lush figure running ahead up the path. Her small, powerful body was well muscled with ample curves. The rising sun silhouetted the indentation of a small waist. Her hair had begun to dry and flowed behind her like a dark cloud.

If he didn't regain the upper hand and stop the tightening in his groin, he might do something he would regret.

In one long stride he caught up and pulled her to the top of the rise so she could see his armed men surrounding her workers. Francois pushed and shoved them into small groups and tied their hands behind their backs while the rest of the crew stood guard. Cries of dread pierced the air.

"No." Marie's quiet plea tore at him. She turned, a grim look on her face. "Please don't hurt them."

"Then, Mademoiselle, you will dress and tell them you are coming with me."

"Are you nothing more than a stick man with a mango for a head?" She scorched him with a glare. "I cannot leave now. If I'm not here to manage the harvest, I could lose my home. And it is *Madame* Galante. Do not forget yourself."

"Of course — *Madame* — but, like the mango, I am sweet inside. If only you would taste the fruit. Unfortunately, I am too short of time to accommodate you." He gave his best theatrical bow and saluted before switching to a more menacing tone.

"Enough. My men await my word to begin punishing your workers." He curled his hand around her arm and squeezed tight. "You will pack a few things and prepare to come with me, or I will order the killing of your people to begin."

Marie wrenched away from Jean and turned to walk toward Galante House, her confidence battered. She stomped through a stand of dwarf palms and pushed back limbs slapping at her face. A flock of magenta-feathered birds burst from the trees above and rose in a raucous body.

She arrived out of breath at the rear portico with the bastard close behind. When she hesitated, he jerked her through the back entrance into the house. Once inside, he tucked her so close, she could feel the hard ridge of him pressing at her backside.

When she whirled to complain, she feared arguing with this dark, forbidding man was a mistake. His eyes, green as the sea beyond the reef, dragged her down into their depths.

"Leave me alone, please. I will pack as quickly as possible. I promise." She sucked in a deep gulp of air just to maintain her balance.

"Yes, you will do as you are told," Jean assured her, clasping her closer to him. "But just to make sure, I'm coming with you."

She tried to wriggle free, but he only tightened his hold and pushed her up a staircase to the second level. When she turned to lash out at him again and his eyes darkened, Marie stifled the retort bubbling inside.

"Take me to your room," he said, his tone more insistent.

Once inside the house, the walls closed in around them, and she couldn't escape his scent – a touch of sandalwood – overwhelmingly male and possessive.

"No," she said, defiance in her voice, and tried to make herself as small as possible to shrink from his touch.

"I tire of your nonsense, woman. I do not want to hurt anyone, but if I must…" His expression hardened. "I could leave you here and convince your people to persuade you."

"They would never help you."

"Maybe not, but I think you would change your mind if I tell my men to begin the slaughter."

She clamped her mouth shut, her heart pounding so hard in her chest, she was sure he could hear. Her stomach was rock hard, as if she'd eaten an under-ripe plantain.

"Which one should we start with?" He tilted his head and raised one brow. "Maybe the small boy, or better yet, the fierce old grandmother?"

Her jaw tightened. "Since you've given me no choice, I will do as you say, but you needn't come with me." She turned to race up the staircase only to be snatched back to his side.

He grabbed her chin and pulled her face close to his. "I promise I'll wait outside your door, but if you try anything, anything at all, I will carve one of your people like butter with my knife."

Horrified, she swung her head away and climbed the stairs with him close behind. Marie swiped at a tear sliding down her cheek. She would obey for now, but revenge would come later.

At the dark mahogany door to her bedroom she stopped and raised her face to her captor. "I suppose when you are done with me, you will kill me."

"If you do exactly as I say, I'll return you within the week." His firm promise surprised her, along with the light returning to his eyes.

Everything else about this strange man was dark and forbidding. His curly black hair, slashes of brows, deeply tanned skin, and warning glare all made her uneasy for reasons she didn't want examine too closely.

"Can you at least give me an idea of what kind of illness I will have to treat?"

"Of course." He placed his boot on a bench outside her room and leaned toward her. He paused for a few moments as if deciding how much to tell her. "My men are falling victim to a peculiar, debilitating disease, and I was told the wise woman healer of this island is the only one who can help."

He glanced at the floor and then braced his arms against the back of the bench and lowered his head as if embarrassed to meet her eyes. "Please hurry. Gather a few things so we can be gone."

She slipped through the door, slammed it shut, and leaned against the other side. Closing her eyes for a second, she regained her composure and formed a plan.

Marie crossed the room and opened a wooden chest in front of the window. She ticked off all the possible ailments that could be claiming Jean's men before stuffing packets of St. John's wort, sarsaparilla, dried soursop and guava, devil's claw, and mint into her small bag of medicines. After a moment of indecision, she also included a large stone jar filled with a dark, thick liquid.

From the wardrobe in the corner she pulled out a plain muslin work dress and apron. If he were telling the truth and meant to return her in a week, one dress would suffice. If he planned to dispatch her to the depths of the sea once he had no further use for her, then more than one dress would be a waste. Her morbid thoughts made her laugh in spite of the dire situation.

Throwing the frock over her head, Marie fastened the front bodice buttons, her fingers cramping in haste. She couldn't deal with a constricting corset. Finally, she wrapped a linen scarf around her neck and arranged the fabric for modesty. After grabbing her bag of medicines, she headed for a pair of her older son's discarded half boots near the door.

As an afterthought, she sidetracked to the bed, knelt down, and swept her arm beneath until she felt the cool metal of a small dirk hidden there since her husband's death. She slipped the knife down into the side of her left boot before fastening the buttons.

After a few minutes, Jean slid onto his haunches outside Marie's bedroom and settled in for a long wait. For reasons he couldn't explain, he was ashamed of threatening the healer. He would give her as much time as she needed, within reason.

A smattering of voices drifted across the still morning air from the front of Galante House where his men guarded Marie's workers. He tried to relax but the memory of her soft curves in his arms made his body tighten again.

This unwise yearning was almost painful. *Mon Dieu* — his life was complicated enough. The last thing he needed was to take the healer to his bed. How old could she be? Her clear skin and lithe body put her anywhere from twenty to thirty. Yet how did a woman so young come to own such a large sugarcane plantation?

Marie banged open the door, interrupting his thoughts. There she stood in a baggy, old dress, clutching a leather pouch. Her feet were clad in a misshapen pair of men's boots.

"I'm ready," she said, and quickly averted her eyes.

If he were a gambling man, he'd bet she was hiding something. Between his rough band of smugglers and the small boy in his care, he was an expert at ferreting out secrets.

He stood and towered over her, his arms tightly crossed. "You have everything you need?"

"Yes." Her voice shook a bit, but she steadied and continued. "I have no idea what will be required of me, so I brought a little of everything."

"I'm curious." He raked his eyes over her worn clothing. "For a woman who owns such a large plantation, you dress as if you were a poor urchin off the streets of St. Pierre."

"You come to my home, threaten my people, and expect me to dress prettily for you? I think not."

"Your ugly clothing is probably for the best. I'll have no need to protect your honor. My men won't give you a second look in that rice sack of a dress." His stern speech belied the clutch in his gut telling him his men would be the least of his worries. He couldn't help remembering what the baggy dress concealed.

"Not that my personal business is any concern of yours," she said, fury ringing in her voice, "but I am a widow, thirty-eight, with three grown children." She adjusted her neck scarf, covering all evidence of the breasts he'd already seen. "You are maligning a woman who has no use for your oily charms. The joke is on you."

"Enough." He grasped the back of her dress and rushed her down the staircase toward the front entrance of the house. When he forced her across the cool, polished wood floors, a strong gust of wind unfurled the thin white curtains at the front windows. They danced like specters, and a cold shiver coursed through Jean. He released her at the entry.

"Remember, only you can decide how this morning ends." He leaned close, studied her face for a moment, and tried not to dwell on her full lips, swollen from all her nervous chewing. "Their lives depend on what you do next."

When he saw her shoulders tense, he relaxed a little inside. Finally. The healer believed he would follow through on his threats.

"I will do my best to help your men, but whether they live or die," she said, "you must promise me you will have me back within a week." Marie clenched his hand. "I will lose my home if I cannot be here to ensure the harvest of the cane." Her voice trembled, the fear she would not admit shining in her eyes.

"I promise to do everything in my power to help you keep your home, but not before you save my men," Jean said, and led her out into the sunlight.

CHAPTER THREE

Marie stood next to Jean on the steps of Galante House. She faced her kitchen and field workers, the early morning sun behind them.

Although she hardly knew this man, the thread of commitment in his voice when he promised to have her back in a week gave her a glimmer of hope. She plunged into an explanation for her workers.

"My friends, *Monsieur* Blanchard requests my help to nurse his crew through a fever." She gestured toward him and then stopped talking and fiddled with the wide brim of her straw hat.

After a long pause, she added, "I have agreed to go with him."

Voices raised in anger, the loudest that of *Tante* Luz. Her housekeeper stepped forward, hands on hips. "Dis man is a *contrebandier*, a liar, a thief, Marie. I beg of you, do not go with him. He could harm you."

Marie touched her old friend on the shoulder and said, "All will be well," in a low whisper. To the rest of her workers she said, "While I am gone, *Tante* Luz will be in charge."

She stopped, unable to go on, and tamped down a shout of refusal. Even though she pressed her shaking hands to her thighs, she couldn't block the visions of what he and his men could do to her. The only thought that kept her strong was the horror of what his crew might do to the defenseless older slaves, women and children in her care if she didn't cooperate.

When she caught Luz's attention, the look on her housekeeper's face reflected all the fear rushing through Marie.

Jean began to speak. "Any of you who would like to throw your lot in with ours, come back with us to Dominica. My first in command, Francois, is an escaped slave who has done well with our small band." He extended his arm toward his first mate.

Her workers exchanged frowns.

Marie stepped forward, her hands fisted to her sides. "What *Monsieur*, the thief, does not realize is that everyone who wanted to leave is gone. They left when my husband died. They knew I wouldn't stop them. Any others who wish to leave now may do so, with my blessing." She glared back at Jean with a silent curse on her lips. None of her workers stepped forward to accept his offer.

"I'm sorry to leave with the cane harvest just beginning and so much work to do, I will return as soon as possible."

When Jean's men began releasing the workers, many drifted toward her old nurse, *Tante* Luz, for direction, and for comfort. Several women drew close to Marie and grasped her hand before she turned to walk away with Jean.

He motioned to the rest of his men to follow and led her through the scrub pines and bushes lining the path down to the sea.

She whirled on him when he brushed her arm and reached for her heavy bag. "Do not touch me again, or I swear I will kill you in your sleep." Her hands clenched, and she couldn't stop the words tumbling from her mouth. "How could you try to steal my workers after making me believe you want to help me keep my home?"

Jean remained silent but raised his arms in the air and backed away. He strode forward along the hard packed sandy trail to the head of the line of smugglers making their way down the bluff.

Midway down the steep hill, Marie shaded her eyes with her free hand and eyed their ship at anchor in the cove. Her heart stuttered. Maybe this would be her last view of her home. What would happen to her sons? If she couldn't get back in time to supervise the cane harvest, she might not be able to save the plantation for them.

And would she ever again see her daughter and grandson on Martinique? Envisioning the toddler's small, chubby face strengthened her. This lout could do what he wanted with her, but she was determined. She would return.

Marie tamped down her feelings of dread but couldn't banish the lump in her throat. The smugglers rowed ever closer to their sloop swinging at anchor in the morning breeze, ever closer to her imprisonment.

She hadn't dared look at Jean since he handed her aboard the shore boat, but behind her his body heat seared into her.

"Cure my men and you'll be back in a week, two at the most." He leaned forward and whispered into her ear. Marie started at the warmth of his breath and the brush of his whiskers.

"I warned you not to touch me," Marie said and lifted her hand to shove his face away.

"Why? Are you afraid you might come to desire me and never wish to return to your lonely little island?" he asked in a tone that taunted, and pulled her back into his lap.

When she drew the dagger from her boot and slashed at his face, his men erupted into laughter. He grabbed her wrist and pressed her to him in a painful embrace. The knife clattered to the bottom of the boat, useless.

"Is your healer more than you can handle?" Francois asked with a chuckle.

Jean gave his first mate a dark look and threw her weapon overboard and caught a line thrown from above. When they pulled close to the hull of the smugglers' long, sleek ship he secured the shore boat next to a rope ladder.

After boarding the sloop, Jean handed off Marie to one of the sailors waiting on deck. "Make sure she stays out of trouble," he ordered, "but should any harm come to her, sea creatures will pluck the flesh from your bones."

The young man blanched, his eyes wide, before he touched her arm to follow him below.

Marie shivered at the barely checked rage in his voice and decided against further complaints.

After being pulled down a companionway and shoved into a cabin below decks, Marie winced at the sound of a lock sliding into place.

Her wrist still ached from the wretched smuggler Blanchard forcing her to let go of her dagger. Cursing at the fool she'd been, Marie flexed her fingers and circled the cabin, seeking another weapon.

In the light spilling down from above decks, she crossed the room to examine a bank of bookshelves with restraining slats. Navigation books, charts, and plotting tools jammed side by side with authors ranging from Shakespeare to Cicero and Homer. Surely those volumes couldn't belong to the ship's current unprincipled devil of a captain. They must have been taken from the poor soul he murdered to steal his ship.

The bark of shouted commands and the creak of hoisted sails drew her closer to the cabin portal. She sucked in deep breaths and listened to Jean's men haul up the anchor. With the movement of the ship, she knew the last view of her home was sliding past. Beyond the cove, she could feel a fresh wind lift the sails and they picked up speed. With all her canvas flying, the sloop cruised quickly out to sea.

Marie sighed and pulled away from the opening, too drained from the past few hours to shed any tears. She collapsed onto a chair bolted, along with six others, to the cabin floor.

When her eyes gradually adjusted to the soft light, she noticed a simple platform built into one corner of the compact quarters. Mosquito netting tied to each side revealed a tidy sleeping berth.

At the sight of what she assumed must be his bed, her jittery nerves forced her off the chair and toward a desk. It wouldn't hurt to sneak a look to take her mind off her fears.

She touched a row of sorted, sharpened quills and then picked up a miniature of a young boy with Jean's unruly dark hair. Sea-green eyes stared back at her from the painting. She sensed her captor's presence a split second before she replaced the tiny oil and whirled to face him.

"What are you doing?" he demanded, and pushed her away from his desk. He took a key from a chain around his neck and locked the miniature into one of the drawers.

"Is that your son?" Marie asked.

"Yes," Jean said without hesitation.

His sharp reply so stunned her into silence, she didn't complain when he dragged her toward one of the chairs.

They sat, and she matched his glare.

"Where is his mother?" she asked.

"That is of no concern to you." The volume of his voice increased with his warning.

"Will I see her when we get to your island?" Marie ignored his agitation.

"Perhaps, if it suits my purposes," he said with a dark look.

"Are you going to hide me from her?"

"What makes you think I would need to do such a thing?" A slow grin creased his tanned face. "You are my healer. Your only purpose is to treat my men." His smile widened. "You have too high an opinion of yourself. There are many younger women in the islands more to my liking, if I decide to take a mistress."

"How long before we arrive and I can begin my work?" Marie had to bite her lip to keep from challenging his arrogant baiting. She would find out what ailed his men and not one more day, not one more hour than was absolutely necessary would she spend with this pompous man.

"Three hours," he said, and left the cabin. The clatter of his boots became muffled as he scrambled up to the deck.

"That wretched thief," she said, and spit in her hand, mimicking one of *Tante* Luz's spells against evil. She kicked the chair next to her and bruised her foot before she remembered the furniture was bolted to the floor.

CHAPTER FOUR

Jean steadied the wheel and the ship surfed through huge waves crashing against the northeast side of his island. If he hadn't used this escape hole a hundred times before, mostly under cover of darkness, he might fear they would run aground. Without the perfect timing, the perfect tide, they would crash onto the rocks.

At the last minute, the sleek vessel slid into calm waters through a small, nearly invisible inlet.

Jean tapped Francois on his shoulder to get his attention. "Strike the sails and then have all hands take their places on deck with the poles."

"Aye." His first mate moved from his side with a rolling gait, treading carefully on the heaving deck.

The momentum of wind, waves and current continued to carry them forward. Branches and large fronds slapped at the sides of the hull as the ship glided slowly through a thick mass of underbrush and jungle. The crewmen pushed with the poles to keep the vessel in the center of the shallow channel.

With the worry eased of getting them safely through the inlet, Jean considered what to do with Marie. He hadn't planned beyond seeking a healer and bringing her back with him.

Now he would have to find a place where he could keep an eye on her. In spite of his teasing earlier, he was certain she would be a temptation for his men. At the thought of how the other smugglers would leer at HER, his gut tightened and then dropped like a lead weight to the depths below. Francois would have to warn them to leave her alone.

An ideal place for his prickly healer jumped to mind — his own house and bed — but he rejected the idea before the thought could lodge in his head. Although he was tempted, giving in would end in disaster. He could not risk letting her spend time with Elisabeth and Gerard.

He'd handle Marie the same way he'd handled the crowds during magic shows he'd performed on the streets of St. Pierre. People always see what they expect to see. She would be no different.

"We're almost there." Francois was back at Jean's side.

"As soon as we dock," Jean said, "I'll take her to the sickbay. The quicker she discovers what disease attacks the men, the quicker I can get that hellcat back to her island."

"But, where will she sleep?"

"Put a pallet in the infirmary for her." Jean prayed his face didn't show the feelings he wished he could deny.

"Don't you think she would be more comfortable in my bed?"

Francois's good-natured grin made Jean want to throw him overboard.

"If you touch her, I'll kill you." Jean leaned close to the other man's face and hoped for a neutral glare.

His first mate acknowledged the threat with a half-smile. He was not fooled by Jean's feeble efforts to hide his need for Marie. Francois whistled low before turning to see to the mooring of the ship.

Marie jarred awake to the boom of waves and the slam of the boat's hull. The disgust she felt sprawled on Jean's bunk was nothing compared to the staccato thump of her heart, which pounded in time to the smacking of the ship from one huge roller wave to the next.

Fear made her stomach heave like a drop from the top of the masts to the bilges below. They would crash onto the reef and sink. Death visited her soul and tightened cold fingers around her neck.

She crawled to an upright position and braced herself with a handhold rail. The day's events had sucked away her strength, and she was still groggy.

Dominica. She'd seen the shore many times from the comfort of the deck of a ship on her way to Martinique to visit her daughter. She could not imagine Jean and his crew could land on that rocky coast, let alone make their homes there. A ship would have to head in toward a nasty line of rock outcrops and shallow reefs to either side of their path before finding a safe anchorage.

The volcanic nature of the island created jungle-covered peaks that soared above the sea floor. Mists covered the tops and nestled in occasional valleys.

At the very moment she was sure they would smash on the rocks, the boat calmed and appeared to slide into a quiet inlet. Easing her grip on the polished wood handle, she slumped back onto the bunk and splayed her hands over her chest until the thunks of her heart slowed. How many times would this despicable man push her to the brink of apoplexy?

She lay there and tried to remain calm until Francois appeared in the cabin entry. Jean's next in command leaned against the opening, an impudent grin on his face.

"Gather your things, and I'll take you up on deck. We'll be headed to shore soon." He stopped and tilted his head, studying her. "You've nothing to fear. We would never harm an innocent woman," Francois said in a voice full of honey. She felt anything but safe.

Marie knew better. She couldn't trust anyone until she was home again. "I have no choice but to follow you and find out, do I?" she said, with courage in her voice she didn't feel.

"I pity Jean if he thinks it will be easy with you in camp," Francois said, and burst into laughter. "He will be deviled by both you and his wife."

Marie shivered at the edge in his voice in spite of the banter. He was a very attractive man, but she sensed he could be cruel.

She refused to accept his taunts and picked up her bag to follow him out of the cabin.

◦◦◦

Jean was already ashore when Marie pushed away Francois's arm and clambered into the shore boat on her own. Her foot slipped, and she smacked into the bottom. The way she snapped at Francois when he tried to help retrieve her scattered belongings gave Jean a perverse sort of pleasure. His first mate finally gave up with his hands behind his back, defeated.

While observing the drama between Marie and Francois, Jean failed to notice a young boy dart out of the bushes. The child tackled him around the knees and they went down in a heap.

"Gerard…" Jean picked up the giggling child and staggered to his feet. Twirling him above his head, he laughed and said, "You caught me again. Some day, you will make a fine smuggler, sneaking through the trees."

Time seemed to slow for Jean when he played with the boy. His heart opened and he could forget for a while the heavy burden weighing on his shoulders.

"Jean-pa, please stop. I'm dizzy."

"You're dizzy? How can that be?"

Instead of releasing him, Jean held the child by his feet until the boy's face flushed red. They tumbled onto the sand and rolled about and tickled each other until a woman appeared out of the woods with a light branch in her hand.

Jean scrambled to his feet and faced her.

"What kind of man encourages a boy to disobey his mother?" she demanded. Warning sparks flashed from her eyes. "And what kind of son sneaks off to play while his mother thinks he copies his lessons?"

"It was my idea, Mama." Gerard ducked his head. "It's not Jean-pa's fault."

"You were supposed to be in your room, not down here at the cove."

"I'm sorry, Elisabeth, but the boy needs to play too," Jean said.

Gerard followed his mother, head down, while Jean lingered behind. He swung around to steal another glance at Marie, but she was gone. He kicked at the sand and then disappeared into the thick jungle undergrowth.

Marie shoved the memory of the domestic scene between Jean and his family out of her mind and concentrated on her surroundings. Francois followed a serpentine route through the smugglers' compound, a ruse she assumed he chose to keep her confused. If necessary, she would steal one of the boats beached along the shore of the cove and escape back to her island.

Their compound consisted of a series of clearings, each with a cabin and vegetable garden. She tried to memorize the complicated patchwork of paths between the houses on the way to the sickbay.

"You are quiet, *ma petite*," Francois said. "What vengeful thoughts swirl through that pretty head now?"

She said nothing but continued to plod along the jungle path.

"I'm afraid our notorious captain doesn't care what happens to you, *cherie*," he said, and leaned close. "I, however, will take very good care of you."

"*Monsieur*, you would do well to remember why I am here." Marie jerked away from him. "And bloodthirsty or no, I believe your captain is most concerned with the welfare of his sick men."

Francois laughed and then led on for a while through the tangled brush. He stopped abruptly when he slammed into a solid mass. Jean stood in the middle of the path, barring his way.

Marie blinked her eyes. One moment, there was nothing ahead of them and the next, Jean materialized out of the thick undergrowth.

"*Madame* Galante no longer has need of your company. I will take over from here." Jean glared at his first mate until Francois dipped his head in salute and thrashed off into the jungle.

Jean wanted to throttle Marie. Why could she not just do as she was told and stop snapping hatred out of those dark eyes?

She could argue with him as much as she wished, but Francois was different. His temper could flare at the smallest imagined slight.

At least now her tempting body was covered in a baggy linen dress, but he could still imagine the woman beneath. Even wrapped in shapeless clothes, she seemed to have captured the attention of the rest of the crew. He'd overheard some of the men talking about her.

"Just show me the way to your sick men. Do not let me keep you from your charming little family," Marie said, at last breaking the silence between them.

"You are jealous?" He threw back his head and whooped in laughter.

"Fidelity to your family is a humorous matter to you?"

He didn't answer her question.

"After you finish with my men, you will come to dinner with us, he said."

"You intend to flaunt your captive in front of your poor wife and child?"

"Since we do not often have guests on the island, they will be delighted to spend an evening with such an interesting woman. Gerard will be filled with excitement. He wants to be a physician when he grows up." A teasing smile tugged at the corners of his mouth. "You are not a captive. As soon as you discover a cure for my men, you can return to your home. You have my word."

"Oh, yes, the word of a pirate."

"*Madame*, I am not a pirate."

"Then what *do* you call someone who kidnaps an innocent woman from her home?"

"A desperate man," Jean said, and made an abrupt turn up a side path. Stones loosened by her boots rolled down the steep hill in her scramble to keep up with him. When she paused, panting with exertion, he sneaked a glimpse back long enough to observe her drop one of the combs from her hair at the crossroad of the trails. He stifled a chuckle at her pathetic attempt to outwit him but admitted the stubborn little healer had a surprising streak of courage.

Antoine Courbet stood in front of Galante House and fumed in silence. He would not let the remnant of workers guess the extent of his anger.

How could simple-minded Marie have run off with that worthless smuggler, Jean Blanchard? She could not have picked a worse time or worse companion. He'd counted on her people's loyalty and her determination to complete the harvest. Now he would have to step in.

"*Tante* Luz — come here," he said.

"*Oui, Monsieur* Courbet?" Luz confronted him, her chin jutting in insolence.

Once he was master here, she would learn her place.

"Why has work not begun on the harvest?"

"*Madame* Galante said she would be back within the week. The men do not listen so much to an old woman like me. She has a better way with them." She swiped at a bead of sweat on her forehead and slid her gaze away from his eyes.

"Do you think I'm stupid? She has run off like a whore with that thief, Blanchard. You plot to cover for her."

"You do not own this place yet, you," Luz shot back. "Go away, and come back when *Madame* Galante is here."

He motioned to his guards, and they set fire to the cane with rags soaked in oil and mounted on long, broom-like sticks. Courbet stood close to the first section of field exploding with flames and smiled at the old woman.

She spat on the ground and made the sign of the evil eye, pointing at him.

"You gonna have to answer to dat thief Blanchard now," "He won't like you messing with what belongs to Marie."

Courbet stepped back. "Indeed. I hope he gets angry enough to come after me."

CHAPTER FIVE

Marie hesitated at the crude wooden door to a low, stone house the smugglers used as a sickbay. Only a trickle of a breeze stirred, and she squinted in the late afternoon sun winking low through the jungle brush surrounding the clearing.

The stench of sickness and misery overwhelmed her the minute she stepped through the entrance. She hastened toward the beds where seven men lay, all in severe stages of wasting.

A young man knelt beside a pallet and spooned broth to one of the patients. The ailing man's face was the shade of the belly of a dead fish, and beads of sweat dotted his forehead. A gaping red sore covered one of his cheeks.

"How long has this illness lasted?" Marie asked. Her insides clenched, and she rubbed the cold sweat from her hands. If this horrible disease was infectious, the entire crew of smugglers could be wiped out. Everyone in the compound could die, including her.

"Two weeks," Jean said, holding up two fingers.

"Have you lost anyone?" She softened her voice and turned away from the men lying on the beds. Some moaned in pain. Others stared at the ceiling, too weak to complain.

"Just three in the last week, but the malady spreads. I don't want to think of what another week might bring if we don't find the cause." Jean leaned over a cot and placed his hand on the forehead of one of his crewmen.

"Have you been to other islands recently? Could these men have been bitten by mosquitoes?"

"No – it's the dry season." Jean stretched his arms above his head, weariness in his voice.

"Is there someone who could describe the stages of the disease?"

"What do you want to know?"

"You?" Marie stared at him. "You've been with them from the beginning?"

"Why not? They're my men. They would do no less for me." He beckoned her to follow him outside. A large pot of broth steamed from a tripod over an open fire.

"This is all we've been able to do for them," he said with a shrug. "Although I will you tell you, my remedy has not worked so well. When the disease first hits, they cramp so severely that most of them can't keep the broth down."

"And then what happens?" Marie asked.

"They develop sores around their mouths, lose all the fluid in their bodies, and then they die." He looked away from her, his hands clenched.

"Could this disease spread from man to man?" Marie ran through the possibilities, thinking aloud. "Have any of them had severe headaches, a rash or delirium?"

"No," he said with conviction. "It's just a sudden, overwhelming attack on the stomach and bowels."

"Could your drinking water be fouled?"

"Of course not," Jean said, and pounded his fist against a tree. "Would not all of us be ill at once if the water were bad?"

Marie ignored his question and turned on her heel. "I must speak to each of them quickly. I have an idea, but we must hurry."

He followed her back into the sickbay where she walked to the first bed and sank to her knees. "Let me see the inside of your mouth," she said, and began a meticulous examination of the patient.

Behind her, Jean sucked in a sharp breath and laid his hand on her shoulder. "Don't—."

When Marie swung her head around at the warning, he moved his hand to her cheek.

"Please, Marie, be careful. Don't put yourself in danger. I meant every word when I promised to bring you home safely."

The butterflies inside her stomach warred with dry-mouth terror. This man could kill her if she didn't save his crew, this man could tear her from her home forever.

This man could make her care for him.

Jean leaned against the sickbay wall near the door. The murmur of Marie's voice rose above the low sounds of his men's pain while she questioned them. He could not imagine what she asked. His mind buzzed with questions.

Then he chastised himself. What had he expected of the healer? That she would walk in and know immediately what was wrong? Worry and lack of sleep had pushed him to idiocy. Idiocy that had made him touch her. Now his mind flitted like a starved hummingbird from fear for his men to longing for her.

Guilt overlaid with need pushed him back to the healer, like a dolphin fish to dangling bait. He walked over and touched her hand. "You must be tired and hungry. I was not thinking. Come with me."

She glared at him and rubbed the back of her neck. "Please, leave me. I'm not hungry. There is much I must gather before I decide what to do."

Jean stepped back, his chest tightening. "I will send someone for you in an hour to bring you to my home."

"You want your men to recover, and I want to return to my plantation as soon as possible." Marie surged to her feet and faced him. "I don't have patience for pleasantries," she said.

"But you do have to eat. Finish what needs to be done here," he said. "You must stop when I send for you."

When she opened her mouth to disagree, he extended the palm of his hand. "You will not deny me."

Marie wanted to argue, but Jean disappeared, slithering off into the night like a lizard. Why did he irritate her so?

Just then, her stomach growled with a vengeance, and she glanced around, hoping no one heard. She turned to the patient she'd begun to question about his eating habits before illness had consumed him.

"Tell me your name." She coaxed the young man gritting through his pain.

"Louis," he answered weakly.

Her gut went rock hard, and her heartbeat surged. He was about the same age as her elder son in France – Louis. This smuggler was so young, and corrupted already. Now he might die.

The moment of panic subsided, and she drew from a reserve of calm she didn't know she possessed.

"Try to remember, Louis. What did you eat just before the pains began?" Marie placed her hand on his clammy forehead and leaned down to hear his answer. He doubled over in another spasm of pain and could not finish his reply.

The smuggler working in the sickbay rushed over to hold the young man's head while he retched into a pan next to the bed. Marie used a wet rag to cool his face after the seizure passed and noticed some tiny red blisters around his mouth.

"*Madame*, if there is anything you can do, please help. I don't think these two can last much longer. I can't get them to keep down any liquid."

"Maybe you can assist me." The young man seemed to be able to remain calm in the midst of chaos, and that was what she needed. "You've been caring for them all this while. Surely you can tell me something about what happened just before this calamity struck."

She searched his face for a clue. "What was different? Where did they go they hadn't been before? What did they eat they hadn't eaten before?"

He slowly shook his head. "One day they were all well, and the next, this scourge began to take them." He stopped and seemed lost in thought for a minute. "We been laying low, we have, since we stole guns from the French and sold 'em to the English."

"Go on." She avoided the urge to smile quirking at the corners of her mouth.

"Tell me what you usually eat," she prompted him.

"Our cook is a proper one, she is. Makes good, simple food, and lots of it. Nothing special, and nothing different."

"But what? Meat? Greens? Fruit?" Marie desperately sought to drag details from him. "Have you eaten anything new, or something that didn't taste quite right?"

"I don't know — I just don't know." He hung his head.

"It's not your fault. You've done all you can to help them."

The young man sighed as if a heavy yoke had been lifted.

"Even though we do not yet know the cause of this sickness," Marie said, "I have some things that might make them feel a little better. You can help. Empty the broth out of the pot and prepare some boiling water."

She led him to where she'd dropped her bag in the corner and pulled some packets of herbs from the depths as well as a square of linen. "Put these into the cloth, tie the ends and then dip into the water until the color deepens. We'll try to get them to take a little."

He sniffed at the contents of the packets and frowned. "What is this?"

"Whitewood fig bark tea." She smiled and waved her hand for him to continue with her instructions.

Although she kept her voice low and calm for the sake of the patients, her anger at the looks of suffering on the smugglers' young faces bubbled its way from her fingers all the way to her shoulders and chest. A tight band of pain sharpened her resolve. The horrifying malady that had invaded the lives of these men could not be allowed to continue.

CHAPTER SIX

Marie had no idea how much time had passed before Jean stood in front of her again. He reappeared just as abruptly as he'd left earlier.

"I thought you were going to send someone else for me." She squatted at the side of a low cot, supporting a patient's head while he sipped at the pungent-smelling tea.

"Come with me, now," Jean insisted. "You need to rest. I don't want you to become a victim of this sickness."

"You have no choice. You forced me to come with you, and now I've thrown my lot in with yours." She tilted her face toward him and continued with venom in her voice. "God willing, I will survive, but if not, it will be on your head alone."

He pulled Marie to her feet and dragged her outside before she had a chance to protest.

"Why did you do that?" she asked, anger rising in her voice.

"Abner will take care of them. If your medicine is going to work, it will work just as well coming from his hands as yours," Jean said.

"And where did Abner come from? Why have you forced him to join your band of thieves?" Marie demanded.

"I can't imagine why you care, but he came to the British Navy by way of a press gang. He chose to join us one night when he found us relieving the British of some ammunition they didn't need."

"Oh," she said with a huff and hurried up the trail into the darkness, away from him.

"Where are you going?" he asked, a hint of laughter in his voice.

"Anywhere you are not."

Jean said nothing but simply gripped her arm and steered her in the opposite direction.

Marie groped through total darkness and had to rely on his firm hold to keep from tripping over the gnarled roots of the thick rows of trees along the path.

She fought the urge to give in to despair in the suffocating darkness and trotted on. She had no choice but to trust the strange, infuriating man she'd known less than a day. Whenever she stumbled, he hauled her up and pulled her close before proceeding again.

She vowed to step more carefully and avoid colliding with his solid chest. Marie resented the warm feelings he incited in her and tried to remain angry, without much luck.

She nearly shrieked as a solid mass brushed against her. Jean swore an oath and stopped abruptly.

"Francois, this had better be good," Jean said with a snarl. "Do not make me kill you tonight."

"We must talk, Captain," Francois murmured. "And soon."

"Very well. After I take Marie to the house, I will meet you back here."

"Your wish is my command, Captain," his first mate answered in a faint, mocking tone.

Marie held her breath for several long moments while a strained silence continued between the two men. Jean finally broke away and yanked her along at a fast clip.

"What does he want?" she asked.

"When I find out, Marie, I'll tell you, and then we will both know," Jean said.

Ahead of them, lights seemed to float among the tangle of trees and brush. As she drew nearer, she could see they were actually clusters of candles in the windows of a cabin just off the trail.

"We are here," Jean said. "Welcome to my home." The boy Marie saw earlier on the beach came rushing down the path.

"*Madame* Doctor, *Madame* Doctor, please come with me. Mama has fixed you supper, and you will stay with us, and–"

"Gerard, please. Give *Madame* Galante some time to get to know you before you drown her in questions."

"But, Jean-Pa, I want to be a doctor too. Maybe she can show me what I have to do."

"There will be plenty of opportunity for you to learn," Jean chided him. "First, you must eat so you can grow up strong. And then you can do whatever you want."

Gerard turned and scampered back up the path to the cabin door, stopping several times to look back and urge them on with a sweep of his arm.

"That was Gerard." Jean turned to her with an apologetic, wry smile.

"He is just a boy," Marie said with a grin. "Gerard reminds me of my sons when they were that age, so full of life and curiosity."

"And where are your sons now?" Jean asked.

"They are at school in France. I pray I can keep the plantation for them until they return," Marie said.

Jean pulled open the door Gerard had just dashed through.

A tall, willowy woman with haunting green eyes stood waiting for them.

"Marie, this is Elisabeth. Elisabeth, *Madame* Galante will be our guest while she nurses my men."

She reached out and grasped Marie's hand warmly. "I am so glad you came to help us."

Marie bit her tongue to avoid a caustic reply. She was by no means a willing guest in the thieves' compound, but something caused her to remain kind toward this poor woman. After all, she probably was an innocent victim of her husband's crimes.

Jean hesitated for a moment in the doorway while an odd look passed between him and the woman. Then he disappeared with a short salute.

As soon as he was out of earshot, Elisabeth turned to her and said in a conspiratorial whisper, "He's not really my husband."

⁂

With the light steps of a smuggler, Jean padded barefoot along the trail to where Francois waited for him.

"Ah, so you return quickly. Have you lost interest in your healer so soon?"

"What do you want, Francois?" Jean demanded with a hiss. "I tire of your games."

"Perhaps she would like to know that today Courbet paid a visit to Galante House," Francois said.

"How do you know what is happening there?"

"One of the men we left behind got a message to me a short while ago."

"Now what is that old fraud, Courbet, up to?" Jean wearied of the constant drama of his dealings with one of the wealthiest men in the islands. Sometimes Jean and his men relieved Courbet of things he didn't need. Sometimes they procured things for him.

"He came looking for Marie to warn her he will collect on her late husband's gambling debt as soon as the sugar harvest is complete. When he discovered his little bird had flown, he torched the cane in a fury."

Jean bowed his head, frustrated. He could not see Francois's expression in the darkness, but he was fairly certain the man was smiling.

"What are you going to do?" his first mate asked.

"I'm going to send a few more men to guard the place until I can get her back to her people."

"That won't help Marie. Sending more men to her island will only weaken our defenses here. We already have a group of men away raiding an English warehouse on Guadeloupe tonight." Francois leaned closer to Jean's face. "You know Courbet will eventually seize her plantation no matter what she does. Marie is doomed."

"You forget," Jean said through gritted teeth, "only I decide where and when my men go." He shoved hard at his first mate's arm. "Not you."

"And besides," Jean added, "it doesn't hurt to torch the cane before harvesting. As long as the old man didn't burn down her house, Marie can still prevail. She is a very determined woman. You should not count her out yet."

Francois turned his back to Jean and stared toward the cove.

"Now quit being a naysayer and send one of the ketches back to the island." Jean shoved him again. "They should be there by morning."

Francois turned away and headed for the anchorage in the cove.

Marie stood for a moment, her stomach roiling, after Elisabeth's blunt confession.

"You do not have to make excuses to me," Marie said. "It's not your fault you've been caught in that man's web. He takes what he wants without considering the consequences."

"You don't understand," she interrupted. "Jean is my brother."

"Why? Why are you telling me this?" Marie asked and then demanded sharply, "Did he father your child?"

"No," Elisabeth continued in a soft voice. "I've had no one to talk to for years, and I think the two of you may have feelings for each other. I saw the looks you exchanged today at the cove. My brother has lived alone too long with nothing but the need for vengeance to warm his soul."

"What are you saying?" Marie snorted in disbelief.

"There was tenderness on your face as you watched him with Gerard at the cove today. He has been my protector ever since our parents disappeared years ago and we became orphans on the streets of St. Pierre on Martinique."

"So, who exactly is Gerard's father?" Marie asked, and then, horrified at her own words, added, "I'm so sorry. That is not my concern. Please forgive me."

At that moment, the subject of their conversation clattered down the stairs and raced over to Marie to show her his collection of bird feathers.

Marie's heart softened. She knelt to the cabin floor while he placed the brightly colored objects with care across the room. She crawled from one specimen to another, touching and exclaiming while Gerard beamed at her.

Elisabeth set out a large crockery bowl of chicken stew on a well-worn wooden table and called to them. "Come on, Gerard. Leave *Madame* Galante alone. You're exhausting her," his mother chided. "Come have some stew — both of you."

Marie clutched at her skirts and rose from the floor while the boy retrieved his feathers.

His eyes grew heavy as they finished their supper, and when Jean's sister came around the table to pull him to his feet, he did not complain. She led him to the upper level to bed.

Marie was bone-tired after a day of one disaster after another, but she hung on, determined to return to the patients as soon as Jean reappeared.

Elisabeth came back down the stairs and settled into the chair across from her. She was quiet for several minutes and then continued the story interrupted by her son's appearance.

"I'm sorry to have confused you, but I was overcome by finally having someone I believe I can trust."

Marie covered Elisabeth's hand with her own and looked into her eyes. "You do not owe me any explanation. Please do not trouble yourself."

"But I want to tell my story," she insisted.

"Very well," Marie said. "Begin. Tell me everything," she said, accustomed to many confessions over the years on her rounds as a healer.

"We came to Martinique as children. Our father was captain of a merchant ship, and our mother sailed with him. They came from Nouvelle Orléans with gold to purchase land in the islands and start anew." When Elisabeth paused, Marie motioned for her to continue.

"Shortly after we came to St. Pierre, our parents left one night to meet with a landowner to negotiate for some property on the island. They never came back."

"What did the two of you do then?" Marie asked, and sat forward, agitated.

"At first, our nurse stayed with us, but she ran out of money and had to leave us at an orphanage."

"How long were you there?"

"We left the first night." Elisabeth hung her head. "They wouldn't let Jean stay. They said he was too old."

"How old were you?" Marie asked.

"I was six, but Jean was fourteen."

"Where did you go?" Marie struggled to keep the pity out of her voice.

"We hid on the streets of St. Pierre," she admitted.

"What did you do for food and shelter?"

"At first, all we could do was beg, but older youths would beat us and take whatever money we could collect." The young woman's face burned in embarrassment. "And then we met some people who helped us."

"Thank God," Marie said.

"They were street performers." The blush on her cheeks turned scarlet. "They taught Jean magic tricks to help bring in more money on street corners, and me..." She paused to catch her breath. "They taught me to dance and tell fortunes."

"Did you live with them?"

"For a few years, but when the caravans moved on, Jean and I stayed. My brother refused to leave St. Pierre without discovering what happened to our parents."

"How did you survive all those years, and when did you give birth to Gerard?"

"I was eighteen." A tear squeezed out of the corner of Elisabeth's eye. "A man's servant came to one of our performances and offered us a great deal of money to come and perform at his home." She grew quiet and stared at the wall.

Marie reached out to clasp her hand across the table. "Go on."

"He had Jean beaten and thrown into the street. Then he came after me." Her lips trembled and she looked away.

"Who was he?" Marie asked.

"I don't know. He wore a mask, but I will never forget the sound of his voice."

"The community on Martinique is not so large," Marie said. "It shouldn't be that difficult to find your attacker."

"Jean is so set on revenge, I'm afraid to find out." Elisabeth quieted for a moment and then added, "I'm terrified he might kill him and then end up in prison. He's all Gerard and I have."

"That's why you and Jean maintain the charade of being married?" Marie asked.

"Yes." Elisabeth bowed her head. "He blames himself for what happened and still tries to protect me."

"Does anyone else know?"

"I don't think so," she said, "but sometimes I get the feeling Francois knows something's off." She paused for a moment and stared into the distance. "He's not really such a bad man. He just irritates Jean."

"Does he know you're not really married?" Marie asked.

"I'm not sure, but I think he suspects."

Jean waited outside the cabin and listened in the dark. The thick jungle undergrowth pressed in on him, squeezing his heart and lungs until the only thing left was the pain in Elisabeth's voice, the pain of betrayal, the pain of her loss of innocence. She'd wasted eight years locked in a lie to keep her son safe.

This was the first time he'd heard his sister's entire story. She'd never been able to talk about that night, until now.

He sat on the ground, slumped against a tree, and waited until his breathing returned to normal. He was too upset to confront his sister now, but if she could remember any small detail about her attacker, any description of the man beneath the mask, the islanders would finally see Jean Blanchard deserved his reputation as a bloodthirsty killer.

CHAPTER SEVEN

Jean retraced his steps down the dirt path a short distance and then stomped to the doorway to give Marie and Elisabeth ample warning of his approach.

His sister came to the door with a candle and peered out at him. "Is all well with Francois?"

"Yes, he is always well," Jean said, irritation in his voice. "He's invincible."

"Something important must have happened for him to seek you out this late at night."

"It's nothing for you to worry about." Jean ran his fingers through his hair and peered around her to the table where Marie sat. He motioned for her and said, "Marie, could you please come outside for a moment?"

As she followed him into the darkness, Jean worried about how to tell her and then decided to be direct. "Courbet showed up at Galante House after you left."

"Did he hurt anyone?" she asked, and put her hand to her mouth.

"We just got word from a man we left behind to make sure no one tried to follow us. He'll stop at nothing to get your plantation, Marie. You must know that by now."

"What did he do?"

"No one was hurt, but he threatened your workers and then torched the cane when he discovered you're with me."

Marie sucked in a breath and sagged against the trunk of a palm tree. Jean closed the distance between them and placed his hands on her shoulders.

"I sent Francois to guard the plantation, and of course, it doesn't hurt to torch the cane before beginning the harvest. Courbet and his men were just trying to frighten and intimidate you and your people."

"He's certainly succeeding," she said.

"You can't let him win, Marie."

She withdrew from his touch and asked, "Why are you troubling yourself over my problems?"

"I feel responsible for you."

"Then let us return to your sick men, and I'll try to relieve you of all your burdens at once so that I can return to my plantation."

"Do you know yet what disease sickens my men?" Jean asked.

"No, but I have some suspicions," she said.

Marie had not slept since the night before, and a thin slash of pink was beginning to show between the dark, still ocean and the blackness of the sky as they climbed back up toward the sick bay.

At a sudden cry in the dark, she lurched to a stop and clutched her chest. He turned abruptly, his face close to hers, with a wide grin on his face.

"Only roosters," Jean assured her.

"Wh—, what?"

"Roosters – they're fighting."

"Of course," Marie admitted with a puff of breath. "How silly of me."

"No. It's dark, you're in a strange place, and that sound unsettled you."

"Nonsense. I hear them constantly on my island."

Pulling a water-filled gourd from the sling on his shoulder, he turned, squeezed her hand and made her sit on a boulder along the trail.

Once she stopped, she began to shiver, even though the night was warm, covering her like a heavy, velvet blanket. Jean sat next to her and held the gourd to her lips. The cool water slid down her throat, lining her parched throat like silk.

"We've been working you too hard. You haven't had a moment to yourself." Jean put his arm around her and added, "My family probably wore you out with their endless chatter."

"I did not mind talking to your sister and Gerard." Jean stiffened next to her, and she added, "I know all about your little arrangement." She placed her hand over his. "I understand, though, and I promise not to reveal your secret."

"I have to keep Elisabeth and Gerard safe," Jean said, and jerked his hand away.

Marie began to think he might leave, but he suddenly returned, placed his hands to either side of her face, and pulled her to him. He drank from her lips as deeply as she had drunk from the water jug.

After a short hesitation, she sank into his kiss and let him pull her closer. Marie was lost. She took what he offered and could not pull away.

Jean ended the embrace and gave her a long look. "That was unwise."

She shoved him away and said, "Bringing me here to begin with was most certainly unwise. Let me finish quickly what needs to be done so that I can return home and forget we ever met."

She rose from her seat on the boulder and tugged on his shirt to drag him with her.

⁅ ⚓ ⁆

As he climbed up the trail with Marie swaying ahead of him in the early morning light, Jean tried to make sense of one of the weirdest nights he ever spent. He had no idea how his feelings had spiraled out of control. He would have to maintain his distance from this sea siren.

"Are you really a devil, as my workers believe, or is everything you do just an illusion?" Marie asked, turning toward him.

"No, I don't think so, to the first question, and yes to the last, maybe," Jean said.

"Can you make people disappear?" she demanded.

"That depends."

"On what?"

"On whether or not I want to see them again – or whether they ask too many questions," he added, unable to keep the playfulness out of his voice.

"I don't know why I bother to ask you serious questions," she said, and jammed her hands on her hips. "We can't afford to waste time," she said, and continued walking. "I need to check the insides of their mouths again to make sure, but I believe I can make something that will relieve the pain and swelling of the blisters I saw earlier."

When they entered the cabin, she turned to Abner, the young man caring for the patients, and asked him to fetch a bucket of clean water from the well.

Out of her large bag she pulled a mortar and pestle as well as a bag of soursop. She set the items on a table and began mashing the dried fruit flesh.

Jean watched her and shuddered. "What are you going to do with that?"

"This is the base for a poultice to put on the sores around their mouths. When Abner gets back, I'll add the water to the fruit," Marie said.

"Then you must know the cause of all this suffering," Jean said.

"There is a murderer on your island." Marie pounded harder on the soursop and shoved an escaped tendril of hair behind her ear. "Someone is poisoning your men."

Jean grabbed her by the arm and pulled her to face him. "How can you possibly know such a thing?" He tightened his grip when she tried to turn away. "You accuse my men without any proof. You'd better tread lightly."

Marie dropped the pestle and wrenched her arm from his grasp. "Would you rather disbelieve me and risk your entire crew?"

"For all I know, you made up a quick explanation so you can get back to your plantation." He stooped and retrieved the pestle.

"*Mon dieu*, but you are such a stubborn man." She snatched the implement from him and returned to her pounding. "They all have the symptoms of having eaten apples from the machineel tree. Ordinary stomach complaints are not accompanied by blisters around the lips and inside the mouth."

"I can't believe someone went to so much trouble to hurt my men." Jean shook his head, his tone still skeptical.

"You'd better believe," Marie said. "The tree is so poisonous, you cannot sit beneath its branches in the rain. Drops of water sliding off the bark and leaves can burn your skin. The men who survived contact with the fruit are very lucky. If eaten in even small quantities, those sweet apples can cause death."

Jean watched while Marie and Abner mixed the dried fruit with water to form a thick, sticky mass. They went from patient to patient, applying the mixture to the red, weeping blisters. After a few minutes, he took part of the poultice to the others and mirroring her actions, smeared the soothing concoction on their chests and faces.

Once they'd treated all the men with the soursop paste, she made more of the tea of the bark of the whitewood fig tree and urged the patients to sip the hot, bitter drink.

"How do you know you're doing the right thing?" Jean asked.

"For every poison occurring in nature," she explained, "there are always antidotes nearby." She shrugged and added, "A tea made from this bark is the only way to alleviate the effects of the deadly toxin."

"Perhaps the same could be said for people. For every evil monster we encounter, maybe there are good souls to counteract the effect," Jean said. "But you avoided my question. You still haven't explained how you know what to do."

"Your men aren't the first to fall victim to the machineel tree," Marie assured him. "They're everywhere along the shores of the islands."

"Enough. You need rest," Jean ordered. "Come with me." He curled his hand around hers, and she followed him without argument. "No more talk of poisoning. I still can't believe anyone would deliberately try to kill my men. There must be some other explanation," he said.

Eyes heavy from the need for sleep, Marie followed Jean blindly as he led her through a thicket of sharp-edged succulents. Occasionally, she had to use her free hand to pull her dress free of the prickly stems.

Uncertainty gnawed at her when they broke into a clearing in front of a cabin on stilts. He squeezed her hand still nestled in his and strode up the wooden steps. She stopped midway through the climb, fatigued. When he turned and scooped her into his arms, she did not have the strength to protest. She wrapped her arms around his neck and buried her head on his shoulder to shield her eyes from the rising sun.

With her last conscious act, she sank onto a large bed filling most of the room at the rear of the tree-house cottage. And then there was a kiss so soft on her forehead, she thought it might have been a butterfly before the mosquito netting closed around her. The final thought fluttering through her mind was she should try to escape.

Jean twisted and turned in an attempt to adjust his long legs and arms to the confining hammock on the porch where Gerard slept when he spent the night. He comforted himself with the thought that Marie had so quickly discovered the source of the strange illness.

The sooner he could deliver the vexing woman back to her island, the sooner he would get his life back. However, he had serious doubts there could be a murderer among his crew.

He fell asleep mid-turn and spent the next few hours in uneasy dreams of voluptuous sirens beckoning him to follow them to the bottom of the sea.

CHAPTER EIGHT

Marie woke suddenly and for a few seconds could not remember where she was. A gauzy canopy covered the space above her while a deafening rush of water muffled the outside sounds of the jungle. Had she heard this same waterfall before she fell asleep in the early dawn hours? Oh, yes. Reality crashed in on her. She was in Jean's bed.

She sat up in a rush when he stepped through the door with a plate of fruit. She tugged the sheet up to her neck and asked hesitantly, "Did I...? Did you...?"

"No, you didn't; nor did I." Jean held up his hand, palm toward her. "You fell immediately to sleep, and I spent the night in the hammock."

"How are the men responding to the treatment? When can I go back to see them?"

He sat next to her, pressing two fingers against her lips. "Quiet. Eat first. Questions later."

"But how...?"

"Close your eyes."

"Why?"

"Just close them."

Marie squeezed shut her eyes and felt the ripe flesh of a mango pressing against her mouth.

"Eat," he said.

She opened her mouth and savored the sweet fruit while the juice ran down her chin and throat. She swiped at the drip but was intercepted by a soft cloth wielded by her jailer.

"Why...," she started, and opened her eyes, only to be silenced by a chunk of coconut followed closely by another slice of mango. This time she accepted both offerings into her hands. Sticky juice ran down her fingers. She took slow, careful bites and sat in wary silence. He scooted closer to her on the bed.

"Why are you being so nice to me?" She finished the coconut and reached for the cup of water he'd poured for her. "What do you want?"

"I want to make up for your first day here. I'm afraid I was not a very good host, since good will and charm are not my strong points. But I will answer one question for each bit of food you eat," Jean said. "You slept all day yesterday after treating my men."

"But I need to return to help." She half-stood before he gave her a gentle push back down to sitting.

"You're interrupting," he said, putting his fingers to her mouth. "Abner is following your instructions, and the patients are responding well, thanks to you."

"What about the blisters?" she asked.

"Fading."

"And the stomach complaints?"

"Slowly improving," he said. "Perhaps I can return you to your island tomorrow."

"Don't be so quick to let down your guard," she said, and plucked at his sleeve. "We still don't know how the fruit of the machineel tree ended up in their food."

"What are you suggesting?"

"Can't you see? We need to find the person trying to destroy your crew."

A cold sliver of alarm lanced through Jean. What if Marie were right? Someone meant to destroy him, even if they had to kill his men. He'd suspected as much but still was sickened at the weapon his shadowy enemy had chosen.

Right now, all he wanted to do was while away the morning with Marie. If they could put aside the dangers lurking around them, he would sink into her softness and taste the pleasures of her sweet body.

"We have to start right away," Marie said.

"What?" By all that's holy, he'd missed her entire thread of conversation.

Marie stared at him, her dark eyes wide.

"We have to examine the hands of all your men," she repeated slowly, as though he were a dolt.

"Because?"

She gave out a loud huff and answered, "Because whoever slipped the machineel apples into your crew's food might still have blisters on his hands."

CHAPTER NINE

Marie and Jean made their way down a tightly overgrown wooden walkway toward a patch of light. She coughed and swatted at cobwebs, wondering how he and his men navigated the intricate maze of the island compound. She'd given up dropping small bits of cloth ripped from her petticoat. They'd covered too much ground.

Another tickling on her neck and she swept a hand across her shoulder to clear a wisp of web, only to see the indignant spider scrabble off into the underbrush. Marie could understand the creature's plight. She too would be angry if someone destroyed her home, which was exactly what this arrogant smuggler might do.

"Slowing down this early in the morning, are we?" Jean turned at the sound of Marie stopping on the trail and quirked a brow. "You were the one who didn't want to linger in my comfortable bed."

"Insufferable man."

"There's not much farther to go. Our communal kitchen is just ahead." He kept moving forward, leaving her to finish brushing the rest of the poor spider's home from her dress.

A few minutes later she stumbled into a clearing with cooking fires, stone ovens and a thatched shelter over rough-hewn tables and benches. Several of Jean's men tended large simmering pots while a tall, slender woman stood at a table with a huge bowl filled with dough. Her hands were buried deep as she rhythmically punched the mixture down, over and over.

She turned her head and smiled at Marie as Jean brought her under the shelter.

"Marie, this is Cecile, our head cook. She can tell you whatever you need to know," Jean said, and then without stopping, passed beyond the women to fade back into the jungle.

Marie stared after him and then turned to the woman with a shake of her head. "Is he always so mysterious and abrupt?"

Cecile gazed for a moment in the direction of Jean's disappearance as if she too were puzzled, then faced Marie.

"I owe dat man my life," she offered, as if that were explanation enough. "Me, I come from a plantation on Guadeloupe. When my boy died, I ran off and came here to cook."

Cecile returned to kneading the dough, her hands still covered in the sticky flour mixture. She wore a long, sashed dress made of a deep red batik fabric, and a bright yellow turban covered her hair. The caramel tint of her skin glowed in the early morning sun.

The tall woman rolled the bread dough out of the mixing bowl and slapped it onto a narrow chopping board covered in flour. Marie listened to the comforting sounds of her folding and shaping the mixture into a loaf form.

Cecile finally broke the companionable silence. "What think you happened to the men?"

Marie thought a moment before answering the cook's abrupt question. "I believe it's something they ate, and I'm trying to find out what foods they've been given over the last few weeks." She dragged a finger through the heavy white flour overflowing onto the sides of the board while Cecile continued working the loaf. "I would guess whatever it was would be a favorite with most of the men, since so many of them are ill."

"I am the only one who cooks here every day. The men take turns working the fires, tending the vegetable gardens, and preparing food." Cecile paused and gazed at Marie, raising and jutting forward her chin.

"I need to talk to all the men who have had a hand in the preparation of food," Marie hastily added, her stomach suddenly queasy at the turn of conversation and the look in Cecile's eyes.

Cecile broke out into an unexpected peal of laughter and pointed at the circle of smugglers who had gathered around them near the fire. "You believe one of us, we poison the men?"

Marie's face flushed at the accusation. This she had not expected.

"You must look at everyone's hands," Cecile said.

"Why?" Marie demanded. "That will take way too long."

"If you check only the crew who work in the kitchen, what if the poisoner works somewhere else? He will know you suspect him." She paused and added, "If you look at everyone, no one will know what you suspect."

"You're right. Spreading around the suspicion does make sense," Marie admitted.

"And besides, how do you know the bad food was not an accident?"

"If it had been an accident, the malaise and deaths would have happened all at once, not gradually over a period of weeks."

Maybe so, maybe not," Cecile said, and gave the bread dough one last punch.

Jean slid down the slope behind his sister's cabin and headed around the property to find his nephew. It was Gerard's turn to work in the kitchen gardens, and he wanted to make sure the boy didn't shirk his chores.

He stopped abruptly at the sight of Francois talking quietly with Elisabeth, their heads close together. For a moment the earth shifted beneath his feet, and he took a deep breath to keep from charging between them to give his first mate a beating. While he was debating a course of action, he saw something he had not seen in a long time: His sister smiled, and happiness shone from her eyes.

Jean decided to drop back behind the house to monitor the situation from afar instead of killing Francois. This unexpected development would require more thought.

ANDREA K. STEIN

Marie had warmed to Jean's mysterious cook in spite of her evasive, forbidding reaction to her questions. Once she'd given up asking about the possible cause of the men's sickness, Cecile had turned out to be a treasure trove of information and advice. She'd shared the lore of the flowers, plants, and herbs on the island. They'd talked for several hours and compared treatments for various complaints.

When the cook invited Marie back to her cabin, she had made a great show of meticulously washing her hands clean of flour and sticky dough. Her hands were smooth, soft, and clear of any blemish. It would have been extremely difficult for her to prepare the machineel apples without suffering severe burns herself.

"Cecile, tell me again – where do you find the plants you use for the tea to ease the pain of childbirth?"

"There is a waterfall near the top of the old volcano. You will find the small plants in the shade of the river rocks. There's a pool up there, too, if you'd like to bathe," she said, and then added, "The men, dey stay away from there – too much work to climb," she added, with a smile that didn't reach her eyes.

"Then maybe I shouldn't try either?"

"The path is simple to follow, and you are a strong woman – I can tell," Cecile assured her. "I'll take you to the beginning of the trail."

Marie's doubts about finding the waterfall grew with every labored step up the mountain. She nearly laughed at her original need to bathe. Whenever she found her way back down, if she didn't break her neck, she would be filthy again. She sorely missed her early morning ritual of swimming out beyond the point on her own island.

Every step on the sandy trail swirled up more grit to coat her feet and legs. She kept a wary watch on the encroaching jungle at the edge of the path, imagining eyes watching her from the thick, waxy green undergrowth. The smell of death and decay assaulted her nose. Occasional animal snorts and shrieks slowed her forward progress while she held her breath and wondered.

After hours of winding through the confining leafy tunnel, she emerged into a clearing, and a steady wind lifted the cloud ringing the volcano. Her breath hitched. This must be like the view from the top of the world. The ocean below spread out like diamonds sparkling in the sun.

At the sight of the shadow of her home island in the distance, sadness and regret stabbed at her. She hoped Luz and the others were preparing for the cane harvest. Even more, she hoped Courbet would leave them in peace until she could return.

Turning away, she moved toward the sound of water thundering to the valley below. The light bag Cecile had given her to gather plants had begun to feel as though it were filled with potatoes. When she finally reached the clearing, she sank onto one of the rocks ringing the clear pool at the base of the falls and pulled off her old work boots.

Marie massaged her feet for a few moments and then lowered them into the cool waters. A sigh of pleasure escaped from deep in her throat. She studied the clear depths of the pool and then rose to slip out of her dress before diving cleanly into the small basin. She resurfaced under the falls and let the rushing water batter her body until all her worries and fears seemed to flow along with the water into the valley.

After what seemed a lifetime, she reluctantly pulled herself out of the pool and found a flat rock in the sun where she could stretch out. In that moment, the hairs on her scalp tingled. She swung around, sure someone watched from the jungle. No one. She sighed and sat down, awkwardly finger-combing her hair. Spreading her wet, dark curls out around her, she drifted off to sleep.

When she awakened with a start a while later, the sun had lowered toward the sea. She was terrified of being in the jungle alone after dark and scrambled to her feet to gather her things before starting the perilous trek back down the mountain.

As an afterthought, she began checking around the rocks ringing the pool for the plant Cecile had described to her. A plant she could grind into a tea for the pain of labor would be a wonderful thing to bring back to the women of her island. Then she remembered with a jolt how many of the younger men and women had stolen away. She couldn't blame them, but she probably wouldn't be delivering many more babies.

After working her way around most of the pool without seeing anything of the medicinal greenery the cook described, Marie gave up. She refused to dwell on why Cecile would mislead her. Her overactive imagination already had her jumping at every sound.

She reluctantly turned to make her way back down the steep path. Maybe she could coax Jean into returning and finding the plant for her. After all, he owed her, and her people, a lot.

She moved down the mountain as quickly as she could, hoping to make it to the base before sunset. That was her last thought before she woke up in terror at the bottom of a small cliff. Her head throbbed, and blood trickled down the side of her face. The darkness of the night settled like a heavy, velvet glove over her eyes.

When she tried to push up onto her feet, pain stabbed at her right ankle. She thumped back down and ignored the ominous skitterings and slitherings nearby. She was not alone in this impenetrable green hell. She clenched her teeth against the pain and ordered her imagination to shut down while she tried to come up with a way out of her predicament.

Jean cursed and kicked at a rock on the trail. He'd looked everywhere for Marie after having spent most of the day on Guadeloupe. He'd negotiated with the English garrison quartermaster for some particularly fine wine. The minute he returned, he'd sought her out to tell her about his great trading coup at the expense of both the French and the English.

If one of his men had helped her escape, he was a dead man.

"Francois — how can you not know where she is? This is, after all, a very small island," he insisted.

"She was headed to Cecile's cabin the last I saw her this morning. Maybe she's still there. You know how women are – they could still be talking. Maybe they've forgotten the time." His first mate's gaze slid sideways and he lifted his shoulders in a shrug.

"Marie would not have left without a word to me, or without checking on the men in the infirmary." Jean tried to convince himself as much as Francois, but his doubts grew with each moment he couldn't find her.

"You never warn any of your other women before *you* disappear," Francois reminded him.

"This is different," Jean gritted out, and then added with a snarl, "Take me to Cecile."

CHAPTER TEN

The air hung heavy with the scent of the flowers on the small orange trees guarding the path to Cecile's small cabin.

Jean rushed along the stone walkway, ignoring the dense masses of fruits and vegetables brushing against his legs. As he raced against the dusk that would soon cover the island, his boots caught and crunched on dried vines winding across the footpath.

Francois followed, his steps more slow and deliberate.

Jean pounded on Cecile's door, shaking the ring of blood-red lilies surrounding the frame, and then waited. After a few moments, he raised his fist again just as the door opened a crack.

"Whatever has happened? Has the kitchen burned down?" Cecile asked. She peeked cautiously around the door before letting them in.

Jean pushed his way into the small cabin and pointed angrily at her. "Where is she? If you're hiding her, I will exact retribution."

"Who?"

"You know who — Marie — you were with her this morning."

"Yes," Cecile answered, her voice even and calm.

"What did you do with her?"

"Nothing. She wanted to see the kitchen and what we cook for the crew. Then she asked me about the herbs and spices I use in food preparation, so I brought her back here."

"Where did she go after that?"

"I don't know," Cecile replied. "She said she wanted to bathe, so I gave her directions to the waterfall pool near the summit of the volcano."

"The volcano? That's a three-hour climb, straight up the mountain." Jean ran his hands through his hair and then slammed his hand against the wall. "What were you thinking?"

"I told her the cove was easier and safer. But she said she wanted privacy. She was afraid someone would spy on her."

"I have to find her. We can't leave her alone up there. Maybe she's lost, or hurt," Jean said, and glared at Francois who leaned against the wall with a bored expression. "You should have watched her more closely."

"Me?" Francois extended his hands, palms up. "You were the one who didn't trust me to take care of her. Remember last night? I thought you banned me from escorting her."

"I didn't mean for you to leave her totally alone, either, without a guard." Jean ground his teeth and clenched his fists. "Come with me. Gather some men in case we need help, and bring torches and lines from the boats."

Within a short while, the small band of searchers headed up the mountain, waving lighted torches and shouting for Marie.

Jean berated himself for assuming she would stay close to the small compound, and out of trouble. He went over everything she'd said that morning and then remembered their last conversation before he'd left her at the communal kitchen. She believed there was a killer among his men. A bolt of fear seized him. Maybe she'd found the culprit, and now she was in danger, too.

Jean and his men moved steadily up the trail for about an hour and a half. When Jean first heard a weak cry, he had them aim their torches down the side of the precipice until the flickering light revealed a crumpled form on a narrow ledge.

"We need more light," he shouted. "Bring the torches closer together."

Marie lay sprawled on the rocks, waving her arm at the rescuers. Jean scrambled down and pulled her into his arms while Francois and the other men rigged a sling to haul her back up to the trail.

"Why did you leave without telling me?" he asked, and rubbed carefully across her blood-matted scalp.

She didn't answer, but her whole body shook from exposure. Her eyes were wide, her pupils dilated.

Even as the bile of fear rose in his throat, Jean's anger surged like an uncontrollable storm at sea. How had one small woman upended his existence in such a short period and stirred warring emotions within him?

When he gathered her to him and stood, she sagged, unable to stand. He held her battered body tight and vowed to keep her safe.

"What happened?" he demanded.

"I don't really remember," she said, "but I think someone pushed me." She groaned then. "My ankle. It hurts. I may not be able to walk," she said with a whimper.

He bent back down and settled her into his lap while he feathered his fingers along the skin above her boot. There was swelling, but the bones seemed to be in a normal position.

"Looks like a sprain. You'll have to stay off your foot for a day or two, but I don't think it's serious." He turned an anguished look toward her. "Marie, try to remember. Who hurt you?" he asked, and then lowered his voice. "Did the person you suspect of the poisonings come after you?" He glanced furtively up the drop-off to see if anyone was close enough to overhear them.

"I did not see anything." She buried her head on his chest and sobbed. "I, I thought no one would find me," she finally said with a hiccup.

He tightened his grip on her and turned as Francois reached the ledge with the rope sling. "We need to get her back to camp quickly. She can't stop shivering. The head wound isn't deep, but her ankle is swollen. I doubt she can walk."

Francois said nothing but helped Jean secure Marie in the sling and then motioned for the men above to pull her up while they guided the rope from below.

Once back on the trail, they made a rough litter with the sling and two long logs for carrying her back down the mountain.

Jean took the front end of the litter, and the men began the steep descent back to the smugglers' camp.

"Why would Cecile send Marie up here just to bathe?" Jean demanded of Francois with a growl. His first mate had brought the cook to the camp some months earlier, saying she was a runaway he had smuggled off Guadeloupe.

"Captain, you heard Cecile. She told the healer it would be safer to bathe in the cove." Francois repositioned his grip on the other side of the front of the litter and craned his head toward Jean. "Didn't you say the sick men are getting better from her treatments? Maybe you should take her back to her island. *Mon Dieu* — for all we know, it could be bad luck to take a healer away from her people."

"Not so loud," Jean said with a hiss. "Don't spread needless superstitions to the others. You know how quickly such rumors spread."

Jean continued edging his way down in silence, considering Francois's suggestion. Maybe he was right. After all, she was determined to return to her cane harvest, and his men were getting better. He pushed her nagging accusation to the back of his mind. If a killer ranged among his crewmen, he would find him and make sure he never killed again. The last thing he needed was for Marie to find the murderer and risk danger.

"You know I'm right." Francois's voice floated back to him across the still night air.

Jean stole a backward look at Marie. Her eyes flickered open, and when she caught his stare, she made a slight side-to-side movement of her head in silent denial.

She'd been listening to their conversation and didn't want to leave. Jean cheered inwardly and continued the labored passage down the trail.

For now, she could stay, but as long as she remained in his camp, he would not leave her side, not ever.

A dull ache settled in Marie's head. Her scattered thoughts kept waddling away from her like a gaggle of geese. Each time she thought she'd figured out how she ended up on the ledge below the trail, her mind would circle back to the beginning.

Of all the fuzzy details, one in particular was just beyond her reach.

She sat cross-legged on Jean's bed, slowly chewing on a slice of fresh bread. After a day of climbing and then lying in terror on the ledge, she was hungry. But with each swallow, a wave of nausea came over her, forcing her finally to put the bread down and lie back against the pillows.

As Jean moved around the room snuffing out candles, the complete darkness caused Marie a bout of terror. "Jean," she cried, "don't leave me alone."

"I'm here, Marie. Let me get a mat from the porch."

"No. Just come here and hold me. I can't face the darkness again." She paused for a moment and then added with a small squeak, "Please?"

She gulped when she heard him pad across the room and then felt his weight sink down beside her.

"Is this really what you want?" he asked, and rolled toward her, folding her into his arms.

"I don't, I don't know," she replied, her voice cracking with confusion and fatigue.

"Just sleep. No one will harm you, and that includes me," he promised.

Jean could not believe he had just agreed to share a bed with Marie. What was he thinking? He had to stay on guard in case whoever threatened her on the volcano trail returned to finish his wicked plan.

Lying so close to her warm body, he felt her breathing ease when she fell into a deep sleep. He inhaled deeply of her scent – sandalwood soap and the mint leaves she chewed on throughout the day. Her skin... He forced himself to stop considering how it would feel to press into her soft skin, and then pulled her more tightly to him. After that, he lay in silence, hopelessly awake, wondering how in hell he would make it through the night without going mad.

Francois slapped the dust from his hat as he walked through Cecile's garden and then pushed open the door without knocking.

"What do you think you're doing, eh?" She looked up sharply before returning to the herbs she was pounding with a pestle and mortar.

"Do not pretend with me, *Maman*. You know why I'm here." He eased himself down onto a battered wooden bench and watched her. "If you're going to get rid of Marie, for God's sake, do it right."

She stopped pounding and moved toward him, hands on hips. "What say you?"

"We found her injured on a ledge along the path to the volcano. She cried out when she saw the torches and heard us calling her name."

"*Mon dieu*. That woman has to leave. She knows too much, that *sorciere*."

"I told Jean it's bad luck to take a healer from her people to get him to send her back."

"And did he listen to you?"

"No. I think he wants to bed the little healer. After tonight's disaster, you'd better stop causing trouble for a while before Jean or Marie finds out."

"The healer only suspects, she does not know for certain. There is no proof." She stepped back behind the table and resumed pounding. "As long as you are here, though, there is something we need to discuss."

"What would that be?" He moved to a more comfortable position on the bench, then rose and paced toward the door, peering outside.

"You know."

"What?"

"Where were you this afternoon?" She stopped and stripped off the leaf wraps protecting her hands. "Maybe we wouldn't be having this conversation if you would have come along with me to get rid of Marie."

"I have work to do here. I can't just take off with you whenever you need me. People will get suspicious."

"I suspect something already. You weren't working this afternoon at Jean's cabin, were you?"

Francois turned away and stared out the door before whirling on her. "How dare you judge me?"

"You will get yourself killed before we finish our work here," she warned.

"You're probably right," he admitted, "but Elisabeth is a lonely, ignored woman." He turned back to his mother and added, "Did you know he doesn't even sleep with her? They live together like brother and sister. Her days are spent alone with her son. When he wants to take a woman, he goes to another island."

"You poor, foolish boy." Cecile shook her head and moved closer. "Sit down. I have a story for you."

Marie dreamed of the jungle again. This time the dark heat of the night was not the only thing pressing down on her face. She couldn't breathe and struggled awake. Jean was above her, his hand clamped over her mouth. When she scratched his face and pushed back at him, he loosened his hold a bit and raised one finger to his lips. When she propped herself up, he vanished out a window, leaving her alone with whirling thoughts and fears.

A few minutes later, a voice floated in from the front of the small cabin. "Marie — are you awake? Would you like some company? I don't want to intrude."

She fell back onto the pillows and expelled a sigh of relief. It was Elisabeth. "I'm back here," she managed to croak.

Jean's sister appeared in the doorway, a wide grin on her face. "We were worried about you yesterday, but I see Jean has taken good care of you. He and Gerard are outside, catching lizards. I asked him to give us some privacy."

"Is something wrong?"

"I'm not sure." She lifted her heavy honey-blonde hair from her neck and wound it into a knot, pulling pins from her pocket to secure it. "It's Francois. He said Jean will probably order him to go back with you to help with the cane."

"But I already told Jean I'm not ready to go. The men in the sick bay—. "

"You mustn't upset yourself, Marie. Your treatments are working. The men are getting better. Jean should keep his word and get you back to your island." Elisabeth paced to the other side of the room and back, stopping before Marie. "You have to tell me, though. Do you have feelings for Francois?" She burst into tears and sank onto the edge of the bed. "I saw him with you. He stood close to you…"

Marie folded the young woman into her arms and rocked her as she would a child. "Does Jean know you care for Francois?"

"No. Please don't tell him," she said with a sob onto Marie's shoulder.

"You needn't worry. Have you considered perhaps Francois was pretending to be attracted to me to cover up his feelings for you? In fact, I'm going to have a little talk with your brother. I don't need or want a *contrebandier* helping me with the harvest. I have challenges enough already. But more importantly, I am not ready to abandon the men. I believe they're being poisoned, and I intend to find the one who is culpable before I leave."

Francois strode toward the cove, still furious at the memory of his mother's words the night before. He was late for his watch and still seethed at Jean's continuing interference in such a cruel manner in Elisabeth's life. He came through a tunnel of undergrowth and stopped short. A familiar ship hove to outside the treacherous, rocky inlet. Her small boat, loaded with men, rowed with steady strokes toward the headland.

Mon dieu. His treacherous father, Courbet, could not wait. He'd given up on their sabotage plans and was coming to finish the job.

Francois turned and ran back to a large conch wedged onto the branch of a tree. He lifted the shell to his mouth and sounded the alarm.

CHAPTER ELEVEN

The blast of the conch shell shattered the silence of the compound and brought Jean to his feet. He scooped up Gerard and raced into the cabin.

Both Marie and Elisabeth turned to him, uncertainty on their faces.

"You should be safe here for now," he said, and pushed Gerard toward his mother. "Elisabeth, you know what to do if I don't return. Go to the refuge on the other side of the island. Don't wait for me."

He barely glanced at the two women again while he unlocked a chest in the corner and grabbed weapons, shoving them into his boots and belt. He took the shirt he'd left behind earlier, when he was convinced there was a spy outside the cabin.

He gave each of them a small pistol before turning to crush his sister in a fast embrace. He pulled Marie close, and lightly kissed her cheek. When he gazed into the well of her warm, brown eyes, he saw a stubborn retort forming. Pulling her more tightly to him he warned, "For God's sake, do as Elisabeth tells you. Don't take any chances. As soon as I return, I'm taking you home. I can't expose you to any more danger."

Without further delay, he ran out to the porch and jumped down onto the ground to join his crew in the rush to the cove.

Marie crawled to where her old work dress hung over the back of a chair. She pulled herself up and threw the dress on over her nightshift.

The still keening conch shell nearly drove what little reason she had left from her head. Leaning on the table to steady herself, she began to form a plan. As she sifted through the possibilities, her grogginess gave way to resolute determination.

"Elisabeth," she snapped. "Here is what we will do." At that moment, the wail of the shell stopped abruptly only to be replaced by the sound of gunshots coming from the cove.

Elisabeth's eyes widened, and she moaned and collapsed onto a chair. "Francois must not die before I tell him how much I care," she said.

"Stop that and banish such thoughts from your head," Marie said.

Jean's sister turned her tear-streaked face toward Marie, confusion in her eyes.

"You are scaring your son. He has no idea what is happening, and does not understand the little deception you and your brother have been playing. You must calm yourself for his sake," Marie added in a whisper.

Gerard had dashed outside and was leaning over the rail around the porch as much as he dared to hear what was going on at the cove.

"Also," Marie said, "we will find our way to the infirmary to check on the sick crewmen. They must be frightened by the commotion." She laid her hand on Elisabeth's shoulder and leaned close. "You have to show me the way. I don't think I can remember which of the paths to take."

"But you cannot walk on your injured ankle," Elisabeth said.

"Yes, I can," Marie insisted. "Get me a long, sturdy tree branch for support, and I'll make do."

Elisabeth called Gerard back into the cabin and set him on a search of nearby trees and brush for a branch Marie could use. When he pouted, she reminded him of the responsibility Jean had given him to watch over them.

Once the boy trotted back with what Marie needed, they collected food and jugs of water from Jean's kitchen.

When they were ready to leave for the sickbay, Gerard complained again. "*Non, Maman*," he said, and stamped his foot. "I want to fight with Jean-Pa and Francois."

"You must come with us." His mother grasped his wrist and pulled him down along the path.

Suddenly, he sat down, arms crossed, refusing to move.

Marie leaned over on her rough, homemade cane and smoothed his damp, dark hair back from his eyes. It had not been that long since she had dealt with headstrong boys.

"If you go to fight with the men in the cove, what will your mother and I do?" She tried to keep her tone as soothing as possible despite her own jangled nerves and pounding heart. "We need your help to get to the sick bay with all this food and water. If you leave, who will protect us?"

He returned a gaze as steady as her own and without a word rose off the path, taking the water jugs from his mother.

Marie's work dress she'd thrown on before they left the cabin stuck to her legs in the wet heat of the day as they made their way toward the infirmary. It seemed a lifetime since she'd last had her morning swim off the headlands of her home. A bag filled with fruit, bread and her medicinal herbs swung from her shoulder and banged against her back with each halting step.

After a series of twists and turns, the path opened into a clearing enclosing the familiar whitewashed sickbay. An unnatural silence greeted their approach. Even the raucous, wildly colored birds had ceased their shrieking.

On an impulse, Marie plucked at Gerard's shirt and motioned Elisabeth back onto the path. She leaned down and whispered in his ear, "Do you know of a way through the jungle off the path?"

He nodded, eyes wide.

"Take your mother and stay out of sight until I come back to give you the all-clear. Watch for me."

Elisabeth grasped at Marie's arm and pleaded with her to hide with them. She brushed her away with a firm squeeze of her hand. Jean's sister faded with her son into the foliage along the path as if they'd never been there.

With her bag slung over one shoulder, Marie straightened before limping toward the infirmary. By then, even the pops of gunfire and shouts from the cove had stopped.

Marie slipped through the door of the sickbay and breathed a sigh of relief at the familiar scene of Abner administering cool, water-soaked cloths and her healing tea.

He glanced at her, an apology in his eyes, as rough hands grasped her from behind. Her makeshift crutch clattered to the dirt floor.

Courbet moved from a dark corner of the room and confronted her, pinching her chin to pull her face close to him. "Marie, Marie," he said in a low, husky whisper, "you've made this so difficult. Why, at the beginning of harvest, would you follow that thief, Blanchard, like a common whore?" He abruptly released her chin and began to stroke her neck with his fingers, stopping just short of her breasts.

Marie tried to swallow the lump in her throat, but she couldn't manage enough spit. Instead, she freed one of her hands from the guard's grasp and swatted Courbet's hand away, scratching his arm. He drew back, shock in his eyes, and delivered a loud slap to the side of her face, sending her sprawling into the corner.

As she lay there, dazed with the room in a blur and tried to regain her senses, Courbet squatted at her side and began stroking her hand. "Why do you put yourself through all this pain? He isn't worth even one of these pretty fingers."

She sucked in a strangled breath when he suddenly grasped her thumb and bent it painfully. An involuntary cry escaped her lips.

The features on his face bespoke charm and grace, if one did not look too closely. Permanent frown lines etched his forehead above a perfect, patrician nose, and the high cheekbones covered in sun-touched skin led to cruel, thin lips.

His long blond hair, bleached by the sun, was drawn back into a neat queue, and he was dressed as though he had just stepped out for an afternoon tea at the governor's home on Martinique.

He stared at her a few moments longer before releasing her finger and returning to a warm smile that didn't quite illumine his cold, gray eyes.

"You're shaking, Marie, and on such a warm afternoon. Are you sure you haven't caught your patients' malaise?" He turned with a sweeping motion of his arm to indicate the men on pallets throughout the room. "Come back with me, and I'll leave some of my men to help you with the harvest. At my expense, of course. See how benevolent I can be?"

"I cannot trust you and yours." Marie sat up and swiped at the cold sweat on her nose and forehead, never taking her eyes from his reptile-like smile.

He bent closer, his foul breath making her want to gag. "Give up," he said with a hiss. "There's no one left to help but old men, women, and children. You know you can't prevail against me. The markers I hold on your husband's gambling debts are too high."

"I will pay off the debt, and you will produce those markers with suitable signatures, or I will go to the commandant on Martinique," Marie insisted.

"I've already talked to the governor," he said. "He holds your beautiful daughter and grandson in high regard." Courbet reached out and brushed her wilted hair out of her face. "And we are in agreement. Give up. It wasn't your fault. How were you to know his gambling debts were piling up?"

She barely heard what he was saying, her skin crawled so. She jerked away when he laid his hand on her arm again.

"You should acknowledge my right to the plantation and accept my kind offer of marriage. It isn't right for a woman like you to be alone."

"You cannot force a widow still in mourning. There are laws," Marie snapped.

"I can bring the priest from St. Pierre," he said.

Bile rose from her stomach at the memory of the day after her husband's death, when Courbet had forced her to sit with him while he rubbed her hands and explained how she would have no choice but to marry him. His fascination with touching her made her want to run outside and gulp in fresh air.

Just then, one of his men charged through the front door and shouted, "Fire! They've torched your ship."

Courbet gave her a sharp look before turning to hasten after the man toward the cove. He pointed at her over his shoulder. "I'm not finished with you, Marie. I'll be back. There's nowhere you can hide. And if Jean and his men try to interfere, I will destroy them."

With that, he raced out of the cabin, taking all of his men with him.

Marie sat shaking in silence, clutching her arms around her waist.

Abner rushed to her side with a gourd full of water and was urging her to drink when Jean burst into the infirmary. Soot covered his face, and small burns and cuts riddled his hands and arms.

"Let me put some ointment on those burns," she insisted, when he strode across the room, retrieved her tree branch cane, and pulled her to her feet. She cradled his hands in her one free hand to assess the damage.

"It's nothing," he said, when she made Abner bring her packet of herbs and salves she'd left in a corner before her face-off with Courbet.

After Marie treated his hands, she leaned against the wall and glared at him. "Now, tell me what's happened. Whose idea was it to attack Courbet's ship, of all things? Are you mad?"

"Francois…" Jean bit off the name of his first mate and frowned.

"Thank God," she said. "At least now we know he's on our side. We can take him off the list of suspects," Marie said with a sigh.

"That shows how much you know," Jean said with a weary sigh.

She tilted her head, a question on her lips.

"Yes. I've suspected Francois for some time. He's been trying to undermine me for the last year," Jean said.

"But that doesn't make sense," Marie said. "Why the sudden need to help you?"

Jean broke out into a wide grin, his teeth unnaturally white in his dark, sooty face. "I think he's developed a *tendresse* for my sister."

"What makes you think he hasn't become loyal to you?" she asked. "I'm serious. You have to let go and trust eventually."

Jean pulled her to him and silenced her small speech while he rubbed her shoulders and surveyed the state of the sickbay. "We were lucky today. He won't be so civil again." After a few moments of silence, he asked the question she'd been dreading. "Did he hurt you?"

"No."

"Not in any way?"

"He tried to frighten me, as he always does, but I stood my ground."

Jean pulled her face close to his and warned, "You must not enrage him. He's capable of great cruelty. I won't allow it."

Marie pushed herself back from his embrace and gave him an assessing look. "Since when have you become my protector?"

The scowl on his face softened when she finally smiled.

"I'm glad," she said. "I need all the protection I can get. Who better to keep me safe than a magician who's a thief?"

Jean fought the urge to bang his head against a sturdy coconut tree. Every time he set a plan in motion to deal with Marie and keep her at arm's length, something, or someone, intervened. He had been ready to return her to her island so that both of them could get on with their lives.

Now, Courbet had escalated his campaign to destroy Marie and take her plantation. He had to do something. He couldn't just take her back to her home and leave her at the mercy of that monster.

He glanced where she lay in deep slumber and came to a decision. There were forces at work here even he could not circumvent. His need for this woman had become almost painful. He had decided. Regardless of what she believed, he would have her. He would keep her safe. Now all he had to do was convince her she needed him, too. That's all.

Tomorrow would be hard. He would have to return Marie to her island and convince her she was on her own. God help him when she discovered his deception.

Marie was so excited, she wanted to throw her makeshift crutch overboard and do a little dance. They were sailing toward her home, fairly surfing into heavy waves as they beat into a stiff, easterly wind.

Jean had been strangely silent. He hadn't even tried to talk her out of her scheme again.

She went over and over in her mind the harvest steps, refusing to dwell on the dangers. The mere act of bringing in the cane took a great deal of courage, strength, and blind faith. From the heavy, sharp scythes to the mountainous grinding rock powered by oxen, the possibilities to be seriously injured were endless.

In fact, a strong man with a machete always stood by the grinder in case someone caught a hand or an arm. Amputation was infinitely preferable to death by suction into the relentless, turning stone crevice.

Before her husband died, he and the overseer had managed the harvest, and her father before them. Marie had tried to ignore the terrors of the harvest, only assisting with clothing, food and treatment of injuries. When she'd fired the overseer after her husband's death and he went to work for Courbet, she was left to face the challenges of the cane alone. She had to carry on. None of them would have a home if that bastard prevailed.

CHAPTER TWELVE

While Jean's men scrambled to anchor his ship in Marie's cove, he faced her and struggled to hide his feelings.

Weak, late fall storm clouds half-heartedly scudded past above them while he searched for the right words.

"You are home, *Madame* Galante, in less than a week, just as I promised." He averted his eyes and leaned over the side to study the sparkling aqua depths for signs of the heavy anchor chain dragging in the white sand below. "I wish you luck with the harvest."

When he straightened and turned back to her, she caught him off-guard. Dropping the tree branch, she wrapped her arms around his neck and planted a quick kiss on his cheek. His arms closed around her as if of their own accord, and he pulled her to him.

"Marie, please come back with me and let us protect you." He buried his face in the depths of her soft, curling hair and brushed the tender part of her ear with his mouth when he whispered his entreaty.

"I will be fine," she said, and jerked away, pulling her bag over her shoulder. "Courbet hungers for control, but he'd be a fool to take over a plantation with so few workers instead of getting his money back." She straightened and headed for the small boat where Francois waited. "And besides, I can go to the governor on Martinique if he refuses to honor payment of my husband's debts. My son-in-law is the fort commandant, and he would plead my cause."

Jean grasped her shoulders and held her in front of him at arm's length. "God speed, Marie Galante. I owe you my men's lives. If there is anything I can do to repay this great debt, you must get word to me. And I will be here."

"I am a healer," she said simply. "It is my calling to relieve suffering. But you still don't know who poisoned your men."

Her accusation turned like a knife in his gut. "Perhaps they know we're on to them and will be afraid to try to poison the men again."

The doubting look she gave him expressed more than words. Turning abruptly, she moved to the side of the ship.

Jean watched as Francois swung her down from the deck into the shore boat and continued watching as they rowed quickly to the beach in the cove where a number of her workers waited to welcome her.

The sour old harpy, *Tante* Luz, stood in front, tears streaming down her face. She had expected her mistress to be abused while in his care. Guilt pricked at his conscience when he saw how frightened island folk were of him.

When Francois returned, Jean motioned to his first mate to follow him down to his cabin.

Once inside, Jean sat down hard onto one of the chairs at the chart table and stretched out his long legs.

He lifted his head to gaze directly at Francois. "We must make plans," Jean said. "I can't let her face this harvest alone."

Marie allowed *Tante* Luz to enfold her in a long hug before breaking the embrace to drop her bag to the sand and brush the tears from the cheeks of her old friend.

"What happened?" Luz asked, her voice sharp, and pointed to the tree branch Marie still used to keep her weight off her slowly healing ankle.

She waved away her housekeeper's frantic question and said, "Come, Luz. Let's put this behind us and get to work."

"Come here, my pet. Let me rub your shoulders," Cecile murmured in almost a purr to the man glowering at her cottage door.

"None of your lies today," Courbet said, and stepped past, roughly pushing her out of the way. He stalked across the cramped living area and sprawled onto the bench, shoving her away with his foot when she tried to approach.

"You can't do anything right. Jean is still in charge of his band of smugglers, and even though you tried to kill her, that French *putain*, Marie, still lives."

"*Moi*? I don't know what you're talking about."

"You heard me – I know what you've been doing." He took a deep draught from the cup of rum she'd pushed into his hand, and then continued, "I don't know why I take you and Francois into my confidence."

Cecile knelt at his feet and covered his hand with her own. "Sometimes, *mon cher*, you make things too hard on yourself. With all Marie's dead husband owed you, the land should be yours if anything happens to her. And," she continued, "with her gone from dis island, we can finish poisoning Jean's men without anyone to treat dem. Den, Francois can take over the smuggling."

"Ah, sweet Cecile," he said, and crushed her hand tightly between his until she moaned in pain. "All you had to do was follow my instructions. Exactly. You cannot possibly know my plans. We need to destroy Jean totally. And Marie's plantation is the last piece in the game. Then I will be the largest planter in the islands. I can control prices, but not without respectability. Marie will provide that."

"What piece is Jean in your game?"

"He has the power to destroy everything," Courbet said, with a deep sigh.

"And Marie?" Cecile asked sharply, hatred boiling in her heart.

"How did you think this would end?" he asked with a bark of incredulity.

"Francois and I are the only family you have," Cecile insisted. "We belong at your side."

He stood suddenly. An ugly laugh erupted from deep inside him, and he pulled her to the tiny back room of the cottage.

Cecile's heart began to turn, even as it broke.

Marie's arms felt as if they were being pulled from their sockets. One day blurred into the next while she stubbornly continued the harvest of the cane. A week after she'd bid Jean farewell, she could not believe the progress her small rag-tag band of workers had accomplished. Each night, she collapsed into bed with a rush of hopelessness. But each morning she would discover they'd accomplished far more than she would have thought the night before.

A hesitant hand touched her arm, and she whirled to discover Luz's grandson, Yancey, patiently waiting to lift the water jug for her. *Mon dieu*, she had been daydreaming – staring at nothing while everyone else did their share. Before she could take a sip, a cloud of chattering sugar birds flushed from a nearby tangle of brush exposed their yellow bellies to the morning sun.

Courbet had actually helped the harvest along when he had his men burn her fields to terrorize her and demoralize her remaining workers. She smiled at the thought of outwitting him in one small way. The fire burned away all the dry, dead leaves, leaving the water-rich stalks and roots unharmed.

Courbet didn't realize she'd spent many hours riding with her father across the plantation during harvest. He'd been a hands-on planter, and had explained the process to Marie.

Marie and her small, loyal band had been using machetes all week to cut the standing cane just above the ground. Several of the men took turns shoving the freshly cut cane through the huge stone rollers turned by oxen.

Marie had spent an entire day with her workers and had questioned them endlessly to add to what she already knew about harvesting the cane.

A stone channel moved the cane liquid away from the press, to ovens where the juice cooked down and drained to an evaporator outside. The cooling mixture eventually dried to crystals. The end product was loaded onto oxen-drawn wagons and delivered to St. Marais to be taken by ship to refineries in France.

A small, polite cough interrupted her thoughts.

"You should drink some water, *Madame*. *Grand-mere* sent me to make sure you stop to rest." Yancey held out the huge pitcher, his arm shaking under the weight.

Marie knelt quickly and took the water from him, pouring a glass of the cooling liquid. She fondly ruffled his hair and gazed into his light, hazel eyes. "And what is your *grand-mere* preparing for lunch today?"

"Coconut soup with fried plantains," he said, and leapt to his feet. "I get to help."

As Marie watched the child skip away, a single tear slipped down her cheek. She hated the plantation life into which she'd been born, but she'd never had the courage to insist on change. Poor Yancey was a victim of that life. *Tante* Luz's daughter had made the mistake of attracting the attention of Marie's late husband. She'd died giving birth to Yancey.

This was the last year the cane could be harvested before a new planting. If only she and her small band could glean enough to pay off her husband's gambling debt with some extra to give the remaining slaves a portion to begin new lives. Her sons would be returning from their studies in France at the end of the year. The land would still be theirs, and they could do as they wished. She would sell her mother's jewelry and buy passage back to France, where her aunts would welcome her into their households.

As evening fell, Marie shaded her eyes under her broad-brimmed straw hat and surveyed the work accomplished that day. Even though her old linen work dress was drenched with sweat and clung to her after a day of backbreaking chopping, more than half the cane in her southern-most field still stood. She'd already sent the workers back to Galante house for a late supper.

A cloud of despair enveloped her like a swamp as Luz moved silently from the path and wrapped her in her arms. Together, they turned to watch the sun settling low over the island. Marie breathed deeply of the salt air, grateful for the freshening breeze.

An upstart parrot swooped down to a nearby branch and berated her in raucous squawks. In the heavy silence following the outburst, Marie's senses went on full alert.

"Luz," Marie whispered with a hiss, and stuck out her arm to halt her friend's progress toward the jungle path to the house.

"What?"

"Shhhhh — listen."

"For what?" Luz repeated.

"Something is out there."

"Of course," Luz said, with a snort. "Spirits always wander in the dark."

Marie shook her head with an indulgent smile and motioned to her old friend to follow her home.

When darkness fell over the field, a pile of brush near the worn path moved imperceptibly, and a creature with a blackened face moved out into the field.

Jean stood and stretched his sore muscles while reaching for a machete hidden in the wagon one of his men rolled forward. They gave each other weary looks before moving toward the remaining cane.

Jules was a newcomer to his band of smugglers who had escaped from a plantation on Guadeloupe the week before. The elderly man had appealed to Jean to take him on but was reluctant to cut cane again. He changed his mind when Jean offered to pay him a share of the smugglers' pot if he helped harvest Marie's crop.

For weeks, Jean had been laboring every night after Marie's workers left the fields. He sailed back to Dominica every few days to check on his men and exchange cane cutters. Many of Marie's workers suspected his presence, and even Yancey sneaked out at night to bring him water. Marie, however, stubbornly clung to the hope that along with her remaining loyal workers she could manage a miracle and harvest the cane before she had to pay off the debt.

He began to question his own sanity after the first week. Why he continued to return each night he couldn't say, except for his shameful nightly excursions to Marie's bedroom, just before dawn. All he needed to continue was another glimpse of Marie curled around her pillow like a kitten one small foot rubbing the other. Her thin muslin nightgown twisted around her legs each night from her restless dreams, but she slept the deep sleep of an angel. Maybe tonight he would steal a kiss. Maybe.

She wouldn't wake; it would cost her nothing, and with any luck, she wouldn't remember when Luz came to get her at first light. His rambling thoughts had brought him to the back entrance to Galante House before he had a chance to talk himself out of what his treacherous heart wanted.

Marie struggled to shake the fuzziness out of her head when she surfaced from the clutches of a nightmare. A soft step in the hallway brought her fully awake. She slid out of bed, palming the knife she kept on the floor, and lit a small candle by the bed.

She crouched in the shadows by the hinged side of the door in readiness to lunge at the intruder. When the door opened slowly, a familiar head appeared. She quietly laid the knife on a small table and then jerked Jean into the room by his arm. He grabbed her tightly by her other hand and slammed her into his chest.

"What are you doing sneaking around in the middle of the night?" he demanded.

"What am I doing?" she managed with a sputter. "This is my house. I get to ask the questions here. I could have slit your worthless throat," she added, and pushed hard against his chest. "Why haven't you let me go?"

"Because I don't want to." Jean spun her around easily and kissed her chin before working his way down her throat. When she tried to push him away, he tightened his embrace.

She couldn't breathe for a moment, and fought the urge to let go and sink into him.

"You're the 'spirit man' who's been helping us every night. Aren't you?" She tipped her head back and glared at him.

"And what if I am?" he challenged her.

"My battle with Courbet is my own," she said stubbornly. "You should stay out of it. He is a dangerous man to have for an enemy."

Jean released her suddenly and began to chuckle. "So you think you're the only reason Courbet hates me?"

"Don't mock me. I'm warning you."

Jean wandered over to a small table holding a bowl of water and a cake of soap. He bent to splash the cool liquid on his face and then began washing away the dirt of the field. After drying with a small cloth towel, he settled himself on her bed.

"What are you doing?" Marie asked and plucked at her night shift. "Don't get comfortable. You're leaving soon."

Jean stared at her and rubbed at his hair where the water had splashed. She approached cautiously, skirting the edge of the bed and the reach of his arms. She misjudged the latter and found herself pulled onto his lap.

"Now, now, my fine Puss. I think I liked you better sound asleep." He took her hands into his and began to kiss each finger. "I may have to cut these claws for my own protection."

"You – you've been taking advantage of me while I slept," she said with a gasp, snatching her hands out of his grip.

"I've never taken anything you'd miss," he assured her with an impudent grin and smoothed the still wet cloth over the black smudges on her face and neck where he'd touched her.

With his hands occupied, she slithered out of his grasp and escaped to a corner of the room.

"You have to go back to Dominica before Courbet discovers you've been helping me."

"Now that my magic is no longer hidden, you and I can continue the cane harvest together."

"But, but what will people think?" she asked.

"They'll think I am a fool, and you are a very lucky woman," Jean said. He wet his fingers then and pinched out the flame on the candle next to her bed.

"What about Courbet?" Marie insisted, her voice sounding childish and petulant even to herself. The silence felt heavy and profound in the warm tropical darkness while she waited for Jean's answer.

The mattress creaked with the weight of his body sinking into her bed before his reply floated across the room — "He'll just have to find his own woman."

Against her better judgment, she padded across the room and gave an exasperated sigh before lying down beside him. Although her breasts were heavy with aching and need, his breathing already had the deep, measured sound of a man dead asleep.

Marie jerked upright, her heart pounding, to morning light streaming through her bedroom window. Luz would catch her. She squinted at the far side of the bed. She was alone.

Wrapping her arms tightly across her breasts, she fumed at the thought of yet another chaste night in the same bed with that maddening man.

CHAPTER THIRTEEN

Luz knocked and then pushed open Marie's door, balancing a tray with coffee and biscuits. Marie could swear a fleeting, sly smile crossed her old friend's face as she set the tray on the table next to the bed.

"I trust you slept well," Luz said, glancing at the mussed sheets.

"Quit pretending to be so innocent," Marie said. "He's gone." She picked up a biscuit and dabbed some mango jam on the warm crust. "You've known he's been here all along," she added, and flashed an accusatory look at the older woman. "I'm curious, though. When did you stop hating the 'devil man' and start being part of his underhanded plans?"

Luz opened her mouth as if to protest, but Marie stuck her hand out to forestall any excuses. "You betrayed me in my own house. Explain."

Luz pulled a chair to the side of the bed and settled in, smoothing her apron and picking at a small piece of lint on her skirt.

"Marie, you and me, we been together a long time. I was with your mother, helped when you were born. When your sweet mama died, I raised you like my own. Your papa meant well, but he didn't know the kind of man he gave you to as wife. Dat was the saddest day at Galante House when he came."

Marie leaned over and rested her hand on Luz's arm. "I know you've suffered for his sins, and I'm so sorry. If only…"

Luz laid her hand over Marie's and interrupted. "What happened was not your fault. I gave Leia too much freedom, and…" Luz stopped and rubbed away a tear rolling down her cheek.

"Let's not talk about him," Marie said. "He was a careless, hateful man, but now he's gone, leaving us to clean up after his mistakes." Marie finished her biscuit and took several gulps of coffee before replacing the cup and squeezing Luz's hand.

"Tell me where Jean and his men stopped last night. Which field do we start with today?" Marie gazed steadily into Luz's eyes, daring her to deny she knew Jean had been secretly helping them at night with the harvest.

"You should ask him," Luz shot back with a smile. "He's downstairs pretending he didn't spend last night under those sheets."

≈

Jean leaned on his elbows at the worn wooden table in the outdoor kitchen, watching two parrots squabble over a chunk of bread he'd set out. Dawn was beginning to brush the horizon with a narrow, pink stroke.

He'd sent Jules to the far south field to cut cane with Marie's other workers. Jean was resigned to face her wrath before joining them. He felt like the dark waves rolling out in from the ocean only to crash against the headland. His life was just as tangled around Marie's, like seawater drenching the rocks.

One of the plantation roosters crowed and covered the sound of Marie's footsteps as she came up behind him to rub his shoulders. When he turned his head, she smiled and took his hand, pulling him to the path to the fields.

After a few steps, she stopped to raise her arms and tie back her long, dark curls with a cloth. "You know you are a very naughty boy to watch an old woman while she sleeps," she said with a teasing lilt.

"I'll show you a naughty boy," Jean said. He pulled her to him, and she yielded, opening her mouth for a lingering kiss. His tongue explored her soft heat and his lips feathered kisses across her face.

He made a vow when she broke away and walked toward Luz's group of workers. That night, he would not let exhaustion claim him before he tasted more of Marie's sweet body.

When the sun climbed higher and hammered down on the field, Marie hitched up her skirt between her legs and tied the excess with a piece of rope. Her old straw hat felt like an oven perched on her head, but she couldn't give up the shade of the wide, floppy brim.

The midday heat finally drove all thought from her head except the next stalk of cane. She was ashamed of how little she accomplished in each row compared with the rest of the workers, but she reasoned her meager attempts at cutting cane were the least she could do to let her remaining people know she was determined to prevail. She'd even given up sneaking furtive looks at Jean at the far side of the field.

He'd stripped off his shirt, his tanned back slick with sweat. He and one of his men slashed their way through row after row as if the stubborn cane were no more than mounds of butter.

She looked up at a shout from Luz and gratefully walked to the shade of the foliage at the edge of the field.

"Why you stay out there in the sun so long?" Luz asked, furiously fanning her own flushed face. "Your skin goin' look like leather before long." A sly smile crept onto her face as she added, "Then that fine man won't want to stay and work his self to death for you."

Marie swatted at Luz in mock censure but couldn't help laughing. "I'm sure he has some deeper reason for staying on."

"Uh-huh."

"What?" Marie demanded.

Luz just rolled her eyes as they made their way to the kitchen outside Galante House to bring back the noon meal of plantains and cassava cakes.

CHAPTER FOURTEEN

Shadows had inched across the field when Jean stopped for a moment to take a deep swig from his water jug. He surveyed what his small band of cane cutters had harvested that day.

Only one row remained, but the workers' heads were bowed in fatigue, Marie continued her stubborn hacking of the cane. Her dress was soaked with sweat, and the fabric clung to her breasts. In spite of his own exhaustion, he vowed he would stay awake that night, and so would she, even if he had to force *cafe'* down her throat.

Neither the backbreaking cane cutting nor the heat of the searing sun could erase the memory of her body pressed close. If he had to spend another restless night craving Marie, he would go mad.

"What do you want me to do now, Captain?" His crew member, Jules, stopped next to him and swiped at the sweat pooling on his face as he awaited an answer.

"We're done for today. Come back to Galante House for some food, and then find a place to sleep tonight in one of the empty cabins down by the cove. The breezes will be cooler there."

"We're not staying in the brush tonight?"

Jean swung around, irritated, only to see a broad smile on the man's face. "No, we're not," he replied firmly, and tossed the scythe into one of the wagons on his way up the path to Galante House.

⸎

Tante Luz and the other women who helped prepare food for the next day carefully ignored Jean as he strode through the outdoor kitchen. No one stopped him when he pushed through the back entrance of the plantation house and shed his dust-covered boots.

On the way up the polished, mahogany staircase, he rehearsed what he wanted to say to Marie. She needed his help and protection. She needed him in her bed. He hadn't quite worked out the last part, but he was convinced she wanted him too. In any event, he would never leave her to face Courbet's wrath alone.

He knocked hesitantly on the entry to her bedroom, then pounded when there was no answer. The door opened a small crack, then widened as Marie pushed her head outside.

"Oh, it's you," she said, face flushed, a sheet clutched around her. She jerked him inside by his shirt and slammed the door shut before padding back toward a tin tub in the corner, trailing wet footprints. When Marie reached the side of the tub, she carelessly tossed the sheet to the floor and lowered herself into the tub with a groan.

Jean's heart pounded so hard, he was afraid it would climb out of his chest. All he could think of was the first time he'd seen this confounded woman emerging from the surf like a mermaid.

Her back to him, she slid further down into the scented water. Satisfied little sounds came from deep in her throat.

"Hmmm – humph"

"Is that all you have to say?" Jean demanded, anger bubbling in his voice.

"Hmmm? I would offer to share the tub, but I don't want to. This feels too good. Get your own." She reached for a sponge and soap on a small table nearby.

His control snapped at the sight of water sluicing down her back. When she leaned out of the tub, one pink-budded breast dripped water while she stretched further to grasp a small brush on the far side of the table.

Just when he thought he'd lost the ability to breathe, there was a small scratching at the door. He paced back across the room and opened it a crack.

"What?"

Luz stood outside, two men behind her with another tub full of water. "Dat woman, she won't share," she said.

Jean opened his mouth to protest, but they shoved past him and dragged the tub inside, leaving before he had a chance to complain. Shame burned at him from the inside out. How could he ever face her servants again?

Marie turned at the commotion and stared at him for a moment. "Well? Aren't you going to strip off those filthy clothes and get in the tub?"

"I can't." Jean's courage failed him. Ironic for a man so fearless in daring raids against British and French garrisons.

"Of course you can." She turned her head and gave him an assessing look. "My husband's clothes will fit you – maybe they'll be too loose, but they'll do."

"No, you misunderstand," Jean said. "I can't let you do this. You'll be shunned by the other planters. What will they think? We're on your home island now."

"Wait. Aren't you the one who said people would think I'm a lucky woman?" When he continued to stand, moving from one foot to the other, she added, "*Mon Dieu*, we've already shared the same bed, and you've been living here for days. My reputation is in tatters. Don't you think we should at least enjoy ourselves?"

He stared silently at Marie and with slow movements pulled off his breeches and shirt before easing into the soothing water. For a moment the pleasure was so great, he thought he might never move again. But when Marie rose from her tub on the other side of the room to come to him, he lost his ability to reason. All blood abandoned his brain when she climbed from the bath and walked across the floor to stand before him, water dripping from the warm pink curves of her body. With sponge and soap, she knelt behind him and began to scrub his back.

"Don't," he pleaded, and reached for one of her hands.

"Let me wash you," she insisted gently. "If it weren't for you and your men, we would never be able to harvest enough cane to pay off the debt."

"I'm not the man you think I am. How do you know I won't take everything from you?"

"I know all I need to know about you, Jean Blanchard."

"But…"

"Shhhhh." She quieted his protests by brushing his lips with her fingertips. "Tonight, you are the captain of my heart, and I am the keeper of your soul. Nothing bad can happen while we are together within these walls."

In a sudden movement, Jean reached behind him with one strong arm and pulled her to the side of the tub. Half-raising himself from the soapy depths, he grasped the back of her head and brought her close for a kiss. He slowly explored the depths of her mouth with his tongue, urging her along on a dizzying descent into pleasure.

He pulled her closer as he stepped from the tub, feeling the soft pressure of her breasts on his chest. She clung to him and wrapped her legs around his waist. Water dripped from their bodies and pooled onto the polished floor.

"Tante Luz will never forgive us," Marie said with an impish grin. She pointed at the puddle of soapy water at his feet.

"No, Marie. That conniving woman has been pushing us together ever since I got here. Now that she finally has her way, I think she'll be happy to overlook a little water on the floor."

"But nobody knew you were here."

"Everyone but you."

"But…"

"It doesn't matter," Jean whispered with a smile against her lips as he lowered her down his body.

She slid against his erection, encasing him in her warmth. He let out his breath with a groan and pulled her the last few steps toward the bed where he lowered her gently and wrapped her in a cool sheet. He knelt at the side of the bed while Marie scrabbled back, reaching for her night shift.

She let out a small squeak of surprise when he suddenly grasped her ankles and pulled her back to the side of the bed. When he began kissing the tender skin inside her thighs, her whole body stiffened, and she tried to sit up.

"Non, ma petite," Jean said, his voice a soothing rumble against her body. "Tonight I am going to pleasure you slowly and thoroughly, and as long as we share a bed, you will not need this." Snatching her shift lying on the bed, he tossed it to a far corner of the room.

"A trifling piece of cloth could never keep me from possessing you."

Marie stopped struggling and relaxed with a sigh. Her senses must have gone to mush in the long soak she'd allowed her aching muscles. She didn't have the strength, or will, to deny Jean whatever he chose to do.

She didn't care about the consequences. This headstrong woman she'd become was not the obedient daughter who had always been ruled, first by her father, and then her faithless husband.

The closer Jean pulled her to his mouth, the more she sank into pure sensation. Her bones melted into the featherbed while he assaulted her senses with the swirl of his tongue. At his insistent thrust, her pleasure was so fierce, she stiffened her body and tried to pull away.

"Shhhh," Jean insisted, and grasped her hips, positioning her closer. A sudden wave of need shocked Marie into silence, and she shuddered at the intensity of feeling flowing through her.

He moved onto the bed, pulling her toward the soft pillows beneath the mosquito netting. His warm breath tickled at the sensitive skin behind her ear while he feathered soft kisses up her neck.

Jean stopped for a moment to whisper, "I knew from the moment I saw you emerge from the sea. I knew how you would taste." He pulled her body beneath him and covered her.

Heat suffused her flushed face, and Marie was grateful for the darkness and a cool breeze freshening off the ocean. She enfolded him in her arms and pressed into him, pleasure pulsing with every breath. He suddenly rolled over, taking her with him.

"What?" Marie demanded, annoyed at the pleading tone of her voice.

"You are too beautiful a feast to gorge upon and then hurry from the table."

"You make me sound like poached fish," Marie complained.

"I am decided. I will not rush," he said.

"But…"

Jean leaned over, put two fingers to her lips to quiet her, and then began to stroke her thighs with feather light touches of his calloused hands. He moved on to her breasts, slowly bringing each small bud of a nipple to attention before suckling the perfect mounds.

While Marie writhed and bucked under the gentle teasing of his mouth, all she could think was this was nothing like the duty of the marriage bed she'd suffered through for many, long years.

Jean leaned back on his elbows at the foot of the bed and stared at her, his cock distended and swollen. She sat up and reached for him with her hands.

"*Non*, not yet," he insisted in a hoarse voice, pushing her back. He crawled slowly toward her, bringing his face so close, she could feel the heat of his breath. After taking her mouth in a long, probing kiss, he moved back to the apex of her thighs and slid a finger into her heat.

Her face flamed and she jerked away. She could almost hear the slickness of her moisture when he withdrew. He laid his hand on her stomach.

"What do you wish of me, Marie?" he asked, his body warm and heavy against her.

"How do you expect me to choose?" she demanded, pressing closer to him with a small moan. "You have taken over my mind as well as my body."

"I am yours to command," he insisted, and pushed away from her embrace. "Tell me what you want."

"Please. I want you to love me. That's all. Don't make me beg."

He moved quickly back down the bed, snatched an extra pillow and cradled the soft underside of her thighs. He separated her legs with his knee and then thrust slowly into her.

Marie took a sharp intake of breath as he withdrew slightly then slid back into the deepest part of her soul. Tears leaked out the side of her eyes and flowed down her cheeks. She'd never been loved so thoroughly, never had such feelings flood through her. She might as well have been a virgin. And then thoughts abandoned her when an intense stab of pleasure overwhelmed her senses.

She clung to him and tried to imprint her body with the sound of his rough breathing, the touch of his calloused hands, the scent of the bottomless need drenching both of them.

She moved with him as if in a race and then they both fell over an edge from which she knew she could never return.

The sound of Jean's ragged breathing brought her back to the bed they shared and the reality of what existed outside the walls of her room. The reality she would have to return to soon.

He withdrew and moved rapidly away from her, off the bed, and then just as abruptly returned to enclose her in his arms and explore her mouth again.

Marie reached up to touch his lips, confused. "Why did you leave?" she asked with a pout.

He sat up, taking her with him, and held her at arm's length. "Surely you wouldn't want the child of a thief," he said, softening his harsh words with a boyish grin.

"Maybe you don't know what I want," Marie answered.

"I know what you wanted a few minutes ago," he replied, and ducked to avoid a swat from the back of her hand. He grasped her mid-swing and pulled her back to the bank of pillows.

Hours later he gave her bruised lips one last kiss before they both sank into a deep, dreamless sleep.

Marie awoke slowly, stretching her sore limbs, and then looked toward the other side of the bed. Jean was gone. Her heart thudded hard for a moment before she reasoned he'd probably left early to finish the last part of the field from the day before.

A clean muslin work dress lay across the bench at the foot of her bed as well as a pot of coffee and plate of biscuits sat on a tray. Luz must have come and gone already.

She slipped out of bed and jerked the well-mended dress over her head before taking her breakfast to a small table at the window. She shook her head and noted Luz had provided two cups. She poured one for herself, and in the midst of savoring the first hot sip, there was a sharp knock.

Marie opened the door to a frazzled Luz.

Without explanation, she barged into the room and demanded, "Where is dat man?"

"What man?" Marie asked, backing away from the doorway. She gave her tiny, energetic housekeeper a smug smile.

Luz straightened her small stature to full height. "How many men you got in here?"

Marie giggled and leaned close to her housekeeper's ear. "I think there may have been one or two in here last night," she confided in a loud whisper.

Luz sobered again. "Well, where is that smuggler captain now?"

A sudden wind battered at the bedroom shutters, and a chill crept up Marie's back. She put her hand on her friend's shoulder and insisted, "Something's wrong, isn't it?" When Luz didn't answer, the chill turned to fear, and she raised her voice in anger. "Tell me. What's happened?"

"His man, he come to eat and asked me where Jean goin' to." Luz dropped her eyes from Marie's questioning look.

Marie's gaze hardened. "Of course, he's gotten what he wanted. Now he doesn't need to help me anymore. *Mon Dieu*, but the lengths he went to..." She stopped herself at the stricken look on Luz's face.

"Then why'd he leave his man here?"

"He was probably in a hurry to put distance between us. After all, what does a young man want with an old woman?" Marie sank down onto the bench with a sigh and hid her face in her hands. "I can just hear him bragging to his men about me."

"Stop," Luz said, pulling Marie's hands from her face. "You're wrong. If he left, he had a good reason."

"And what would that be?" Marie asked.

"You just wait, you. You'll see," Luz said, muttering to herself as she backed out of the room with an armload of linens.

Marie refused to give credence to Luz's excuses for Jean and his betrayal. Feeling used, she sat with her head in her hands while a fierce rain rattled against the shutters.

CHAPTER FIFTEEN

Jean awoke with a start. His arms and legs ached from the chains and shackles pinning him to the damp, dark cell walls of Martinique's French prison in St. Pierre. He might have been able to gauge how long he'd been there by the height of the sun in the sky if it weren't for the deluge outside the small barred window.

Angry breakers rolled in on the nearby shore, their crashes obliterating even the harsh pounding of the late season storm.

Gradually, he sorted out the pain and discovered the lump on the back of his head won the battle for the most thought-numbing intensity. The knock he received from an unknown assailant when he left Marie's bed early that morning had blotted out what little memory he had of the sudden attack.

The thought of Marie unprotected on her small island forced him to remain awake and clear his head. He had to come up with a plan and soon. He'd escaped the French so many times in the past, they would make him suffer. He had no doubt a firing squad, or hanging, loomed in his future. He'd heard about the St. Pierre jail but this was his first unfortunate inspection from the inside.

The most horrifying part of this particular cell was its single crude opening. The bar-covered window faced the ocean, with freedom tantalizingly close but completely out of reach. Once the accursed storm subsided, his heart would break when he glimpsed the bright blue sky and sun drenched green waters.

He sagged against his bonds and fought despair. As his eyes adjusted to the darkness, he began to look for something, anything he could use to pry his way out. His gaze seized upon a pile of rags in a corner of the small cell. God knew what he would do with them if he could extricate himself from his shackles, but the exercise of thinking kept him from losing his grip on sanity.

Suddenly, the rags moved and a faint sound emerged from the filthy pile.

"Qui etes vous?"

After starting softly, the voice boomed surprisingly strong for a bundle of tattered cloth.

"Je suis Jean Blanchard," Jean replied indignantly. *"Qui etes* vous*?"*

The pile shuffled closer and formed into a small man whose feet were shackled together instead of being chained to the wall like Jean's.

"So, you're the great Jean Blanchard," the wizened creature spat out. "How come you to be brought so low?" He leaned against the stone wall and then slid down and squatted in front of Jean.

"Your name first, sir," Jean insisted.

"My name means nothing anymore, but you can call me Abelard." He continued as though Jean had not interrupted. "They say you take escaped slaves into your band of smugglers. Treat them fine, like they're one of you."

"How long have you been here?" Jean stared curiously at the wizened man.

"Long enough. I stay low, out of the guards' way." His cellmate shifted slightly and re-adjusted his cuffed ankles, scuttling sideways, like a crab on the sand evading predators. "But I hear things."

"What plantation did you escape from, and why haven't they claimed you?"

"Courbet…"

That one word invoked so much for Jean. "And he's leaving you here to rot." It was not so much a question as a statement.

The old man smiled, revealing the few teeth left in his mouth. His arm also hung limply at his side from an old break that probably had never been set.

"Better I rot here than die slowly in great pain there."

"Do you remember Francois and Cecile?" Jean asked, to keep him talking as much as to stay awake. "They're my first mate and cook. They escaped from Courbet's place and came to work for me."

"She's his woman, and Francois..." The small rag pile of a man hesitated for a moment. "Everyone knows. Francois is his son."

"Courbet's son?" Jean said, stunned. He sat down hard and swallowed against the bile rising in his chest. He'd been duped from the beginning. And his sister... He'd seen the attraction growing between her and Francois, and yet he'd done nothing to protect her. He'd held his counsel against his first mate. He'd let concern for his sister's happiness sway him. Elisabeth deserved a love of her own.

Now there was nothing he could do but strain against his shackles and curse.

⁘

Marie hacked at the cane in the new field with all the fury she felt toward Jean. The depth of her fury grew with each succeeding whack. The longer she didn't hear from him, the more her imagination painted scenes of how he indulged himself while she pounded away at the cane with a heavy scythe.

Even though she fell into her bed each night exhausted, muscles aching more each day than she thought possible, her dreams betrayed her with visions of the soulless Jean. He came to her with the same endearments and tender touches he'd plied her with that night, only to have him disappear the next morning.

She gave Luz warning glares whenever she thought her housekeeper was about to launch into another defense of that black-heart. No wonder everyone thought he was a devil. Why hadn't she taken heed when she had the chance?

One week had passed since the night of the "great betrayal," as she'd come to think of what had passed between them. Only Jules of Jean's men remained to help in the Galante fields. No one seemed to know what had happened to Jean, and the other smugglers had gone back to Dominica when he didn't return.

Her daily ritual of bathing in the ocean had fallen by the wayside in lieu of an extra hour of sleep in the morning. *Mon Dieu,* but she could not get enough sleep.

Marie brushed away a thread hanging off her old muslin dress as she and Luz walked toward the far field they'd been working for days. Already, the intense sun filtered through the heavy canopy of greenery above them along the path. A small bird, bright with green and yellow feathers, swooped onto the path in front of them and refused to be budged.

"On, you. Go, before we pick you up and throw you in a pot for our next meal," Luz shrieked at the small, winged fellow. His only response was to cock his small head in interest at the outburst.

"Luz, Luz. Don't frighten him. It's not his fault our lives are so hard." When Luz gave her an annoyed look, she added, "All right, then. Shall I run back and get an ax?"

They glared at each other before Luz was the first to collapse in laughter. Marie joined her, and they both sat on a rock and giggled until their small nemesis flew away.

They stood again and stoically headed toward the field, arms clasped around each other.

"Why do you think Jean abandoned us?" Marie finally broke the companionable silence. "Was it my fault?"

"Why do you ask such a question?" Luz turned and put her finger beneath Marie's chin, gazing into her eyes. "Dat man loves you. If he had to leave in a hurry, den he had a good reason. Don't give up on him."

"If he loves me, then where is he?"

Moisture pooled on Marie's back in the stillness following the morning storm. Luz supervised a small band of children who relayed buckets of water from the well to the field. Marie dipped a cup from one of the buckets, and looked up at the sound of Luz's grandson Yancey shouting for her.

He stopped in front of her and hopped from one foot to the other and gasped. "*Madame* Darroc. She come to visit. She's pretty mad dere's no one but me to answer the door."

Marie leaned on her scythe, resigned. She would have to deal with the island's worst gossip or there would be hellish consequences. "You didn't tell her we were all down here cutting cane, did you?" She raised an eyebrow at the small boy, the question hanging between them.

"No," he assured her, a slow grin spreading across his face. "I told her you had a headache and were still asleep."

Marie bent over and hugged the small urchin while his grandmother frowned.

"Yancey, you saved me," Marie said. "Now run back and tell her I'll be there in a few minutes."

As he passed Luz, she bent over and swatted his backside before he tore back up the path. Marie kicked off the clogs she wore in the field and ran through the brush out to the sand along the shore. She picked up speed as she looped back around away from the front drive of Galante House.

Once she gained the backside of the house, she found a toehold in the vines climbing toward her bedroom window and scrambled up the two stories. After slipping in through the window where she always left the shutters open, she rushed to her closet to pick out the least confining dress she could find that would still pass *Madame* Darroc's inspection.

Marie had never been able to understand the way most planters' wives dressed in the islands. She'd returned to France only once when she was very young to visit her mother's sisters. Even though she kept several dresses of the latest fashion, she'd worn them only on the rare occasions her husband had seen fit to drag her along to social obligations. She always sought to have the dressmaker in St. Pierre sew her frocks in the lightest fabrics she could find.

She bypassed all underpinnings except a corset she could lace up the front, hastily attaching panniers under the skirt. With no time to bath her filthy feet, she jerked on stockings and garters before jamming her feet into soft leather slippers. A quick glance in the mirror next to the door as she rushed out to the landing revealed she would pass a cursory inspection, so long as she didn't stand with sunlight behind her.

Marie raced down the stairs, pausing only long enough on the bottom landing to compose herself before entering the drawing room. Even as she rounded the corner, she dreaded the reason for *Madame* Darroc's visit. Most of her neighbors had given up any pretense of social protocol after her husband's death. She was a pariah, especially after everyone on the island heard about her husband's huge gambling debt owed Courbet.

In fact, there had been considerable speculation that Marie should beg Courbet to marry her, to avoid upsetting the natural progression of island social mores. The few neighbors who knew her well were more inclined to see Marie giving up and returning to her mother's family in France.

At the last moment, she thought of her sun-flushed cheeks she couldn't hide from her nosy neighbor. There was nothing for it but to face the old gossip.

"Good morning," Marie said, and managed a cheerful smile. "Please accept my deepest apologies for keeping you waiting, but as you've probably heard, most of our workers chose to leave after my husband's death." She tried to hide her shaking hands by smoothing her skirts. "To what do I owe the great pleasure of your company?"

Madame Darroc's face always looked as though she'd sniffed something exceptionally bad. And now she was peering around the drawing room and beyond through the windows where the shutters were thrown wide.

"Are you looking for something?" Marie asked tentatively.

Her guest whirled mid-look and skewered her with a malevolent glare. "You go too far, Marie Galante."

Marie held her ground. "Of what am I accused?"

"You know. Respectable women should not have to discuss such things."

"I see." Marie stood silent for a moment, casting about for some excuse to end the senseless exchange. "Then I suppose I couldn't interest you in some refreshment?" Marie asked, and prayed for Luz to materialize. Her housekeeper's normally annoying habit of interfering would be a welcome interruption.

As if conjured, Luz appeared in the doorway, balancing a tray of floral-scented limewater and small cakes. Marie wanted to hug her old friend, but instead found her voice.

"Please sit, and tell me what troubles you."

"It's that smuggler and despoiler of women."

"I beg your pardon?"

"Don't be evasive. We all know what's been going on since your husband's death."

For a few moments, Marie toyed with the idea of revealing all that had happened to her in the past few weeks but dismissed the thought. Who would believe her?

"Jean Blanchard came to ask my help with a sickness claiming his men, and of course I could not refuse to treat them. He has been a perfect gentleman from the moment I met him."

"Then it's true you went willingly with him to Dominica without a chaperone?"

"Please. Do not exaggerate. I'm a widow and the mother of three grown children. Who could possibly object if I travel to another island to relieve pain and suffering?"

"*Monsieur* Courbet."

Marie blanched and busied herself pouring drinks while she digested the unexpected turn in the conversation. "What does *Monsieur* Courbet have to do with my affairs?" she asked carefully.

"Why, at least half of this plantation belongs to him now. He wants to do the right thing and provide you with a respectable way out of your husband's gambling debts."

She prattled on as if she didn't see Marie's warning glare. "Everyone on the island knows what's been going on here. The idea of you trying to bring in the cane with the worthless group of slaves left after you foolishly let the stronger men and women escape…"

"*Madame* Darroc," Marie interrupted. "I'm going to have to ask you to leave. You go too far. How I live is none of your business, or anyone else's, come to that."

The woman banged down her glass on the tray and stood. "Thank God *Monsieur* Courbet is a benevolent, forgiving man. He assured us now that Jean is in prison and out of your house, he would be happy to call on you and make arrangements to help you with your late husband's debt."

Marie's heart stuttered, and she struggled to hide her warring emotions. Jean was in prison. He hadn't abandoned her. That accursed Courbet had somehow waylaid him after he left her arms that night.

She pointed a finger at *Madame* Darroc. "You must leave. Now. Before I lose what patience I have left. You are not welcome here. Do not return."

"I will go," she said, "but do not think you can continue living in sin, taking criminals into your bed. You shame the good women of this island."

Marie breathed deeply, in and out, and then advanced on the woman whose face glowed bright red from her impassioned speech. The smug set to her lips changed when Marie moved steadily toward her, palm out. When she turned abruptly, Marie pushed hard on her back and *Madame* Darroc did a sort of dancing shuffle toward the hallway where Luz ushered her toward the front of the house.

After the door slammed behind Marie's neighbor, Luz returned and pointed toward the back of the house.

Marie ignored her gesture and vented her hatred of Courbet "That snake has gone too far. I am going to find him and force him to tell me where Jean is being held. I can't let that poor man rot in jail. He risked everything to help us." Her mind racing, she finally noticed Luz still frantically gesturing.

"What?" Marie asked, and finally looked where Luz pointed.

A tearful Elisabeth appeared behind her with Francois.

"Please, come in. Tell me what you know," Marie insisted and rushed to gather Jean's sister into her arms.

"Courbet had Jean ambushed and taken to the French prison in St. Pierre on Martinique." Elisabeth sucked in a breath and hiccupped. "They're going to kill him."

"When?" Marie gasped and her heart beat a wild tattoo as if she were swimming against a riptide. "What can we do?"

"I don't know. They've put him in a jail from which no one escapes, and Courbet is pressing the magistrate to execute him tomorrow."

Marie looked beyond Jean's distraught sister to Francois. "Is this true? There is nothing we can do? There has to be something."

He looked down, refusing to meet her gaze, and said, "I wish things were different, but no, there's nothing we can do."

Courbet was behind all of this, she was sure – why did he hate Jean so? Because of her, because he let his guard down to love her, he was going to die. She had to act.

Marie crossed to Francois and pressed her hand to his shoulder. "Did you sail here in Jean's ship?"

"Yes," he said, drawing his answer out with a question at the end.

"Then this is what we must do. I have a plan. It will be risky, but we have to try."

CHAPTER SIXTEEN

Back in his cell, Jean contemplated his short future. His mind raced as he went over all the ways he might escape. Those thoughts were futile, because he'd spent the past three days scouring every inch of his cell. The simple truth was, he was going to die. There was no way to evade justice.

His cellmate Abelard scrabbled toward him from a far corner. "So you've returned to our humble abode. How is my old friend, Judge Cabasson?"

Jean slanted him a look. "Your friend does very well. From the looks of him, he's not missed nearly as many fine meals as you have since you've been his guest."

"Did you find out why you're here?"

"From all the smuggling I've done over the years — stealing from the French, selling to the English, stealing from the English, selling to the French — they have plenty of reason to end my career." Jean scratched at the beard that had grown wild in the few days he'd been imprisoned. "Courbet was there to gloat, so I imagine he had something to do with my downfall."

"Why would he want you dead?"

"I suppose he wants to turn over my smuggling venture to his son, Francois. That has to be part of the plan."

Silence descended on the small cell as Jean considered all the reasons Courbet hated him. "Of course, there's Marie."

"Marie?" The small man sat up straighter on the dirt floor. "This Marie he wants — is she your woman?"

"He wants her plantation," Jean corrected him, "and she is my friend." Anger swelled in his chest at his inability to act.

"Any sane man would want her with or without her property, but for him, it's the land."

The more Jean considered all the possibilities, the more he wondered if there were something else he'd overlooked at the root of Courbet's crazed campaign. Some other obsession for getting rid of him.

He gave his cellmate a considering look. "How long did you work for that bastard?"

"Long enough to know Courbet has a lot to hide," Abelard said.

"My parents disappeared nineteen years ago, along with the title to their land," Jean said. We'd just traveled here from *Nouvelle Orléans*. My mother and father went to meet with a man to buy a plantation one night and never returned." Jean paced the short distance between the barred window and the back stone wall.

"What did you do?" his cellmate asked.

"What could I do? I had my little sister to think about. Revenge had to wait." Jean smashed his fist against the stones.

"You think Courbet was involved in your parents' disappearance?"

"What do you think?"

"He's certainly capable of all manner of horrible crimes."

While Jean's men set anchor in a hidden cove north of St. Pierre, Marie watched anxiously from the deck of the sleek ship. She hoped they weren't too late to make a difference, but she had to try. The sun was just peering up from the edge of the world, fiery pink and gold streaks heralding a new day.

Once they'd boarded Jean's ship at her island harbor, a stiff northerly breeze spanked from the stern so that they surfed most of the night, their sails full out for the seventy-mile run. With the fast passage, they'd arrived much earlier than she'd anticipated.

The crew used careful soundings in the pre-dawn shadows to hook the anchor onto the narrow shelf along the shore. After a few feet, there was a steep drop-off into the depths of the ocean.

As soon as the hull of the shore boat struck sand, they jumped onto the beach and followed the jungle path into town. Birds screeched overhead as they pounded up the dirt trail. Bright green lizards rousted from the surrounding jungle growth skittered across the path. Marie gave her boot a vigorous shake when one tried to run up her ankle.

After a two-hour walk, they stood in front of the French garrison. With ten of Jean's loyal men looking on, Marie walked up to the gate and rapped hard on the weathered wood. A young soldier peered through the tiny barred window opening.

"State your business," he demanded, "or step away from the gate." He seemed taken aback at the small woman standing in the street seeking entry.

"I am *Madame* Marie Galante, and I have business with your commandant."

"I doubt that. He wouldn't have business with the likes of you. He's married to a beautiful young woman." A second guard standing behind him laughed and added, "A very jealous young woman."

"Enough," Marie shouted, her patience wearing thin. "You must take me to him now. It is a matter of life and death."

"But his wife…"

"…is my daughter."

Just when she despaired of gaining entry, a tall man in impeccable dress uniform and shiny boots stormed toward them and opened the gate.

"Ah, Sergeant Larousse, thank God it is you," Marie said with a sigh. "These men do not remember me, and I must see my daughter."

With a questioning glance, he took in her disheveled dress, Elisabeth's anxious face, and the men accompanying them.

After a long pause, he said, "Yes, *Madame* Galante. I remember very well from when we met at the commandant's marriage to your charming daughter. A very pleasant afternoon." He paused for a moment, as if calculating his effect on her and then added, "I'm so sorry about your husband's death." He stepped through the heavy wooden opening and took her arm, guiding her forward with a gentle pressure on her elbow.

When his eyes strayed to Elisabeth, Marie made hasty introductions.

"Very well, the two of you may come in, but..." he said, with a stern look at Francois and Jean's men behind them. "The lot of you must wait outside the gate." He turned then toward the guards.

"You, Fournet, step lively. Tell Commandant Renaud and his lady they have welcome company." The younger guard took off at a trot into the fort courtyard.

"I must apologize," Larousse said, as he bent down and explained, his mouth uncomfortably close to her ear, "these are new recruits."

After scrutinizing her face again, the first soldier reluctantly stood aside while Larousse ushered her through the gate.

"And, if I were you, I would show a little more respect toward your commandant's mother-in-law," she added with a sniff when she sailed past him, nose in the air, giving her best imitation of *Madame* Darroc. Her composure faltered only when she saw the line of bullet holes in the courtyard wall and the dark brown stains below on the cobblestones.

⁘

Marie raised her face to the early morning wind lifting on the high bluff above the harbor. The ocean salt breezes cooled the sunbaked cobblestones of the inner courtyard of the garrison.

Larousse led her and Elisabeth toward a snug stone cottage inside the military enclave housing the French contingent of guards and cavalry. The men made Martinique their home to protect King Louis XV's interests in the lucrative Windward Islands sugar trade.

A childish shriek sounded, and her three-year-old grandson Maurice raced out of the cottage toward her. She bent low and opened her arms. He giggled and shouted when she swooped him up above her head.

Close behind him was his mother Rianne still in a morning dress, with a cap on her head. She smiled at Marie out of impossibly blue eyes. Tendrils of long golden hair escaped from the cap when she raced to keep up with her son.

Marie embraced her daughter, the child wriggling between them. They separated and stared for a long moment.

"What's wrong, *Maman*? Why are you here?" She put her arm around Marie and squeezed.

Marie turned to Jean's sister and urged her closer. "This is Elisabeth Blanchard, sister to the man in the garrison jail sentenced to die this morning."

"What could his fate have to do with you?" Rianne asked, her eyes wide.

"There is not much time to explain — we must see the magistrate before they put him to death."

"*Mon dieu.* What has he done?"

"He is a smuggler, but he is such a good man. He does not deserve to die."

"But why you? Why do you intercede on his behalf?"

Heat flooded from the roots of Marie's hair to her neck. She looked into her daughter's eyes and confessed. "I love him. Please help me save him."

Finally. Jean had a plan. Now, all he needed was for his men to smuggle something into the prison, the same way they spirited things away. However, he would be dead before he could get a message back to Dominica for his crew.

Just then, Francois and two of Jean's other men walked through the alley next to the jail. It was all he could do to keep from shouting at them. They pretended nonchalance and averted their eyes from the barred window where Jean pressed his face.

He couldn't imagine why they were there, but he didn't care. He would seize the opportunity like a dog tearing at a bone.

Behind him, Abelard stirred from sleep and pushed himself up from his pile of rags in the corner. With a questioning look, Jean held two fingers to his mouth and pointed to the window. The little man joined him at the lookout.

"Three of my men are on that corner," Jean whispered. "We have to get a message to them."

"Looks like they have plans of their own," Abelard whispered back.

In the next instant, the courtyard rocked from the force of an explosion. Both Jean and Abelard were thrown to the dirt floor, covering their heads with their hands while debris blew around. A drummer began beating a cadence, and guards poured from throughout the compound.

Jean picked himself up, brushing dust and plaster from his clothing. His cellmate hadn't moved but groaned a little.

He looked around, expecting to see a huge hole through one of the walls, but the blast had made barely a dent in the thick-walled jail. All the debris had blown in through the barred window.

He applauded his men's daring, but the effort had done little more than alert the garrison to their presence.

At that moment, the cell door burst open, and one of the guards jerked him through. "You've enjoyed our hospitality too long. Come with us."

"What happened?" Jean asked.

"You don't need to know," the second guard growled as each man seized one of his arms and dragged him out into the sunlight.

Whatever his men had intended with the blast, the misguided attempt had served only to anger the guards and probably hasten his demise. His arms felt as though they were being pulled from the sockets, but he still managed a wry chuckle while they dragged him through the garrison.

When they passed through the outer courtyard, a company of the garrison's marksmen sat cleaning their guns. One of them shouted at Jean, "We look forward to target practice with your head. This time tomorrow, thief, you will be a feast for the crabs."

So, Jean thought, they're going to make quick work of me. Probably much less painful than rotting away for months or years in a tiny cell, he consoled himself. When he raised his head to survey the instruments of his eventual destruction, one of the guards struck him on the back of his head, and he sank into darkness.

Marie cradled a cup of tea and stared into the steam while Rianne and her son-in-law, Henri, argued about her defense of Jean.

She tried to concentrate on the delicate china in her hands instead of the harsh condemnations erupting from two people she loved.

Rianne pleaded with her husband. "Henri, tell her. Tell her he is a vicious murderer and thief." Tears spilled from her daughter's eyes, and Marie's heart broke.

Henri took a long pause before replying. He searched the faces of the two women who pulled him in different directions.

"Actually, Rianne, I've sent a message to the judge. He has consented to hear Marie's plea on Blanchard's behalf."

"How could you?" The younger woman pounded the heavy oak table and pointed an accusing finger at him.

Her husband flinched, but held his ground. "All the charges against him were brought by that planter, Courbet." He stood and paced in front of the open window casement in the cottage kitchen. "I don't trust him. I never have. Most of his dealings with our quartermaster seem to fall just at the edge of honesty.

"Yes, Jean's a thief," he continued, "but he's also helped us with information on the movements of English ships." He stopped and turned to Marie. "I'm not convinced he's guilty of all the charges against him, so anything you tell the judge might sway the final verdict."

"My mother should not be involved with this criminal." Rianne stamped her foot and jammed her hands to her hips. "How could you?"

Marie carefully placed her daughter's teacup on the table and stood. She closed the space between her and her son-in-law and embraced him.

"Thank you, thank you for giving him a chance." She smiled and added, "I promise you won't be sorry."

"Then come with me now. He's in the judge's chambers with Courbet. We must hasten." He grabbed his uniform jacket from the back of the kitchen chair and motioned for her to precede him out the door.

"I'm coming too," Rianne said. "Don't leave without me," she added, and raced into a back room calling for her son's nurse.

After she impatiently herded the two of them out of the small cottage, Marie hurried across the cobbled courtyard, trying to will her daughter and son-in-law to move more quickly. When they passed the bullet-riddled wall and the marksmen, she forced her gaze out over the sea where the blazing sun rose relentlessly toward high noon.

The corridor leading to the magistrate's chambers was dark and cool, causing her to blink rapidly to adjust to the extreme contrast from the intense light outside.

In answer to Henri's decisive knock on the door, a solid "Come" sounded from within. As they crowded into the room, the man looked up from his desk where he studied a stack of papers. Courbet sat opposite him, pointing out an item on one of the sheets. Jean slumped against two guards on a bench in the corner.

Marie winced at the state of his face — swelling, bruised, bleeding, mute testament to the treatment he'd received. All because he'd tried to help her instead of staying out of Courbet's way.

She tensed and moved toward Jean with a sharp intake of breath. Henri squeezed her arm and guided her to a bench where he pushed both her and Rianne down with a thump.

Magistrate Cabasson stared out at them through a thatch of thick silver hair falling across his brow. He paused a long moment before breaking the silence.

"Commandant Renaud — why are these women in my court?"

"We wish to speak to the matter I raised in my message earlier today," Henri said.

"But this is a serious case to be dealt with among men. What concern is it of these two?"

"Your honor, this is my wife, Rianne, and her mother, Marie Galante." Henri coughed and shifted his tall frame while he extracted a handkerchief from his pocket.

Marie seized the moment and stood abruptly before her son-in-law could stop her. "Your honor, there are circumstances you should be aware of before you sentence this man." At that, she turned and stretched her arm toward Jean.

The judge continued staring, and for a moment she feared he would order her to leave.

"Please listen to what I have to say."

An almost imperceptible nod from him encouraged her to go on.

"I know the accused is a smuggler, but he is a good man and does not deserve to die. I am a widow who has lost almost everything but my land. My late husband died owing huge gambling debts to *Monsieur* Courbet." At that, she pointed toward her tormenter. "If I cannot bring in my sugar crop in time, I will lose the land too. It's been in my family for many years. I beg you to allow the accused to live and instead sentence him to help me bring in my cane." She struggled to keep her voice from trembling and then went on. "After we harvest the sugar, if you still believe the evidence shows *Monsieur* Blanchard deserves to die, then so be it..." She stopped to gulp in some air.

"*Madame* Galante," the judge interrupted, "do you vouch for this man? Do you swear to this court you will do all in your power to make sure he does not escape?"

Before Marie could answer, Courbet was suddenly by her side. He covered her hand with his and gripped hard. "Your honor, I too hate to see an able-bodied man executed while there is a way he can be useful to the community." He squeezed harder and smiled at Marie. "Since I brought the charges, I agree to suspend them temporarily until *Madame* Galante and the prisoner can harvest the cane."

"It is decided, then," the magistrate said, and pounded the table with his knuckles. "Six weeks from today, we will bring *Monsieur* Blanchard back and finish this trial."

Jean managed to lift his head to receive the verdict.

"But mark me, now. When you return to my chambers, no matter the good you've wrought, you will receive a sentence from this court."

When Marie tried to pull back her hand from Courbet, he tightened his grip. She shivered and imagined his body smashed against the rocks at the bottom of the headlands on her island.

CHAPTER SEVENTEEN

Marie took the kerchief tucked around her neck and mopped at her face. Since the judge had freed Jean to help with the harvest, her own happiness had taken a distinct downward turn. In spite of saving him, at least temporarily, the impossible man seemed to hate her for her efforts.

She bent to slash once more at the cane, gripped the scythe more tightly, and put the entire weight of her body into the swing. She took pride in her toughening arms and calves. The tool stuck hard and jarred her out of her daydream. She'd have one of the men sharpen the blade.

The metal edge had dulled quickly since she'd been pretending the cane she'd been slashing had been Jean's neck. Not only had he ceased coming to her bed, now she had to endure daily visits from Courbet. His cruel black eyes and hard features greeted her across the dining room table each evening. She'd had to warn Luz not to put anything in his food to further annoy him or, God forbid, kill him.

Just then Luz broke through the foliage surrounding the field as if summoned by Marie's thoughts. She rushed toward her muttering aloud, house slippers slapping.

"Dat man — he here again." Her old friend breathed heavily, shaking her head with every step. "He got to leave you alone, or…"

"Luz." Marie interrupted her. "We have to tolerate him a little while longer. What if he complains to the magistrate?"

In truth, Marie was too worn out to think much beyond Jean's current reprieve. She struggled through each day only to fall into an uneasy, restless sleep trying to figure out a way to save him after the cane harvest.

When she glanced to the other side of the field, her shoulder blades prickled from the heated censure of his glare. She was sure he marked Courbet's arrival each day by Luz's agitated appearance.

Enough. She dropped her scythe and stomped toward him, ignoring the warning signs when his eyes widened and his nostrils flared at her approach.

"Why do you give me such looks of hatred every day?" She gripped her fists tightly and refused to back down. "Am I not the woman who saved your worthless skin, who completely ruined her reputation to keep you in this world a while longer?"

"Yet you run to his arms every day." Jean's words came out like hard pellets of rain peppering a tin roof.

Marie leaned back and slapped him so hard, Luz ran to them.

"What now? You two don't have enough problems without making dat man wait?" Luz said. "Instead of hating each other, mebbe you should figure out a way to outwit the firing squad."

Work stopped in the field and every head leaned toward the three quarrelers.

When Marie threw up her hands and spun on her heel to follow Luz from the field, Jean grabbed her by the shoulder and turned her into his arms. She couldn't breathe for a moment, but stilled and drank in the male feel of him and steady thudding of his heart. He held her for a few moments, jaw muscles twitching. Then quickly released her.

"Go," he said, his breathing hard. He grabbed his scythe and returned to the rhythmic slashing of the cane.

⊰✦⊱

Marie bent over her washbasin and sluiced cool water down her face and neck while struggling with the same questions over and over. How was she going to save Jean, and why was Courbet so intent on his demise? When she stretched an arm above her head and sponged water down her back, a thought struck her. Somehow, she would get Courbet to reveal what was behind his great hatred of Jean.

She crossed to the large wardrobe press she rarely opened and peered inside. She picked out two of her best dresses and laid them on the bed. Taking a small bell from her bedside table, she rang for Luz.

Luz appeared quickly and gave her a sly smile. "Bout time you figured out how to get what you want," she said, and bustled over to help Marie choose one of the dresses.

Later, when Marie swept down the stairs, Courbet waited at the bottom with a frown that soon turned into a smirk. Marie had taken Luz's advice and worn her best evening gown, its daring décolletage barely covering the dark aureoles around her nipples. She'd also submitted to the discomfort of a corset over her chemise to push up her breasts.

"To what do I owe this unexpected display of splendid woman flesh?" he asked, and took her hand, leading her to the dining room.

"Do I need a reason?" she asked, and allowed him to seat her while he ogled her breasts. Her mother's diamond ear bobs swayed and sparkled in the waning light - the only jewelry she'd managed to keep from her husband's greedy hands. Luz lit the candles in the candelabra and motioned for the kitchen girls to bring the soup course.

Marie remained silent, waiting for him to pour her a glass of wine. She'd had one of her family's best vintages brought up from the cellar beneath the kitchen. He poured another for himself and then handed the bottle dotted with droplets of moisture back to Yancey. The boy transferred the bottle to a silver bucket of cool water at the end of the table and eyed Courbet warily.

After tasting the light green soup, Courbet looked up at Luz hovering nearby. "Excellent – my compliments to the staff."

For once, Luz kept her head down and demurely nodded at his praise, although Marie had to stifle laughter at her attempt at humility.

Courbet paused and lifted his glass. "A toast to your success in bringing in the cane – may we always enjoy happiness in Galante House." There was a mocking lilt to his voice.

"We?" she asked, with a huff.

"Of course. You don't think I'm going to abandon you, do you?" He shifted in his chair and stretched one booted leg toward Marie's place at the head of the table. "After all, I promised your husband—."

"It's because of the two of you I'm in this horrible predicament, on the brink of losing my family home." Marie's fragile attempt to charm Courbet crumbled. They hadn't finished the first course and already she'd raised her voice.

He stood and threw down his napkin before stalking toward her. "Have you forgotten I have the power of life and death over your pitiful excuse for a lover? One word from me, and the judge will have him executed."

For the first time since her husband's death and betrayal, doubt overwhelmed her. Courbet placed his hand on the back of her chair and leaned low over her face.

"This is as good as my home now, and you will do exactly as I say." He laughed then, a low, ugly sound from deep in his throat. "Keep playing at harvesting the cane, Marie. It will keep your mind occupied until Jean the thief faces the firing squad."

"He is a good man, a brave man — I won't let you destroy him," Marie said.

"Is that what you think?" He laughed and gripped her arm, lifting her from the chair. He dragged her toward the open window and pointed toward the shore. "Look down there."

Bile rose in Marie's throat at the scene. Jean was on his knees with three of Courbet's guards beating him with clubs. Heavy chains bound his feet to his hands behind his back.

"See what your insistence on doing this your way made me do?" He pinched her arm hard and turned her away from the window, forcing her close to his face. "I hate to have my dinner interrupted by unpleasantness, but your prisoner-lover doesn't like to see us together. He somehow thinks he'll escape, and the two of you will live on happily in some kind of dream."

He dragged her back to her chair and pushed her down with one hand on her shoulder before kneeling in front of her. "Surely you know better. When you don't have enough cane to pay off the debt, Galante House will be mine. If I were you,

Marie, I would be thinking of a way to make *Monsieur* Courbet happy enough to keep you with him."

He moved back to his chair, smoothed his napkin across his lap, and shouted for Luz. "*On y va* — dinner has waited long enough."

Luz motioned for the next course as if nothing had happened, and Marie tucked into her soup. The only sign of their heated exchange was the slight tremor in her hand when she lifted the silver spoon to her mouth.

Anger filled her, crowding out better judgment. "What makes you think I would marry you?" she asked, and set down the spoon with a clatter.

Courbet looked up, pursed his lips, and leaned back while Luz set the steamed fish course in front of him. "Marie, you certainly don't think I would make you my wife. I've decided there are plenty of eligible young women among the planters' daughters. I need someone to be the mother of my children. And we both know you're too old."

He chewed on a mouthful of fish and waved his fork at her before swallowing. "You could stay with Luz and your late husband's little bastard down in the cabin by the shore. We'll need help with the household and maybe some lessons for the children." He rubbed his chin for a moment and then added, "If you keep your figure, I might even be persuaded to visit you a few times a week."

Marie leapt to her feet so fast, she overturned her plate of fish. Courbet moved to her side and shoved her back into place. He grasped her shoulders and rubbed them while he stooped to whisper in her ear, "Don't fight me. You'll only get hurt, and Jean will die much sooner."

"Luz," he shouted, "another plate for *Madame* Galante."

A few moments later, the older woman followed a server into the room, her hands hidden behind her back and a murderous light in her eyes only Marie could interpret.

She gave her housekeeper a warning frown and then passed the rest of the meal in a blur, choking back both fear and anger. She couldn't decide what she dreaded more: what he might do to her before the end of the evening or what Luz would do to him.

Outside in the dark, Francois crouched close to the ground. If only Cecile had been there to hear Courbet's words.

He'd had no illusions about the direction of his father's loyalties from the beginning, but had gone along with his mother's scheming. Now he was not so sure. He had some thinking to do.

With one last backward glance at the candlelight streaming from the window above, he faded back into the shadows before racing down toward the beach where Jean still lay.

Marie was so weary from the wine and Courbet's insults, she yearned to lay her head down on her arms at the table and weep. However, she still grasped at the wisp of a chance she might goad him into revealing the source of his great hatred for Jean.

Straightening her back, she took in several deep breaths for courage just as Luz removed the last course.

Marie stood and said, "*Monsieur* Courbet — would you like some of my father's brandy he brought back from his last trip to France?"

"Of course." He tilted his head and searched her face. "To what do I owe this great honor?"

"Since you soon may be the new owner of Galante House, perhaps we should drink a toast to your future." She straightened her back to adjust the unaccustomed tight cinching at her waist.

"Does this mean you've conceded defeat?" Courbet asked, a sudden wariness in his eyes.

"Not necessarily," she soothed, and moved away from the table. "But I know as well as you, our chances are small of harvesting enough cane to pay off such a huge debt." She leaned forward in the candlelight and added, "I may be determined, but I'm not stupid, *Monsieur*."

"'Antoine,' please," he said, and gave her a wide, leering smile, like one of the field dogs when they cornered a lizard. "We need not be so formal," he added. "I'm happy to see you're accepting the inevitable." He stood, came to her side, and palmed the small of her back.

"Let's have the brandy in father's library in honor of his memory," she said, favoring Courbet with an adoring look even as she shivered in revulsion at his touch. Marie jerked away, forcing him to drop his hand from her backside.

Luz waited in the library, candles lit with a tray of two cut-crystal glasses and a decanter filled with a rich, amber-colored liquid.

Marie motioned for her to place the tray on a table between two overstuffed chairs angled close to a stone fireplace. In deference to the stiflingly warm evening, she'd placed baskets full of fragrant sea grasses in the alcove where a fire burned on cooler nights.

"Will there be anything else, *Madame* Galante?"

"No, Luz. Everyone can go on to bed. We'll be here awhile," Marie said, glancing sideways at Courbet. His lean face with high cheekbones, which seemed almost handsome in daylight, took on an ugly, twisted aspect in the glow of the candlelight beneath his chin. He seemed like an eerie skeleton. An old prayer she hadn't thought of since her children were small popped into her head: *Keep us safe, oh Lord, from beasties in the night.*

"What are you plotting, Marie?" he asked. "Do you hope to dissuade me from sending your lover to his death once the cane is in?"

"What an odd question on a night like this," Marie replied, trying to maintain placid detachment in her voice. "You've won. Galante Plantation is practically yours. You can do anything you want, Antoine. Your wealth is such that we all are in your debt." She gave him a broad smile and poured each of the glasses two-thirds full.

"I just wish to be a gracious loser. Perhaps there is room for me somewhere in your vast empire?" She pretended disinterest in his reply and sipped slowly, letting the fiery liquid burn its way down her throat.

He gave her a predatory smile before swallowing a long draught of the brandy. "You know, Marie, I regret I can't keep you as my wife. After all I've done, the risks I've taken to build this empire, I have to pass the legacy on to my heirs."

His head bowed over his glass until she thought he'd fallen asleep, but he suddenly jerked back to attention and continued.

"Too bad. You've always been such a pretty little thing. Your husband never appreciated you. He certainly wasn't thinking of you the night he wagered it all away. Do you know at the very last, he…" Courbet stopped short when Marie quietly filled his glass again.

He tipped back the glass for another long swallow and studied a spot on the wood paneling just above her head. "I shouldn't tell you this, but after all was lost, he offered to give you to me for the night in exchange for another chance to win his fortune back."

"*His* fortune? He gambled away *my* family home." Marie's stomach roiled, threatening to heave up the fish. She clamped shut her mouth, not trusting herself to speak further. She glanced away and replaced the decanter on the tray. The shadows bathing her side of the table hid her quick retrieval of a bottle hidden beneath the ruffles cascading from the cushion on her chair.

"Come on. Drink with me," he said. This is supposed to be a night of celebration. Take your medicine like a good girl. Humility in defeat is balm for the soul."

She gave him a smile meant to dazzle, upended her glass and emptied the liquid in one gulp. Setting down the empty glass, she leaned over the tray for another drink.

Marie noted the watery, rheumy look in Courbet's eyes. Her father's brandy had begun to affect him. When he leaned back in his chair and squinted at the fireplace alcove, she reached below the ruffle for another dose of water to dilute the effects of her own intake.

She'd counted on Luz to remember their old routine to calm her husband on the many nights he'd become abusive. But now she needed to move fast to learn as much as she could from Courbet before he passed into unconsciousness.

"Antoine."

"Hmmm?"

"How did you build your business? Did your family help you purchase your first plantation?"

"No family. Did it all m'self." He leaned forward and grasped her wrist in a painful hold. "Not everyone is as privileged as you and your w'thless husband."

His words increasingly slurred. It was now or never. She leaned into his searing grip and strained to hear. "I so admire a man who makes his own way in the world," she said, "but I can't imagine how you did it." She then took a calculated risk. "Jean is just a thief. But you accumulated wealth the hard way."

"Jean has to die." He spat out the harsh words so loudly, she shrank back into the chair.

"But surely he's no threat to you. Couldn't you just let him return to the garrison jail and serve out a sentence?"

"Knows too much, but doesn't know what he knows." Courbet sank into oblivion and then jerked upright again. "Maybe I could keep you at the house in the hills. Nobody there now but servants and Cecile."

Cecile? Marie thought, and held her breath, waiting for another clue. Minutes passed, and finally a loud snore issued from the recesses of the other chair. She shrugged and rose to go down to the shore. His guards would have to roll him into his carriage and take him home. When she passed the three men lounging near the front door, she motioned for them to collect their master.

Marie hurried out into the velvet softness of the night and tried to piece together Courbet's disjointed hints. Cecile, who might have poisoned Jean's men, was one of Courbet's servants.

Soft moonlight filtered through the trees along the path to the shore, lighting her way to find Jean.

Jean regained consciousness with a start, his arms and legs taut with pain. He'd finally passed out after Courbet's guards had beaten him and left him lying cheek down in the coarse sand.

He awoke to the metallic taste of blood dribbling down the side of his head and into his slack mouth. At some point, they'd released him from the chains securing his wrists to his ankles.

When he struggled to raise his head, a blurry vision of Marie appeared leaning over him. Although the shackles were gone, the pain of the beatings remained.

"*Mon dieu.* How can I help someone who has no regard for his own life?" Marie tisked at Jean as if she were his mother and helped him stand on unsteady feet.

He rolled back down and complained, "What do you care what happens to me while you're up there making love to that devil, Courbet?"

"Is there anywhere on your body they didn't beat you?" she asked.

"I don't think so," Jean said, before adding, "Well maybe here." He pointed to a small spot just beneath his elbow.

Marie drew back and slapped him hard exactly on the place he'd touched.

"Ow. Why did you do that?" he cried.

"You don't deserve all the people who seek to keep you alive. You're like a piglet who's saved from the fire only to rush back in."

"You're the only fire that threatens me," Jean said, and tried to drag her down to the sand with him.

She pushed him away and sat up. Pulling her knees into her chest, she stared out across the moonlit sea. His hands reached for her, but she scooted away.

"I'm sorry. There, I've said it." Jean crawled close to her and forced her to look into his eyes.

"I didn't mean to accuse you of something I know you would never willingly do, but we both know how cruel and persuasive Courbet can be." He placed his hand over her lips when she opened her mouth. "It doesn't matter, Marie," he said, surprised he meant what he said. Two things burned in his soul. He loved this woman more than anything, but his hatred of Courbet surpassed all else.

"If you're done feeling sorry for yourself, would you like to know what *Monsieur* Courbet told me?" Marie asked.

"And just what did you do to loosen his tongue?" Jean's face darkened with jealousy.

"Apparently, he is no match for my father's brandy," she said with a weary sigh and shook her head at Jean's fit of temper. "More importantly, he let slip that Cecile lives on his plantation on the north shore of Martinique. I think there may be other secrets he hides there."

CHAPTER EIGHTEEN

Gerard slept peacefully on his pallet in the cabin on Marie's plantation he shared with his mother. Elisabeth knelt and touched his cheek, her lips curving at the way he still found his thumb in sleep. She rose at a knock, wondering who could be at her door at such a late hour.

She didn't expect Francois that night, as he'd been working with a small crew of Jean's men on a cane field at the far side of the plantation. She opened the door, anticipating his teasing smile, and instead greeted a man who looked as though the world weighed on his shoulders.

"What's happened?" She grasped his hand and pulled him into the cabin.

"I have something to tell you."

"You look like the bearer of bad news," she said. "Please, just tell me. Don't frighten me." Her chest contracted in panic, and she forgot to breathe. She touched her hand to her lips, her eyes wide. "Has something happened to my brother? I knew nothing good could come from him watching Marie deal with that devil every night."

"Do not fear for Jean." Francois covered her hand with his, pulled her close, and held her gaze. "Hear me out. I'm not the man you think I am."

"Stop. You're the man I love. Nothing you say can change that." In spite of her brave words, a small whimper escaped her lips. "What have you done?"

"I've deceived you and your brother from the beginning."

"No," she wailed.

"Yes. Courbet is my father. He convinced my mother to help with his twisted plan, and she begged me to help."

"But who is your mother?"

"Cecile."

"The cook at the compound?" Elisabeth collapsed onto one of the small cabin's crude wooden chairs and gave him an anguished look. "Please tell me your mother hasn't been poisoning our men."

His silence tore at her heart.

"Were you the one who pushed Marie down the mountain?" Her voice took on a harsh edge.

"No."

"But you knew, didn't you?" She jumped to her feet and began to pace. "You knew Cecile sent Marie up there to die, and you didn't do anything to stop her, did you?"

"Elisabeth, I swear to you…"

"Stop, just stop the lies. I don't want to hear any more." She turned away from him and swiped at tears carving a path down her cheeks.

"You've got to listen to me," Francois said. "Come outside. Don't wake Gerard." He stooped to the boy's pallet and tucked the thin blanket around her son's arms.

Outside in the pre-dawn darkness in the cabin's tiny vegetable garden, he told her his story.

"I admit I've lied to you and Jean from the beginning, but I can't tolerate my father's madness any longer." He pulled her close and placed a kiss behind her ear.

"I'm here because I love you and I want to help. I know what Courbet's planning, but I'm not sure why. He has no intention of letting Jean live one minute longer than it takes to bring in Marie's cane. He lied to my mother about acknowledging us as his family. I think I've suspected from the beginning he was using both of us."

"But why?" She ran her hands through her unbound hair and lifted the heavy length off her neck. "Why does he hate us so? And what is his plan?"

Francois hung his head for a moment and then continued. "He claimed he wanted me to take over Jean's crew and divert the spoils to him. He made my mother believe she'd join him as his wife after we helped destroy Jean and Marie.

"Tonight, when I was at Galante House, I stood outside the open dining room shutters and heard him tell Marie his true plans, and they don't include Cecile."

"But what did you do to help destroy Marie?"

Francois dropped his hands and glanced away. "I was there the night her husband lost the plantation to Courbet in a card game."

"*Mon dieu*, no." She interrupted him.

"Let me finish," he said, facing her squarely. "I suspect he put one of my mother's powders in *Monsieur* Galante's drink, to muddle his concentration."

"But we have to tell Marie – she has to go to the authorities. They will set aside her husband's debt."

"We have no proof, Elisabeth, and Courbet probably has the magistrate on Martinique in his debt. We have to proceed carefully, make plans."

She reached for his chin and turned his face toward her. "We can do anything as long as we're together," she said, and placed a soft kiss on his lips.

Marie woke suddenly, her body curled into Jean's. His arm slung over her tightened when she edged toward the side of the bed.

Pink light flooded through the window, illuminating the mussed sheets and piles of clothing discarded on the floor.

She tensed at the thought of a dozen tasks awaiting her. When she scooted catlike to extricate herself from his embrace, he sat up suddenly and trapped her within his arms.

"You're not going anywhere, *Madame* Galante," he murmured and covered her mouth with his in soft possession.

She arched to meet him and cupped his face in her hands, deepening the kiss. All the pressing concerns of a moment before flew from her head.

Later, she sat cross-legged in bed and dabbed salve on the whip lashes striping his face and back. "You stupid, stupid man. What makes you think you are invincible?"

"Because I have a willing wench waiting for me. Nothing can keep me from her."

"Do not be so arrogant. Some day, those monsters might break something we both value. Then what will you do?"

"Do not fear, Marie. As long as there is even one part of my body left, I will use it to pleasure you."

He laughed when her face flushed a crimson to rival an island sunset. She shoved him away and cursed under her breath, pulling on a dressing gown and moving toward the cushioned bench beneath her window. "Come," she said, and patted the space next to her. "We need to plan our search of *Monsieur* Courbet's plantation in the hills."

Jean left the bed more slowly and searched for his clothes. "*We* aren't going to do anything," he insisted. "You cannot be any part of this."

Her eyes widened and she gave him the look she'd used for many years with her sons. "I will not let you do this alone, Jean Blanchard," she said. "And besides, you cannot just walk up to Courbet's house and knock on the door. You need me."

"I hadn't planned on knocking on the door," he said with a wicked grin, "but you've convinced me. Perhaps I do need your help. However, before we do anything else, we must go back to St. Pierre and break into the jail."

"Why?" she asked, and stretched her arms wide, her voice sharp.

"We need to liberate my cellmate from that hell-hole." He leaned over and retrieved his trousers, moving slowly and deliberately. Marie took a sharp intake of breath and pretended to look away. He stared back with a lazy, mocking smile. "He's known Courbet for many years. No one knows more about his sins than my friend, Abelard."

"But how are we going to escape Courbet's notice?"

"I have an idea." Jean moved to Marie's desk and ripped a corner from the bottom of a letter, ignoring her gasp. "I'll send a message to my crew on Dominica to torch one of his warehouses while we're gone. That should keep *Monsieur* Courbet busy for a few days."

At a small tap, Marie opened the door to Luz, who shoved her way in, balancing a tray of coffee and pastries.

"If someone goes along to St. Pierre, it better be me," her housekeeper said.

"Luz, how many times have I asked you not to eavesdrop?" Marie asked.

"How else I gonna find out things around here?" She harrumphed and pointed at Marie. "Not from you."

"Is there anyone in this house who doesn't know my business?" Marie asked, shaking her head and fluffing bed linens to cover her embarrassment.

Luz stopped for a moment as if considering the question and then admitted, "Prob'ly not."

Jean regarded them from the chair where he sat pulling on his boots. "Actually, Marie, it's not such a bad idea to bring Luz along."

"Have you both gone mad?" Marie stood in the center of the room, hands on hips, glaring at them.

Another urgent knock came at the door followed by pounding.

"Pour l'amour du ciel," Marie said, and jerked open the door. Elisabeth and Francois burst into the room, pushing her aside in their rush toward Jean.

Breathless from the long walk from her cabin, she sank onto her knees at her brother's feet. "We must talk, now."

"Don't," Jean said, and pressed two fingers to his sister's lips. His dark eyes hardened into two obsidian points while his glance shifted between her and Francois. "I knew this moment would come." He stood and lifted her to her feet while sending her lover a murderous look. "It wasn't enough for this traitor to undermine my crew; he had to draw you into his web too. I saw what was happening, but couldn't bring myself to stop you." He rubbed savagely at his tousled hair and spread his arms. "What has he done to you? Tell me, or I'll assume the worst and kill him where he stands."

Francois stepped close to Jean and in one smooth motion, pulled a pistol from his belt and turned the barrel into his own chest, the butt toward Jean. "Pull the trigger," he said. "Go ahead. I deserve it." He bowed his head and waited.

The silence in the room thickened until Marie grabbed a poker from the fireplace and knocked the pistol to the floor.

Both men stiffened and drew their fists, but she was faster. She pushed her hands against Jean's chest and shoved hard.

"Enough," she said. "There is no time for your ape-like thrashing of each other. Isn't there something useful we were going to do? Perhaps figure out a way to save your worthless hide or maybe keep a roof over my head?"

The two men backed off a pace or two but maintained their dark study of each other.

Marie turned to Elisabeth. "Now, please explain what was so important that you had to invade my bedroom."

"Francois admitted he and his mother are the ones who have been plotting against Jean and his men. His mother – Cecile – put the poison in the men's food and probably is the one who followed you up the volcano to push you off the cliff."

"But why?" Marie slowly shook her head. "I did nothing to her. I had my suspicions, but I did not accuse her. I wasn't sure." She took a long swallow of dark, hot coffee and slid a glance around the room.

"Courbet is my father," Francois said, "and he is obsessed with destroying Jean. He wants the profits from the smuggling operations for himself, but I'm sure there's more to his hatred."

Elisabeth interrupted. "Francois was there the night Courbet claims to have won your plantation in a card game." She began to pace and then turned, extending her arms toward Marie. "Cecile was there also, and Francois saw her put one of her powders into your husband's drink." She covered her mouth with her fist and whispered, "I'm so sorry."

"And you stood by? Knowing the evil your parents worked?" Jean stepped away from Marie and grasped Francois by the neck. His hand swept the table, smashing a cup to the floor where shards of china scattered to the corners of the room.

"Stop." Elisabeth stepped between the two belligerent men, and Marie grabbed Jean by the back of his shirt. "We must work together to find proof to save Marie's home and stop Courbet," his sister said.

Marie drew Jean into her arms and said, "I guess we're going to have a full crew for that trip to St. Pierre after all."

"Yancey and Gerard are playing outside," Elisabeth said, and raised her hand to her forehead with a sigh. "They'll have to come, too. We can't leave them alone. Courbet might hurt them if he comes to the plantation and we're not here."

Jean covered his sister's hands and nodded to Francois. "The *Lissy Ann* is at anchor down in the cove. Think you all might fancy a sail?"

CHAPTER NINETEEN

Jean rocked back and forth, alternating pressure on his feet to keep the wheel steady through the chop of waves north of Martinique. Marie leaned into him while she held her hands on the wheel, listening to his staccato orders.

She'd begged to help, and he couldn't deny her anything on a day as perfect as this one. Only high, puffy clouds dotted the cerulean sky. Some weather to the west provoked the only wind. the *Lissy Ann* danced on the waves as if spanked by an invisible hand.

Elisabeth had helped Francois hoist and trim the sails while Luz sat grim-faced on an overturned barrel. Gerard and Yancey tumbled and played on deck like small monkeys. One of Jean's men, Jules, stood watch at the bow.

Luz tied her straw hat tightly under her chin, but the wind still snatched and pulled at the wide brim, causing the ribbon to strain under her chin. Her shipboard assignment was one Jean had yet to define. Her main task, it seemed, was to warn all of them to "be careful" and "go faster."

"I don't know why dis boat, she just crawl through the water," Luz complained. "And you boys – you goin' make Gran Luz's hair go all gray."

Jean left Marie to manage the wheel while he made his way to Luz. Leaning over her, he cast a huge shadow. She peeled back the hat brim and gazed up at him, defiant on her face.

"Luz – only God and this ship decide how fast we go. Unless you can make one of them hear you, please stop deviling all of us with your orders," he said.

She gave out a "harrumph" and shoved down the hat brim, shutting him out. He stretched skyward like a cat and then swayed on practiced feet across the tilted deck to where his sister and Francois sat. He scowled at their intertwined hands.

Francois lifted his head and returned a dark frown. "You know I love your sister. You can't make me give her up."

"You won't have any say if I plant you in the graveyard, will you?" Jean said.

Elisabeth stood and slapped her brother, then sat down again in tears.

Gerard stopped playing and ran to his mother. He glared at Jean and Francois and asked, "Why did you make my mother cry?"

"I'm sorry, Gerard," Francois said.

Jean ruffled the hair on his nephew's head before a large gust of wind forced him to help Marie grapple with the wheel. Once he took the helm, he sighted the faint outline of the bluffs on the northern edge of Martinique. They would make the protected anchorage above St. Pierre in a few hours. He'd gather his small band for a war council before they headed down along the shore to the town.

Marie could not stop the tremors. When she finally forced herself to be still, she looked around, hoping no one noticed. She drew Yancey and Gerard to her lap, where both boys tried to wriggle away.

Her fellow crew members sat stiffly in various degrees of tension, except for Luz. Her old friend radiated nothing but determination and anger.

"Luz — you're sure you want to do this? You could stay on the ship with the children until we return," Marie said.

"Dis somethin' I got to do. No more questions." Luz stood and moved to Jean's side. When he put his arm around her, she stood taller and threw Marie a triumphant look.

Marie released the restless boys and crossed her arms, resigning herself to worry. Her annoyance did stop the tremors, though. The sun, high in the late afternoon sky, warmed her.

Jean slowed the ship into the wind and headed toward the shore. All she could see was a thick green wall of jungle.

However, at a look from Jean, Francois went forward to the bow with the glass and finally pointed toward the hidden opening they used on smuggling forays. Soon, the *Lissy Ann* was at anchor in a small protected cove. Marie's tattered nerves gradually calmed as the ship swung gently in the breeze.

"Everyone gather around," Jean said, "and we'll divide the tasks." He crouched on the deck and laid out small shells and bits of driftwood, representing everyone's position that night.

At a shriek from Gerard, he turned a stern face toward the children. "Silence. Your jobs from now on are to remain quiet and obey Jules. You will stay here and help guard the ship while we're gone."

When both boys groaned at being left behind, he added, "What we are going to do in St. Pierre is very important, but all will be for naught if the ship is not still here and ready to go when we come back. I'm counting on you two." He crossed the deck to where the boys sat quiet and wide-eyed at his serious words. Kneeling in front of them, he pulled Gerard and Yancey into his arms and squeezed them hard followed by manly thumps on their backs.

"Now then, for the rest of you." Jean stood and came back across the deck. "Once Elisabeth and I rendezvous with the performers' troupe, Luz will take a basket of food and a bottle of wine to the guards. She'll say she's Abelard's wife, claiming the right to visit him with supplies. They'll be suspicious, because the poor old man never has visitors. You'll have to be convincing and maybe sweeten the deal with an extra bottle of wine."

"But what if they don't believe her?" Marie asked, agitation creeping into her voice. "What if they hurt her?"

"Any one of us could be harmed. Bow out now if you're afraid," Jean said. No one made a sound while he looked from person to person. After a short pause, he continued, "As soon as Luz leaves the wine with the guards, Elisabeth and I will set up across the plaza with the performers." He smiled and added, "There's nothing like a little wine and curiosity to divert attention."

"What about me and Francois?" Marie demanded.

"You will stay out of sight and wait for my signal. You are too well known at St. Pierre's garrison to show your face. Once night falls and the guards have relaxed from the drink and the performance, Francois will use his pickpocket skills to get the key." Jean paused in his instructions and turned to Marie.

"I want you to hide in the warehouse across from the jail. You should be ready with your bag of herbs to help Abelard regain his strength."

Jean stood and leaned into Francois's face. "If you have any notion of betraying us, tell me now. You must swear to me I have your complete loyalty. Swear it in blood."

For an instant, they exchanged angry looks, but then Francois produced a short knife. He slashed the pad of his thumb and clasped Jean's hand hard. "I swear on my life and my love for your sister. From now on, my loyalty belongs only to you, Jean Blanchard."

"If you fail me in this one thing, you will not see another sunrise," Jean said. He turned to Marie and asked, "Are you clear on what you need to do?"

She nodded but added, "You're much more notorious than the rest of us. How do you plan to keep from being recognized and thrown back in jail?"

"Trust me. Not even you will recognize me," Jean said.

Breathless and terrified, Marie watched Jean and Elisabeth disappear into the back streets of St. Pierre. They'd just emerged from the jungle and beach along the shore path from the cove. Francois gave her an awkward pat on the shoulder while Luz impatiently waved an arm and motioned for them to follow.

They'd come at a trot from the cove, but even so, dusk was falling quickly. Francois moved silently from building to building, beckoning to Luz and Marie to follow after he checked each street and alley for soldiers or inquisitive passersby. The cobblestones bruised her feet through her boot soles. Finally, he pointed toward an empty warehouse down the street from the jail. Marie waited a few minutes after he'd picked the lock and then scooted in, the taste of terror in her mouth, and Luz close behind.

Francois signaled for silence while he took a place beneath a window. They settled in to wait, and he carefully levered himself up to the opening every few minutes.

Marie jerked nervously when Luz rose suddenly with the basket of food and wine bottles to set off for the jail. She grabbed at Luz's skirt, but her housekeeper slipped from her grasp.

"Wasn't she supposed to wait for the performers?" Marie asked Francois. He shrugged, shook his head, and then touched his fingers to her lips.

After what seemed an eternity, Francois tapped Marie's shoulder and motioned for her to join him in his vigil at the window. Her eyes had become heavy with fatigue, but she snapped to attention at his touch. He pointed to the town square where a small group of performers rolled a gaudy wagon into place as a stage. They drummed, beat tambourines, and lit torches around the edges of the stage.

As she watched, a tall figure emerged from the shadows and began tossing firebrands in an arc above his head. She drew in a sharp breath when flickering light illuminated his head. He wore a devil's mask with dark eyes glittering through the slits.

A beautiful woman with heavily rouged cheeks and dark kohl around her eyes settled at a table partially covered by a tent near the wagon. She produced a deck of oversized cards and began shuffling them. If that was Elisabeth, she had to be wearing a wig of lush, black tumbling curls.

"Do you see Luz?" Marie whispered to Francois. He clasped his hand over her mouth and pointed to the jail, which was midway between the warehouse and the performers' wagon at the square. Two of the guards had left their posts and were watching the entertainment from just outside the door. One of them held an open wine bottle. So far, so good.

The plan seemed to be working, except for the absent third guard. He must be inside with Luz.

Francois held up two fingers on one hand and just one on the other. He confirmed her suspicions. Only one guard remained inside with Luz and Abelard. As they settled in to wait, the two guards slowly drifted ever closer to the performance, sharing draughts from a bottle as they went.

"What will you do now?" Marie asked, and chewed on her thumbnail.

"It's going to be a lot harder to get the cell key from the third guard if he's still sober."

After what seemed another eternity to Marie, Francois slipped out of the warehouse so deftly, she barely saw him go. She shrank back into the shadows in a corner and tried to ignore the rustlings she knew had to be rats.

No longer able to stand the suspense, she edged toward the window to observe the troupe in the square. Tumblers now rolled in the dust in front of the gaudy wagon. She clenched her hands and dropped to the filthy floor. The masked devil had disappeared along with his torches, and the fortune-teller's seat was empty. There was no sign of the two drunken prison guards either, but the crowd at the square had grown so large, she doubted anyone would be left in the darkened streets to recognize her.

Even though Jean had warned her to stay inside, Marie's sixth sense was crawling like a bug up and down her neck. She had to distract the third guard into moving outside the jail so that Francois could steal the cell key.

Marie tucked her kerchief around her hair and left her décolletage bare to the night breezes. Just as she suspected, the third guard was still stationed at the jail, without having sampled the third bottle of wine.

He was young and seemed inordinately proud of his immaculate uniform. A difficult man to distract.

She leaned in the open door and said, "Such an exciting night, *Monsieur*. What keeps you inside? Your friends are enjoying the performance on the square." She made sure to dip toward him just enough to display the creamy rounded tops of her breasts pushed up above her bodice. With his concentration momentarily shattered, Luz moved from the shadows where she'd been sitting and silently relieved him of the key.

Jean crouched behind the abandoned warehouse and waited for Luz and Francois to emerge from the jail with Abelard between them. Their original plan had been to give the appearance of a guard ushering visitors from the premises. However, too much time had passed. Something was wrong.

He rose and circled around in the dark to get closer to the jail when a sudden boom and sweep of wind threw him backward. His head hit the cobblestones, and he passed out. Seconds later, he awoke to a furnace of flames engulfing the guardhouse and jail.

He jumped to his feet and ran toward the blaze inside the sturdy stone jail. When he reached for the iron handle on the door to the guards' quarters, he jumped back in pain. The heat peeled skin off his palm.

He gagged at the sickening sweet smell of burned flesh floating across the heavy, still night air. When the heat and force of the fire pushed him back across the cobblestone street to the warehouse, he staggered inside and shouted for Marie.

Luz's sturdy arms enfolded him and she spoke soothing words close to his ear. "Marie is safe, and Abelard is with me, but Francois…"

He pushed her away and tried to bolt out the door again.

"It's too late. There's nothing you can do," she said and pulled hard on his arm, dragging him back into the darkness.

Jean suddenly broke away from her and uttered a single word, "Elisabeth." He charged out the door back toward the performers' wagon on the square.

When he raced up the street toward the torch-lit square, Jean's heart nearly stopped at the sight of the table with tarot cards, tools of her trade. The stool she'd perched on earlier was empty, toppled over by the crowd rushing to see the fire.

He whirled at the touch of a hand on his back. His sister stood behind him, shaking. "Francois was in the explosion, wasn't he?" she said. "He's gone, all because he wanted to help us." Jean clapped his hand over her mouth and looked around before pulling her into the shadows at the side of the street.

"We have to get out of here," Jean said, his voice raw from the smoke. "Can't grieve in a public square. And," he said, pulling his hand from her mouth, "we don't really know what happened to Francois. He might not have been in the jail when the explosion hit."

"But what if he was?" She gripped his arm and stared hard while tears carved rivers through the ash smudges on her face.

CHAPTER TWENTY

High Road to Courbet Plantation, South of Marigot

Night closed in around Jean, the stars like silver paint splatters on a black silk backdrop. A slice of a sickle moon threw a pitiful ribbon of light on the last stretch of dirt road up the mountain. They would barely make Courbet's plantation by dawn.

"Is there nothing we can do to cajole them into moving a little faster?" Jean slapped the reins against the wide backs of the accursed slow, plodding oxen as the performers' wagon strained and creaked up the incline. "And stop juggling. How you manage to keep anything aloft in the dark is beyond me."

His companion on the wide seat continued tossing three balls into the air. When one dropped between his feet, he bent down, scooped the offending orb back into his hand and said, "Probably not."

"Probably not what?"

"There's probably nothing we can do to make them move faster."

"Have you never tried to urge them on?" Jean asked.

"No."

"Is that the only advice you have?"

"Yes," the young man replied, and scooted back behind the curtained entrance to the lumbering wagon, pulling his long, brightly clad legs behind him.

Jean shook his head at the ludicrous situation. He was sneaking up on Courbet in a garish-painted street performers' conveyance. Most of the wooden structure was painted a glowing red while turquoise outlined the openings. Gold leaf gilded all, including the wooden spoke wheels, just in case someone might miss their passing.

And if that weren't enough of a challenge, asleep inside the wagon were people he loved and trusted. He refused to contemplate the danger they would face if he failed. The irony bit at him. Jean Blanchard, with a reputation as the bloodiest smuggler in the islands, traveled like a common peddler, trailing his family with him.

The sound of the jail explosion and the light of the leaping flames had alarmed Jules back on the *Lissy Ann*. He'd caught up with them in St. Pierre and delivered the boys who now slept in the wagon with the performers. After seeing the boys safely into Jean's keeping, Jules had returned to guard the ship.

Moments later, Marie emerged from the curtained opening behind him, a smile quirking at the corners of her mouth. "You upset the boy."

"This trip is taking too long. We could walk faster than these oxen," he said with a sputter.

"Yes, we could." She slung one leg, then another, across the high box where Jean sat. "But then we would be too tired to accomplish anything when we get there." Her velvet-soft hand covered his. "You are too tense. Why don't you get some sleep? I can take over for a while."

"No," he bit out and clenched the reins in a tighter grip.

Marie did not argue but instead leaned over and stole a quick kiss.

"What are you doing?" Jean jerked away from her touch, irritated at her persistence. "Do you want us to plunge over the cliff?"

"These poor beasts are not going to move any faster with you gripping the reins as if you could make them fly by your thoughts alone."

"Stop. You endanger all of us." He slung the straps a little harder and made some clucking sounds he hoped would encourage the oxen. When he turned back to rebuff her, she had moved so close to him on the high seat, he could feel the heat of her body through the thin muslin dress. Marie's breath hinted of mint and ocean breezes.

Before he could complain, she grasped his face with both hands and pulled him to her for a lingering kiss. At first she just supped lightly, teasing his lips with her teeth before deepening the invasion of his mouth.

Jean dropped the reins to the footrest where they remained while Marie continued her gentle assault on his determination to remain alert. His arms enfolded her as if they had a will of their own.

"See, the oxen keep moving even though you aren't worrying them." Marie brushed a hand across his forehead, tucking a lock of dark hair behind his ear.

Jean stole a quick glance at the animals as they strained up the mountain road. He bent down and knotted the reins to a hook in the floorboard at his feet.

Without saying a word, he reached over and swept her onto his lap, so that she faced back toward the wagon entrance. Following his lead, she straddled him and clasped him to her, laying her head on his shoulder. She hung on with both arms, her body vulnerable. He could do with her as he wished.

She lifted her head and returned Jean's steady gaze without flinching. He yearned to possess this woman completely. He wanted her to love only him, to cleave to him no matter what lay ahead of them.

With her bare bottom swaying against his cock in rhythm with the wagon, he slid his hand under her, feeling her skin, soft as the inside of the blood red lilies he knew massed along the side of the road. Although the jungle was still cloaked in a curtain of darkness, the summit of the mountain they climbed toward glowed with a stroke of light from the coming sunrise.

He slid a finger inside Marie's heat and felt her already slick with moisture. His heart stuttered, and the tension lifted. Her fingers feather soft worked his trouser buttons loose, and the moment he sprang free, she settled him inside her. She moved with a soft moan and tilted back her head. Jean put his hand to her nape to pull her forward and held her gaze steady. He wanted to see and feel her fall apart in his arms.

When she leaned in to him for a kiss, he claimed her mouth with his lips and stroked at the apex of her thighs. As her breath became ragged, he broke the kiss and cupped her face in his hands. Her dark eyes were wide with desire. "Marie, tell me you love me."

Her only answer was another little moan before she exploded in pleasure in his arms and collapsed onto his shoulder, sobbing. He caught her sobs in his mouth, clenched her hips, and stroked deeply into her body. An intense stab of pleasure seized and took him over the edge.

Jean leaned back and stared up at the stars until his breathing slowed while Marie climbed off his lap, rearranging her skirts and shift. She knelt at his feet and they both remained silent for a long while until Marie finally spoke. "Why is it so important that I put into words what is between us?"

"Because I need you now more than ever. More than the first day I met you and was desperate to save my men."

Marie slowly raised her head. "You are a young man with many years ahead of you. Why would you want to burden yourself with the love of an older woman? You think you need me because you are fighting for your freedom. I bought you a few more weeks to solve the mystery of why Courbet wants you dead. I wish I could do more, but I'm afraid that's all I can do."

"So, what just passed between us meant nothing to you?" The harsh edge of Jean's voice seemed to do what little else had accomplished so far. The stubborn beasts began a slow trot, the top of the mountain drawing close at a faster clip.

"I've risked not only my life for you, but the lives of my men as well. I suffered beatings for you, went to prison because of you and still you deny me the words I need to hear?"

She didn't reply, but turned away from him, the widening light of dawn burnishing the dark fall of her hair.

Marie fought back tears after Jean's declaration. Yes, she loved him, but she couldn't afford to bare her feelings only to have him shatter her trust later. The pain would be more than she could bear.

Jean sat quietly holding the reins without a glance toward her. He distanced himself as far as the seat would allow.

Abelard emerged through the curtain and reached for the reins. Jean grumbled under his breath but left his post without argument.

The old man said nothing for a few miles as the wagon creaked up the mountain.

Marie finally broke the silence. "Thank heaven you made him get some rest." She twisted her hair into a tight roll and jabbed at it with hairpins. She'd nearly forgotten how disheveled she'd look when the sun rose.

Abelard gave her a knowing smile. "Thank heaven he finally wore himself out enough to go inside."

A hot flush spread from Marie's face to her neck. "Did we...?"

The old man reassured her with a pat on the arm. "Fear not, beautiful lady. Your secret is safe with me."

"But—."

"It is only logical that you and Jean should love each other."

"But he is much younger. I should be ashamed."

"Why? Because you fell in love with a loyal, passionate man who is willing to risk everything to keep those he loves safe?"

"He is a smuggler and a cutthroat."

Abelard laughed. "Do not believe everything you hear. Monsieur Blanchard is a man of many faces, one who leads a band of thieves and ex-murderers, but also one who is a fierce protector of those he loves."

"Yes, but which one am I to believe?"

"That is a mystery for you to unravel." The old man clucked deftly at the oxen, and they seemed to pick up speed as they neared the summit. "I believe there is a third *Monsieur* Blanchard waiting for you behind a door only you can open."

He pulled the animals up short at the top before he jumped to the ground and secured the wagon's wooden brake. When he moved to Marie's side and offered his hand, she hopped down to face the dawn.

A hard ocean wind buffeted them from the eastern side of the island, and a bank of dark red clouds lined the horizon. An eerie border of gold edged the roiling mass. A sudden gust flattened Abelard's threadbare cotton shirt to his chest, emphasizing his thin shoulders.

Pressure shifted in Marie's ears as the wind swirled around them, sucking up pillars of dust. When she turned toward the back entrance of the performers' wagon, Abelard pulled her to the side of the road.

"Let them rest a while longer," he said. "You and I need to talk."

Marie bent from the waist, stretching her sore muscles and then sank onto the grass. She flopped down next to Jean's old cellmate and looked at him expectantly. "Why didn't you tell Jean you have a way with the beasts?" She flexed her cramped, bare feet in front of her, frowning at the two-day accumulation of grime.

"If you were in my place, would you have challenged him in his foul mood?"

"Of course not." Marie chuckled and patted his arm. "What do you think will happen when we get to the plantation?"

"I'm not sure. I haven't been there since Courbet decided I knew too much and had me locked away."

"Do you think he could be hiding some proof of the disappearance of Jean's parents?" The gusting winds quieted and an uneasy calm descended on the mountain. She swatted at one of the nearly invisible insects that plagued the interior of the island the minute the wind died down.

"I never mentioned my suspicions to Jean, because I didn't want to encourage hope, but there is something dark and old Courbet hides at this plantation." Abelard leaned over and plucked a tiny purple flower from the grass. He popped the bloom into his mouth and chewed for a moment before adding, "There are raised mounds of earth at different far corners of his cane fields. That man has a lot to answer for, and not just what he might have done to Jean's family."

"But why would he go to the trouble of burying his victims? Why not just take them out to sea?" Marie asked.

"Courbet is a wicked, complicated man." Abelard's voice turned grim. "Maybe he wants to keep the dead close, some kind of control beyond the grave."

Marie shivered in spite of the rising sun's warmth and gathered the courage to ask Abelard a personal question. "There's something about you that puzzles me."

"What, my dear? You can ask me anything."

"Your speech is unlike that of any of the other slaves in the islands. Where were you born?"

"That is a long story. When I was a servant in *Madame* Courbet's house, she tutored me so that I could manage her customers."

"Courbet's mother?" Marie said.

"That's where little Antoine grew up – in a bordello in *Nouvelle Orleans*."

His look silenced her next question.

"You can ask me anything, but I'll reveal only one secret a day."

She reluctantly turned at the sound of their travel companions crawling from the gaudy wagon. Jean was first, with a giggling boy under each arm. Luz followed closely, and then the young juggler and Elisabeth.

Jean stood at the summit, hands on hips, surveying the valley below. Gerard and Yancey darted back and forth, pushing and shoving each other in a game of keep-away.

"What do we do now?" Marie asked, joining him.

"It's simple. We corner the monster in his lair, kill him, and eat him. Then we all live happy lives."

"How can you joke when we're all terrified of what might happen next?"

"I do not jest about such serious matters." He turned to the others and said, "Stretch your legs, take care of creature comforts, and then everyone back in the wagon. Abelard and I will drive from here."

When Gerard and Yancey looked to him as if they were going to complain, he stuck his hand out, palm facing them. "No arguments – get back out of sight."

"You're not going to tell me anything – are you?" Marie said, as the grumbling boys and the rest of the troupe climbed back into the crowded wagon.

"No, I am not."

"Why not?"

Jean did not answer, but instead pulled her to him. His hands slid down her sides to the swell of her hips as if memorizing the contours of her body.

She sucked in a sharp breath and tried to push him away. "Don't..."

He lowered his head and rested his chin on top of her head. "Please, Marie. If you can't give me your love, at least trust me and pretend you love me." He continued rubbing her back for a few moments and then broke the embrace. Striding back to the wagon in a rush, he bent to check the huge wooden brake.

Marie nearly choked on her tears. She still couldn't banish the feeling that Jean would abandon her as soon as he was free. She had to protect her heart.

"Now what you do to dat man?" Luz appeared at her side, a look of exasperation on her face.

"He only thinks he needs me. You know as well as I do. A handsome young man like that...," she trailed off.

Luz raised her eyebrows and spread her arms wide before stomping off toward the wagon, shaking her head.

When the young juggler took charge of guiding the oxen down the last mile, Abelard climbed back inside with the others. Jean pulled hard on the brake to slow the wagon. A chinstrap secured the wide-brimmed straw hat hiding his face.

He studied the scattered groups of thatched huts where Courbet's workers lived. They clustered like mushrooms in small enclaves wherever a flat area could accommodate them. Not a foot of precious land was wasted. Kitchen gardens surrounded each dwelling. Thatched roofs overhung doorways where shade would be welcome later in the day.

When the land leveled enough for a good-sized group of huts, Jean motioned to the young man to slow the oxen. Following Jean's orders, four figures in floppy straw hats slipped out the back door of the performers' wagon and mingled with other workers headed toward the fields. Luz tipped her brim to Jean and leaned onto Elisabeth as they blended in, the boys trotting along behind them.

As the wagon approached another batch of dwellings, Jean again gave the signal. After Marie and Abelard dropped from the caravan, he followed within a few hundred feet, leaving the juggler.

His longer stride brought him close to the others within a few minutes. Luz and his sister slowed to allow the others to catch up. "How far to the plantation house?" Jean asked. He plucked at Abelard's sleeve.

Sea birds circled and squawked above them, making conversation difficult.

"Maybe another mile," his cellmate said, "if we follow the road, but there is a shorter path the house servants use."

"Where?"

"Right here," Abelard said, and disappeared down the side of a steep drainage ditch.

Jean helped the women slide to the bottom of the slope where his old cellmate waited. The boys took the incline with quick lunging whooshes. After he grasped Luz's hand and pulled her to her feet, two tall, fierce-looking men with long cane cutlass blades towered over Abelard. Jean pulled his knife from his boot but re-sheathed the weapon when Abelard clasped one of the strangers to him and slapped him on the back.

"Come here, *Monsieur* Blanchard," Abelard said. "I want you to meet my sons."

"Your sons?" Jean asked, his voice full of disbelief.

"Their mother was tall," Abelard said with a wink. "My old cabin is near here. They still stay there."

"And dere mother?" Luz asked.

Abelard's eyes widened at her question. "She died a few years after Courbet had me locked up. A good woman."

Marie and Elisabeth, who kept their distance at the first sight of Abelard's fierce-looking sons, moved closer. Yancey and Gerard squatted nearby, engrossed in a game of sticks and small pebbles.

"Do they know how many guards are here today, or when Courbet is expected?" Elisabeth asked, her voice quavering.

"The guards are busy in the fields helping the overseers, but my sons promise to send warning with one of the water boys if they leave.

"As for Courbet, he keeps a ship in St. Pierre, but sailing round the tip of the island should take him much longer than our oxen trip over the mountain." Abelard took off his hat and mopped at his brow with a well-worn muslin square. "It just depends on how closely he's following our movements. He has spies everywhere."

Jean rubbed a hand over the stubble on his chin and gazed out over the fields now filling with workers. "Instead of risking the children who carry water, why not have Luz and Elisabeth help the women prepare food? The kitchen is on high enough ground to give a view of anyone coming from the harbor."

"Who I gonna say she is?" Luz asked, crooking a thumb toward his sister.

"Just tell them you're from another Courbet plantation off-island, and put Yancey and Gerard to work too." Jean shrugged his shoulders and urged them on their way. "Tell them Elisabeth is one of Courbet's castoffs. She's been sent to help with housework because her family's disowned her."

"Jean," his sister said through clenched teeth, "you forget. Someone murdered my parents, too." She poked him hard in the chest and leaned into his face. "I'm tired of living in the shadows. I want to know what happened. I've lost nearly everything, and I want my life back." She glared at him, daring him to challenge her right to be there.

Jean raised a brow and stared at his sister, seeing her for the first time. "Everyone has a job to do. Yours is to stay with the boys and protect them. I promise you by the end of today you will know whatever I know, but for now, I need your cooperation."

He turned then toward Marie and said, "I need you and Abelard with me, so I'll know what proof is important enough to take."

Ignoring his sister's silent, angry looks, he bent down to admonish the boys. "Make yourselves useful in the kitchen, and no matter what, do not talk to anyone, not even each other." At the stubborn set to their mouths, Jean softened his tone. "Can you do this one small thing for us?" After a few moments, he added, "It's important."

Luz rolled her eyes as the children nodded in wide-eyed agreement. Jean winced remembering the many times he and Marie had been on the receiving end of that look from the prickly housekeeper.

"Jean Blanchard, you will regret shunting me off like this," Elisabeth shouted back over her shoulder, as the two women trod toward the kitchen, following Abelard's directions. Two subdued boys followed behind.

The rigid set of his sister's back hinted of hell to pay later for sending her away.

Jean eyed his two fellow spies when they finally stood before Courbet's low-slung shuttered house tucked against a hillside. A wide porch with fluted pillars wrapped around three sides of the home, unlike the simple portico entrance and stoop at Galante House.

"What now?" Marie asked, and toed at the gravel on the wide path leading to the front door.

"It looks deserted," Jean said. "All the windows are closed."

Abelard searched around the side of the house and then rejoined them. "He never stays here."

The old man surprised Jean by advancing straight to the entrance and pounding. After a few moments of silence from within, Jean reached around him, turned the knob, and pushed. The door swung open without a sound, revealing a long, dark hallway.

Jean gave Abelard a wry look and then walked in ahead of him and Marie. As his eyes adjusted to the dim light in the front hall, he found a wall sconce and lit the candle with a flint on a nearby table.

"The study is down this way," Abelard said. His companions followed close behind.

They slipped into a room where book-filled shelves lined the walls. Marie inspected the desk while Abelard and Jean opened books and shook out the pages.

"I wonder who this poor fellow was," Jean said, when he stopped short in front of a corner shelf with a human skull wedged between two volumes.

Abelard's voice wavered a bit when he said, "No one knows, but we all had our suspicions."

Marie shook her head and stared at the stark remains. "What kind of man keeps a memento like that?"

Abelard reached past her and twisted the skull slightly. The wall behind creaked and scraped and then swung out smoothly, revealing a hidden alcove behind the rows of books.

Marie gasped. "What's back there?"

"Courbet's secret hiding place is difficult to describe. You need to see and judge with your own eyes."

Jean nearly stopped breathing as he pushed ahead of Abelard, sweeping away cobwebs.

"One thing is certain," Marie said, following close behind. "No one has been in here for a while." She ran into Jean with a thud when he extended his arm behind him.

"Don't," he said. "Let me see what's here first."

"Nonsense," Marie insisted. "You shouldn't have to face alone whatever Courbet has done." She pushed ahead to his side.

Abelard picked up a flint from a table near the door and lit candles in sconces on the wall as they went.

Jean froze mid-stride and let out an anguished groan. A long ebony table with carved legs stretched the length of an entire wall. Fat candles covered the surface. Most of them had burned all the way down to nothing but globs of dried wax. In amongst the tapers were items belonging to his mother. He took in the gruesome inventory: the miniature of her his father had always carried; a comb and brush; a small mirror; and the dusty, tattered remains of the dress she'd worn the last night she'd kissed him goodbye.

Marie came up behind him and took his hand. "Come away, Jean. She's not here. He can't hurt her anymore." She'd guessed the identity of the beautiful woman in the miniature.

He shoved Marie away. "You shouldn't be here. Go. Go back with Abelard. What I have to do is terrible, and you can't be here when Courbet arrives." That twisted bastard had to pay. He would make sure Courbet died slowly in great pain.

Abelard grasped him by the shoulders. "We have work to do. Whatever you're planning can wait." The slight, wizened man motioned Jean over to one of the wall sconces and pulled hard. Behind the candleholder, a small, scooped out section hid a tin box.

Jean dragged the container from its hiding place and pried off the lid. Inside was a sheaf of yellowed paper. He brought the sheets over to the light of another candle and searched the last page. Three sets of signatures transferred the Marigot plantation from an earlier owner to Jean's parents. Another sheet showed a second transfer from his parents to Courbet; however, the signatures appeared slightly different, as if copied.

He tossed the pages onto the table and kicked the empty metal box across the room. Abelard rescued the documents and tucked them inside his shirt. The box he retrieved and hid back behind the sconce.

"What are you going to do?" Marie asked, her voice shaking.

"I'm going to wait here in the dark for that snake to slither back," Jean said with a snarl.

"What about us?" she demanded. "Why can't we help you?"

"I need you to get the others and meet the performers in Marigot. Wait no more than a day for me. If I don't return, go to the magistrate and let him know what's happened."

"I'm not going," Marie said. "I'm not leaving you here alone." She folded her arms and thumped down onto one of the chairs in the alcove.

"Marie, please look at me." Jean sank to his knees in front of her and pried her hands loose from the arms of the chair, clasping them to his chest.

She strained away from him, avoiding eye contact.

"Now we know Courbet is capable of more than mere deceit. He's a murderer. I need you and Abelard to make sure Elisabeth, Luz, and the children are safe."

She shook her head, stubbornly refusing. "You'll wait here till he comes back so that you can kill him." She wrenched her hands out of his grasp. "If he destroys you instead, what will happen to us?" she pleaded. "You must come away. Now."

Jean exchanged a knowing glance with Abelard and then pulled her fingers to his lips. "You have to trust me. I will join you soon. I need a few minutes alone to say good-bye."

The old man came over and took her by the arm. "We have to leave before Courbet gets back with his guards. It will do Jean no good if he has to worry about you when he faces that reptile."

Marie pulled out of Abelard's grasp but finally rose to follow him, giving Jean a dark glance over her shoulder. "Luz is going to be upset when I tell her what you've done." Anger crackled and snapped from her dark eyes.

Jean threw his head back and laughed, softening the tension between them. "That old she-devil would be happy if I never darkened her kitchen again."

"You have to come back to us. We all need you," Abelard said, and gave his old cellmate one last long look before pulling Marie along with him.

Jean watched them retrace their steps back through the swinging bookcase, methodically extinguishing candles as they went. They closed the secret entrance behind them, sealing him in Courbet's hidden hole.

Antoine Courbet drove the farm wagon he kept in Marigot with oxen rented from the town stable. The lack of wind from St. Pierre around the tip of the island up to the port on the eastern shore had left him angry toward anyone unfortunate enough to step into his path.

"Francois, where is your mother?" he asked. "She was supposed to meet us at the ship. The cooks at the east island place will poison us all. We need Cecile."

His son turned to him with a fierce look. "My mother will join us when she is ready. She no longer jumps to your bidding. She thought…"

"That is your problem. Both of you think too much. And look where that got you. Complete failure to take over Blanchard's smuggling business. Do I have to do everything?"

In an awkward move, Francois tried to lean back on the wagon seat with his bandaged hands. "You were the one who decided to stop him by blowing up the jail," he reminded his father.

"Who would have thought those fools would store gunpowder in there? I just wanted to create a diversion with a little fire." Courbet motioned to one of the guards trotting alongside the wagon. "You - run ahead to the kitchen and warn those worthless cooks we'll be staying in the main house tonight."

"Oui, Monsieur, " the man said, and sprinted down the road in the direction of the cane field kitchen.

CHAPTER TWENTY-ONE

Marie scuffed her boots hard along the dusty dirt road leading to the plantation field kitchen and prayed for inspiration. Somehow, she had to stop Jean from killing Courbet. But first, she had to collect Luz, Elisabeth, and the boys.

She struggled to concentrate while raucous gulls flocked along the sides of the road, fighting over bits of carrion leavings. As they rose to escape with their booty, the birds surrendered to the buffeting easterly ocean winds that pushed them farther inland.

Marie fumed in silence at the memory of Jean's feeble attempt to make her believe he wouldn't harm that bastard Courbet. If he thought she couldn't see through his lies, then he knew her even less than she imagined. "How can a man love a woman he doesn't understand?" she blurted out to Abelard.

Jean's old cellmate laughed aloud. "If men refrained from loving women until they understood them, the world would be a very cold and lonely place."

When Marie shot him a withering look, he returned to his careful watch down the trail while he walked next to her.

She knew she should be terrified at the possibility of meeting Courbet or his men. Instead, all she felt was bright, cold outrage. She yearned to unleash her wrath on him. Something twisted within her until one thought crowded out all sensible consideration. Courbet had to pay for what he'd done to Jean's family.

As Marie and Abelard neared the plantation's kitchen behind the cane fields, the skin on the back of her neck tingled from the quiet. At the very least, she expected boys tumbling down the hill toward her. She wiped her sweating palms on the sides of her skirt just as a small figure popped out from behind a flaming pink flowering bush beside the path.

"*Madame* Galante," Yancey shouted.

"How did you get here?" Marie asked, and stooped to his level to hear what he had to say.

His eyes widened, and he gulped for breath. "*Monsieur* Courbet's guards..." He stopped and leaned down, putting his hands on his knees.

"What did they *do* to you?" She pulled the shaking boy to her and cradled his head against her chest. "You can tell me. I won't let them hurt you."

"Not me, but Gerard. The guards took him and his mother, too. I got away."

Marie pushed down rising panic and held Yancey at arm's length to look into his eyes. "You must remember everything and tell us which way they went. What happened to your grandmother?"

"She tole me to wait here for you. She followed the guards." Yancey stopped, wiping at his eyes. "And *Grand-mere* took a big blade with her. She stole one from a cane wagon."

Marie's stomach plummeted at the thought of Luz wielding such a huge weapon in pursuit of men without consciences.

"She waited until they left," Yancey added after a short pause.

Marie knew exactly where Courbet and his men would go: the plantation house where Jean waited. She had to get there first.

She stared hard at Abelard, indecision gripping her. He swept the boy up onto his shoulders and gave him a reassuring pat on one of his legs.

"I know what you're thinking. You go on. I'll take him back to my cabin. Maybe I can get a message to my sons when we pass the field they're working. If I don't hear from you, I'll take the boy to Marigot at first light tomorrow."

Marie trotted up the path and rounded the corner of one of the fields. She saw two overseers and three guards shouting at each other. Courbet must have raised an alarm. If she didn't beat them there, there was no way to save Jean. She abandoned the well-worn path and ran up an embankment, clawing her way through thick undergrowth. Small lizards scattered in her path, skittering across her boots.

She scrambled through a stand of scrubby trees and stumbled into a clearing. Luz was directly ahead of her in the open area, menacing one of the guards. Both her hands grasped the sharp cutlass, weaving it back and forth.

Mon Dieu. Her old nurse would be the death of her. If the guard ran to raise an alarm, all would be lost. She grabbed a fallen branch from beneath a tree, crept up behind him, and swung with all of her strength.

When Jean settled in for a long wait, he hadn't counted on the gentle ghosts in the dark. In spite of anger raging through him, his parents' presence seemed to envelop him with calm and reason. The scent of dried, crushed lily petals Courbet kept in a large bowl on the table reminded him of the night he said his last goodbye to his mother.

In spite of his reassurances to Marie, Jean still planned to kill Courbet. There was no forgiveness this side of hell that man could earn. Jean could not go on living with the knowledge of the bastard's continued success and happiness. He had to die.

But if Courbet died by his hand, what would happen to Marie, Elisabeth, and Gerard when Jean was taken back to the garrison to face the firing squad? For the first time, the thought of abandoning the people he loved made him question his resolve. When had he changed from a bitter man bent on revenge to a man more worried about those in his care who depended on him?

Hot tears welled in his eyes at the memories flooding his senses in the midst of his mother's belongings. He tried not to dwell on how she must have suffered.

Hurt, pain, and fear were not the emotions he channeled from her essence. Instead, a sudden peace came over him, and his unshed tears went inward and cleansed his soul of all the years spent burning for revenge.

He'd never cried as a boy when his parents had disappeared. Instead, the young Jean had hoped over the days, weeks, and finally years that his parents would someday miraculously return and they would be a family again.

The urge for violence gradually deserted him while he waited, crouched in Courbet's hidden room of deceit.

He sat on his haunches, staring at the opening through which the man he despised would soon pass, and noticed a muted glow along the bottom of the door. He estimated the sun had long ago passed its zenith on the long slide back down to dusk. There should not be any light showing through the small crack. When the scent of lilies haunted Jean's senses, he knew what his mother was trying to tell him.

Standing, he squared his shoulders and walked toward the secret passageway. He stopped and checked the armory he carried: a dagger inside his left boot; another knife in his belt; and two small pistols. They were good only at close range, but he wanted to look into the eyes of the bastard who tortured his family when he sent him to hell.

Jean walked to the long table covered with pools of wax and half-used candles. He scooped up an armful of the burned-down stubs he could pry loose before kicking through the door. As the hinges gave way and the heavy slab slammed down, a small metal box fell from a shelf above the door. He snatched the locked receptacle from the floor, stuffed it inside his shirt, and shouldered his way back through the secret passage.

In the dim, late-day sun filtering through the shutters he observed the contents of Courbet's study. Without bothering to close the bookcase opening behind him, he shoved the candles together on the floor and lit all of them with the flint Courbet had so thoughtfully left in the passageway. He rasped the metal piece against a rough stone and used the sparks to flame the wax chunks.

Jean piled chairs and an overstuffed sofa along one wall. After a few seconds' thought, he added armfuls of books onto the pile before tearing down the curtains flanking the windows. In one last step, he ripped a long strip of fabric from one of the curtain panels, stretched it out on the floor, and poured molten wax from each of the candles.

He raced into the hallway connecting the other rooms in the house and kicked open locked doors. Behind the second door he found barrels of gunpowder stacked to the ceiling. Jean whistled. Looked as though Courbet was ready to wage war with his own, personal army. From the dust collected on the barrels, they must have been there for years. So much the better for the surprise he had planned.

He pulled the metal box from inside his shirt to make sure he wasn't carrying something useless and broke the lock with his boot. When he recognized the fragile contents that spilled out, he stopped breathing for a moment. Letters, in his mother's handwriting. He bent and scooped them back into the container.

What he had to do now was simple. He stuffed the metal box back inside his shirt, lit his makeshift fuse, and then ran.

Marie gaped at the guard who turned on her, enraged, after her puny attempt to subdue him with a tree branch. He was tall and young. Outrunning him was out of the question. She pulled the dagger from her boot and sent it slicing through the air into his thigh.

The young man screamed and bent over, grappling with the blade. She slipped behind him and pulled a flintlock pistol from his belt.

He wrested the knife from his leg with such force, the weapon slipped from his fingers and dropped to the ground. Luz rushed over and pushed him onto his knees before she flattened him and sat on the backs of his legs. He shot a look behind him and shouted threats before stopping at the sight of Marie pointing his own pistol at his head.

"Who you tink you are, attacking defenseless women and children?" Luz whomped down on the struggling man and pointed her finger close to his face.

"What do you want from me?" He moaned and reached for his still bleeding thigh. "I know nothing. They just sent me back to slow you down."

"You lie." Marie moved closer and pushed the pistol against one of his ears. His eyes widened in fear, and she said, "Now you will tell us exactly where Courbet's taken the boy and his mother."

"Please, do not kill me. I work for *Monsieur* Courbet to feed my family."

"Pah," Luz bit out. "I know your mother, you. The money dat pig gives you goes to gambling and women in St. Pierre." As if to emphasize her words, she shifted her ample weight and pounded down on his legs again.

He cursed and dropped his head to the grass. After a few moments, he twisted toward her and pleaded, "Let me up, and I'll tell all."

When Luz eased her weight off the man, he tried to scrabble up and away, but his bleeding thigh would not support him. He sagged back onto the ground, rubbing frantically at the wound.

"So you think you don't have to tell us what happened?" Marie bent down and smacked his ear with the butt of the pistol, securing his attention. She cocked the firing pin and pressed the metal barrel against his forehead. "Now you will tell us everything we want to know, from the beginning, and if you leave out anything at all, the whores of St. Pierre will lose a customer."

"All right. I will tell you, but only because you have a pistol to my head. If Courbet finds out, he will kill me."

"Where are Elisabeth and Gerard?" Marie poked hard at his head with the weapon.

"Who?" he asked, as if dazed.

"Don't be stupid – the woman and boy you snatched for Courbet." Luz grabbed Marie's abandoned tree branch and pounded the guard's buttocks.

He screamed and glared at her. "Courbet sent us down to the field kitchen to warn the cooks he'd be staying at the big house tonight, and to bring back some food. He was on his way in the wagon from the harbor in Marigot. Made us run ahead."

"Why did you grab them?" Marie asked, her hand steady on the cocked pistol boring against his head.

"The other guard saw the white woman and asked about her. When the head cook said she was one of Courbet's mistresses, he knew that couldn't be true. So we took her, but she put up a fight, biting and scratching, until we grabbed her little boy and threatened him. The other guard took the captives to Courbet, leaving me to gather the food and head up to the big house."

Marie could not help herself. She drew back and slammed the pistol butt into his nose. Blood flew as he covered his face with his arms.

Luz struggled to keep him under control, but finally snatched the tree branch and knocked him senseless. "Now why you do that to this fool?" Annoyance crept into her voice as she stood and toed over the inert young man. "There. Now mebbe he won't drown in his own blood."

She shook her head and clucked at Marie. "You turnin' into a bloodthirsty old thing. I tink you right. No man gonna climb in your bed. You be killin' him in his sleep." She rolled her eyes and picked up the trusty branch, motioning for Marie to follow her. "Dat cutlass too hard to handle," she said, slashing her new-found weapon through the air. "Dis works much better."

"I'm sorry, Luz. I just lost control when he talked about scaring Gerard. Those brutes go too far." At that moment, Marie's head was snapped back and she cried out in pain. Someone held her by a handful of hair, forcing her up onto her toes.

"We meet again, *Madame* Galante. But this time the power is on my side. Galante Plantation is not going to remain long in your hands."

"Remy," Luz said, dropping the branch with a sharp intake of breath.

Marie moaned and her courage plummeted. Remy, the abusive overseer she banished when her husband died, must have gone over to Courbet.

"That's right. I heard the guard's screams and left the field to investigate," he said. "Now you're going to tell me why you were torturing that poor young man."

On his belly in the high cane, Jean crawled as close as possible to the shouting actors in the tableau unfolding before him. One of Courbet's guards lay still on the ground, his thigh oozing blood while an overseer towered over Marie and Luz.

He stifled the urge to rush to the women's defense and calculated the moment he would make his move. He was determined to control the outcome.

Slowing his breathing, he barely managed to restrain himself when Marie wrenched her hair free from Courbet's overseer.

At that moment an oxen-drawn wagon turned the sharp curve leading to the plantation house. Jean muffled a curse when he saw Francois seated next to Courbet, his former first mate's hands bandaged. On the seat behind the two, Elisabeth cradled Gerard in her lap with two guards holding pistols crowded to either side of them.

Instead of the terror he expected to see on Elisabeth's face, there was anger and determination. Jean breathed a sigh of relief at the signs of his sister's rage. He would need everyone's help to evade Courbet and his henchmen. He prayed he could count on Francois.

"Ah," Courbet said, and pulled up next to the clearing where Luz and Marie struggled with Remy. "Looks like the carefree smuggler has lost the rest of his little family. Now I have them all." He placed the reins in Francois's bandaged hands and climbed down from the wagon seat. Striding to where Marie still struggled with Remy, he taunted, "Marie, Marie – where is your absent lover?"

"He's not here, you soulless excuse for a man." She stood toe to toe with him, as if daring him to gainsay her.

"So you admit you've taken a hardened criminal into your bed. What will your gentle neighbors think?"

Jean ground his fingers into the dirt and gritted his teeth. He wanted to jump up and kill Courbet. But he had only one chance to save those he loved, so he would have to bide his time.

He eased his head to the side and watched a large flock of seagulls ride a roiling, corkscrew updraft. If his knowledge of weather and the sea was correct, all hell would break loose soon. All he could do was keep his silence and hope the others could hold out a while longer against Courbet and his henchmen. However, Jean's vow of silence was sorely taxed by the man's next words.

"I would bet my last gold piece he'll show up if I begin the party." Courbet nodded to the overseer detaining Marie. Remy pulled a whip from his belt in one lazy move.

She flinched as Courbet nodded again and Remy ripped the back of her thin muslin work dress. Marie muttered an oath as he dragged her to a tree. She glanced at Luz and willed her to remain quiet.

"Lean against the bark and stretch your arms around the trunk," he ordered. Marie whirled and grasped the whip, throwing the overseer off balance.

"Who knew that little harridan had so much fight left?" Courbet smiled and turned toward the wagon where Gerard slumped in Elisabeth's lap. "We'll see if this son is more like me than the other." He stood and grasped Gerard's arm, jerking him down off the wagon. Elisabeth shrieked and moved toward Courbet. A guard on the wagon seized and held her.

"Go help Remy with *Madame* Galante. Your papa needs to teach her a lesson in obedience."

"You're *not* my papa, and I would never hurt *Madame* Galante." When Courbet squeezed the boy's arm in a cruel grip, Gerard kicked and thrashed until he let him go.

"This is the thanks I get for rescuing you and your lying mother?" He turned with a sly wink to his overseer. "Maybe the boy needs a lesson along with Marie."

Francois glared at his father. "Leave the boy alone. He is innocent in this vendetta of yours."

Courbet's laugh echoed across the clearing. "As a son, you've always been lacking, but now you're completely worthless. You can't even protect the woman you think you love." He paused and then smirked. "I had her first. You'll always have to live with that."

At a signal from Courbet, the overseer pushed away Marie and came for Gerard instead.

Just as Francois leapt from the wagon onto his father's back, a loud explosion rocked the island and overshadowed his act of defiance. The plantation house burst into flames, and the winds that had been building all day billowed the fire down the hill toward the cane fields.

Courbet easily wrenched away from Francois, whose burned, bandaged hands were nearly useless. He raced up the hill to the house and encroaching flames, motioning for his guards and the overseer to follow.

Jean darted out of the cane field behind them, overpowered one of the guards, and slashed a dagger across his throat. He dispatched the second man with a pistol shot at close range.

When he was certain Courbet's remaining guards had followed him up the drive to contain the fire at the plantation house, he hurried back to the people he loved.

The scene that awaited him chilled his soul.

Gerard sat on the ground, not moving from where Remy had dumped him. Jean could cope with the boy's tantrums, but not the vacant stare, unshed tears glistening in his eyes. Elisabeth crouched over him, touching his face and crooning endearments.

"Gerard, look at me," Jean said, and joined his sister, encircling both of them in his arms. "We have to leave this place now. We have to take care of each other."

Francois had climbed back up onto the seat and looped the reins around his bandaged hands. Elisabeth's back remained rigid while Jean lifted her son from the ground.

She pointed an accusing finger at Francois. "Where have you been? How could you have been in league with that madman?"

"My father nearly killed me when he found me at the jail helping Jean and Abelard. He set a fire to cover our tracks, but didn't count on the gunpowder being stored so close by," Francois explained.

Gerard snuffled loudly before releasing a torrent of tears once he was safe in Jean's arms. Marie moved close to Elisabeth to help her up onto the wagon seat.

Jean's sister whirled and motioned her away. She turned on Francois again. "You haven't explained why you became part of Jean's crew and lied to all of us about your intentions. Your only purpose was to destroy us." Her voice broke. "And then you made me love you…"

Francois slid down to Elisabeth's level and without a word wrapped his arms around her. She tried to push him away, but he wouldn't release her.

Jean turned toward the lead wagon with Gerard slumped over his shoulder, hiccupping with sobs. He motioned for Marie to follow him. When he turned toward Luz with a questioning gaze, she joined Francois and Elisabeth. Marie's housekeeper took charge of pushing the two toward the back seat of the second wagon while she took the reins.

Marie and Jean climbed onto the lead wagon. Gerard's sobs slowed, and he closed his eyes. Marie found an old blanket under the seat and tucked it around the boy.

Jean pulled Marie close, clucked at the oxen, and the wagon jerked into motion. After a long silence, she asked, "Where are we going?"

"Courbet's ship is at the wharf in Marigot with just his captain and a few crew on board." Jean smiled. "His ship's master is a practical man who works for the highest bidder."

CHAPTER TWENTY-TWO

After pulling Marie aboard the wagon, Jean covered her tattered bodice with his vest while they rolled down the road to Marigot. His fingers brushed across her arms as he adjusted her torn shift. She pushed his hands away and pulled the fabric tight across her breasts, shuddering at the memory of Courbet's overseer ripping at her clothes.

"How long were you going to wait before coming for us?" Her voice shook with a tide of contradictory feelings. "I understand you could not show your presence too early, but what would you have done if they'd killed one of us before your explosion went off?"

He sat back on the high seat and stared off in the distance for several seconds. "I had to wait until just the right moment. If I'd shown myself before they were distracted by the fire and explosion..." Jean didn't finish the thought. "When you and Abelard left, I had no way of knowing Courbet was already on the island. His knowledge of what lay in the hidden room must have driven him to return sooner than we expected."

"Did you know Francois was alive and not tell your sister?" She turned to him, stabbing at his chest with one of her fingers.

He grasped her hand and squeezed hard. "We were all there together. I saw what you saw. How could I have guessed he was still alive?"

"You kept things from all of us," Marie insisted. "I just know."

"You're not making any sense. You don't understand."

"Convince me."

"If I had appeared too early, Courbet's men would have disarmed me, and then the outcome would have been unthinkable."

"We were doing fine before you got there."

"Was that before or after the you were tied to the tree?" Jean's laugh filled the silence between them.

"You weren't there," Marie said, and she slid farther away from him. "You didn't see how hard Luz and I fought while you were deciding whether or not to intervene."

"If I had known you were suffering," Jean said as he grasped her hands and pulled her back, "nothing would have kept me from your side."

"Why did you set fire to the house?"

"The truth? I sat in the darkness remembering my mother and thinking only of revenge, and then a strange thing happened. The memories were so strong, I felt her come to me in a cloud of peace. After that, destroying Courbet's house of pain seemed the only sensible course.

"I realized you are my family now, along with my sister and Gerard. The men in my smuggling crew need me to help them find new ways to support themselves. And of course, Luz, Yancey, the workers at your plantation. You're all my responsibility."

Marie opened her mouth to argue only to have him silence her with a kiss.

"I know what you're going to say, but believe me, you are the only woman I want to be with. We'll be married as soon as possible."

"That cannot happen," she interrupted firmly.

"What about our child?"

"There is no child," Marie said, her face flaming red.

"My mother believes we will have a little girl who looks like her by next summer," he insisted.

Marie smacked him on the shoulder. "And I suppose she told you all this while you were meditating in the dark?"

"Of course," he said, an impudent grin on his face.

This time, when she shoved his chest, her hand encountered a small, hard rectangle. "What's in there?"

He reached inside his shirt and brought out the tin box. "I forgot about this," he said, and the expression on his face sobered.

Marie took the reins while Jean pried off the corroded lid.

"These are letters written by my mother," he said, and touched the frayed, faded lavender ribbon tying them together. He replaced the box cover with care and tucked the container in his shirt.

"Should we read them now?" Marie asked.

"No," Jean replied. "We'll wait until we get to the ship," he said through clenched teeth.

An eerie silence settled in from the sea, the waves calming to a glass-like texture. Jean searched the darkening horizon beyond Marigot's harbor for clues to the source of the sudden weather change. Gusts and small squalls had swept across the island all day. Nothing stirred, not even the many flocks of birds that normally swooped, seeking insects and fish in the evening.

In other, saner times, he would have postponed a sea trip, but the risks were too great to stay put. Within hours, Courbet and his men would bring the fire under control. He had to move his family to a safe refuge before the bastards caught up with them. Instinctively, he moved his hand over the metal box still in his shirt. The letters could hold the answers to questions plaguing him since his childhood.

"What do you see?" Marie stood close while he scanned the cloudless horizon with his spyglass.

"Not a sign of a storm approaching, but I can feel the pressure changes. In this season, anything can happen."

"Should we wait?"

"If only we could," Jean said, and turned to Francois. "Lead on to your father's ship."

"She's anchored in the harbor. We'll take the shore boat out to negotiate with Captain Willem," Francois said.

Jean faced Marie and the others. "All of you should stay with the street performers until we return."

"No," Marie said. "What if there's a trap? There could be more guards aboard Courbet's ship, just waiting for you to arrive." She plucked at Francois's shirt. "I'm sorry," she said. "You've been with your father. We don't know if you still owe him your allegiance."

Francois nodded. "I understand why you don't trust me. However, this is our only chance to escape. You have to believe me when I say the most important people to me are Elisabeth and Gerard. I want to regain their trust. Courbet is my father in name only. I no longer call him family."

Just then the lamplighter approached with his torch. Luz pulled the boys close and squeezed.

"Jean, Francois, do what you must. I have no choice but to trust. We will find the performers and wait for you there," Marie said.

Rags muffled the oars as Jean and Francois rowed hard toward Courbet's huge merchant barque lifting on the slight swells of the incoming tide in Marigot's harbor.

Although Francois had assured him the captain would welcome a bribe to take over the ship, Jean left nothing to chance. He would approach the man on his own terms, not at the end of a guard's pistol.

The evening shore breeze nudged the small boat against the larger ship. Jean layered a tattered blanket over the gunnels to quiet their arrival.

The rope boarding ladder hung loose down the side of the ship. Courbet and his men must have been careless in their rush to disembark. Jean grabbed one of the cross lines and hoisted himself upward. Francois followed close behind. The strange, heavy silence caused Jean to place each boot with care as he made his way up the wide-beamed hull.

When he reached for the toe rail, a strong hand tightened on his arm and hauled him aboard as if he weighed less than a fish. He instinctively dropped to the deck in a crouch, his hands up in a defensive pose. Captain Gareth Willem stared down at him, a scowl on his face.

With a sudden bark of laughter, the tall, broad-shouldered man lifted his arms in the universal sign of surrender. "There's only me, Blanchard. Courbet took every last sailor with him to make sure at least one of them killed you." Another rumble of laughter bubbled up from his barrel chest. "Let's retire to my cabin and decide what this ship is worth over a good bottle of rum." The big man's smile morphed into a scowl as Francois pulled himself aboard behind Jean. "So you've changed sides?"

"Yes, he has." Jean spoke quickly to reassure the captain and clapped his arm around his first mate's shoulder. "We've sworn to work together."

Francois straightened and stood tall in the face of the captain's accusation. "My father is insane. I can no longer be his bearer of evil."

Marie slipped through the silent streets of Marigot, keeping to the shadows. The night air hung heavy and warm, like a large cat wrapped around her shoulders. She stopped a moment here and there, casting a look about, before motioning to Luz to follow with Elisabeth and the boys.

Finally, she paused and let her gaze sweep the darkened streets for the performers. How hard could it be to find a large, gaudy wagon full of tumblers and jugglers in a small sea town? A sinking feeling in the pit of her stomach nagged at her. Could something have happened since they left them? She prayed Jean's old friends hadn't been forced to flee across the mountains back to St. Pierre.

At last, from the corner of her eye, she spied a flashing light. Brightly lit torches arced through the air, just one street over. She expelled the breath she'd been holding and sought out her companions crouching down the block behind her. She waved an all-clear sign and pointed toward the fiery jugglers.

Once she gathered the others close, she debated the best way to approach the wagon. No doubt a crowd would have gathered around the street entertainment. For all she knew, Courbet could have spies in the crowd awaiting their return.

A small hand tugged from behind at Jean's vest, which she still wore. Marie jumped at the touch but calmed when she saw Yancey's smiling face.

At her questioning look, he said, "*Monsieur* Abelard and I heard the explosion and saw the flames from Courbet's house." After putting two fingers to his lips, he beckoned them to follow into the dark street behind the torch-lit performance.

Jean followed Captain Willem aft to his cabin. Once inside, he whistled low at the opulence with a sideways glance at Francois. A Turkish carpet in rich, blood-red tones covered the floor while every possible luxury a ship's master could desire crowded the cabin spanning the width of the ship's stern.

Dark-stained teak lined the interior surfaces, including the large desk piled with charts. Light from hanging candle-lit lanterns on gimbals reflected off a polished brass sextant atop the charts. All the chairs and the enclosed bed were stuffed with plump cushions.

Jean shuddered at the thought of how much he would have to pay this wealthy captain to betray Courbet. He shrugged off the negative thought with the vision of Marie, his sister, and Gerard. No matter the cost, he had to ensure their safety.

As if reading his mind, Willem said, "This is *my* ship. Courbet pays dearly for the use of my vessel and my services, but only I decide where my allegiances lie."

The captain extended his arm toward the bench at the end of the chart table and Jean took a seat. Francois followed more slowly.

"Seems you two have run afoul of my business partner," the captain said.

When Francois flinched, Willem gave him a reassuring gesture with the palm of his hand. "We're all businessmen. We're here to negotiate a price." He stared pointedly at Jean. "What do you think your family's safety is worth?"

Jean returned the burly captain's stare. "Just tell me what you want. We've run out of time."

Marie bent over the performers' huge trunk and tossed costumes toward Luz and Elisabeth. She'd decided to use face paint for the boys and let them tumble with the acrobats. The two children loved rolling about and punching each other anyway. No one would take notice of small, tumbling clowns.

Luz took the role of reader of palms. When Marie had broached the idea, her housekeeper waved off any doubts. "I know da lies dose women tell. I got some lies of my own," she'd said, and grabbed at the first turban with gold glitter Marie produced. As soon as Luz had ambled out with a veil covering her face, a long line of Marigot revelers had queued up outside the wagon awaiting her fortune-telling.

A masked Abelard followed close behind Luz, dressed in the bright colors of a jester, bells tinkling from the drooping points on his hat.

Marie smiled in spite of their dire circumstances and dug deeper in search of a disguise for herself. In a fit of inspiration, she'd dressed Elisabeth as one of the male jugglers.

She gathered a pile of gossamer fabric as well as a silver belt, a pile of bangles, and another veil. At the very bottom her hand encountered a silver circlet. She positioned the crown on her head and whirled through the wagon, eyeing the opacity of the layers of her skirts. She didn't want to draw too much unwanted attention.

A giggle bubbled from her throat when she pictured her neighbor, *Madame* Darroc, spying her current incarnation as the lady of veils. She banged down the trunk lid and hurried out to join the others on the stage.

Jean sighed and shook hands with the burly Captain Willem. The big man pulled him into a massive bear hug. *Mon dieu* – what an emotional man. But then, why wouldn't he be? Jean had just agreed to give him a small fortune in exchange for sailing his family to safety.

He'd left what little gold he always carried on his person and his parole that the balance would be paid three days hence in a meeting in St. Pierre Harbor.

He doubted the captain would double-cross him with the promise of so much to come, but he left Francois, just in case. Of course, his former first mate could betray him just as easily, but something in the man's slave-like devotion to Elisabeth made him think not.

Jean barely recognized the man he'd become. He'd just given up most of what he'd worked years to accumulate smuggling. He wouldn't dwell too much on his losses. He had so much more to gain.

After tying the shore boat at the quay closest to Courbet's barque rocking at anchor, he took off at a run. When Jean paused for a few moments to determine his location in the seaside town, he saw the smoky glow of the jugglers' torches and resumed his mad dash to the street where the performers had set up the stage.

A sultry dancer swathed in gauzy skirts swayed to the flute and tambourine players' exotic music. At times, she seemed to hesitate at the steps but then recovered. Torchlight reflected off the delicate circlet holding her dark, tumbling curls away from her face.

He diverted his attention away from the dancer and searched the crowd for Marie, Elisabeth, and the others. Just when he'd nearly given up, one of the small clowns circulating through the crowd for contributions jerked at his pocket. He grasped the small reveler's hand only to see the dancing eyes of his mischievous nephew flash at him.

Jean turned around to stare at the heavily rouged dancer just as men in the audience began tossing coins at her feet and calling out rude incentives.

Anger flushed his face when he realized the tantalizing woman whirling on the stage was Marie. He pushed his way through the crowd and grasped her wrist, pulling her with him toward the end of the wagon where he shoved her through the almost invisible door disguised with an elaborate landscape painting.

Once inside the wagon, Marie broke away from him and began pulling off the layers of her costume and tossing them into the large storage trunk. Arms encircled Jean from behind, and when he whirled to face his attacker, he encountered his sister. Abelard sat in a corner of the wagon cleaning face paint from the two boys.

Marie peeked sideways while re-packing the trunk. "Luz is still out there. Would someone please get her?" Shaking her head, she removed stuffing from the small pointed-toe slippers the boys handed her. "That woman took way too much pleasure tonight misleading the poor citizens of Marigot. After all these years, Luz's gossip found a purpose."

Jean moved to the center of the wagon, irritated. "*Ecoutez—*." His voice cracked through the performers' babble. "We have a ship waiting. I will understand if any of you wish to escape with us." His offer met with silence. "We have to leave immediately."

The chief juggler moved behind him and laid a hand on his shoulder. "It would better if you take your family now and let us disappear into the foothills. Maybe some of Courbet's men will follow us and give you a better chance to disappear."

"I can't let you take that chance." Jean pounded the wall for emphasis. "They're cold-blooded killers."

"And we are the kings of illusion." The man moved away from him, never dropping any of the fruits he'd started to toss through the air. When Jean opened his mouth to protest, one of the juggler's orbs fell to the floor.

"Now look what you've done," he accused Jean with a sly grin. "I'm going to have to ask you to leave and take your bothersome family with you." He winked, softening his parting words, and disappeared out front to harness the oxen and take his place on the wagon's high seat.

"Where are we going?" Marie asked, herding and quieting her charges out into the night. Jean followed close behind but didn't answer her question immediately.

Once behind the wagon, Marie rounded on him, anger in her dark eyes. "Answer me, Jean Blanchard. What have you gotten us into? What terrifying act will you make us perform next?" she demanded.

To avoid a loud, emotional outburst from Marie, Jean spun her around by her waist so that he could whisper in her ear. The crowd passing by would think they were merely two quarreling lovers.

"Your ship awaits, *Madame*," he rasped. "We return to St. Pierre tonight." At a look of fury from his sister, he added, "And yes, your worthless lover awaits you aboard Courbet's barque."

CHAPTER TWENTY-THREE

Marigot Harbor

Jean lay flat behind the seawall in a dark-as-tar corner near the quay. Six other bodies squeezed next to him – more quiet than he'd ever seen them.

The lamplighter had finally illuminated the lantern on the street behind them, the single flare the only glow for several blocks.

He motioned to Abelard and Elisabeth to follow him. They crouched low and scuttled toward where the boat lay tied to a large iron ring at the bottom of steep stone steps.

He sucked in a breath and leaned toward Marie.

"Yes, yes – I know what to do," she said with a hiss. "Just go."

He smiled in the darkness, hidden from his prickly Marie. If this was the worst he could expect for the rest of his days, he'd be lucky.

Jean needed the rowers in place before the others followed, so they could make a quick run for the ship. Minutes would count when Courbet and his men arrived in Marigot. He would not underestimate the man again.

After Jean slipped away toward the boat, Marie counted slowly to one hundred and back, per Jean's orders. Then she and Luz each tucked a boy close and slid from shadow to shadow.

Gerard squeezed her hand once, then twice. Luz and Yancey were on the boat. Their turn to race across the last open space to the safety of the shore boat. She could just see the outline of Jean's face in the reflection off the water. One moment he was staring at her and then his gaze shifted to a point behind them, up the slope next to the quay.

Marie clutched Gerard and ran as if the devil were nipping at her heels.

Courbet and Remy shouted behind them just before she and the boy leapt into the boat. Jean released the single line holding them to the rusty ring, and the three rowers bent hard to put distance between them and Courbet's men.

As pistol shots cracked in the night and spent balls burst into the water around them, Marie covered Gerard's head and shoulders with her body.

Finally, the distance from the dock widened enough that the pursuers' shots fell short of the boat. She sat up gingerly, hugging Gerard close to quiet his shaking.

When she had a chance to look at Jean's sister she saw she was rowing valiantly, but blood flowed from a gunshot crease on one of her shoulders. Her right arm was weak to near uselessness, so that Jean turned to see why her rowing had become one-sided.

Marie took Elisabeth's place and grasped the long oars. When the injured woman leaned away from the gunnels, Luz caught her and ripped a length of her own underskirts to stanch the blood flow.

Marie mouthed a silent prayer of thanks for all the hours she'd spent slashing cane. The muscles in her arms and shoulders responded to the call to row like sturdy little soldiers. Jean and Abelard bent harder on their oars toward Courbet's barque.

The ship loomed larger, and a huge hulk of a man climbed down a ladder hung over the side of the hull. He extended arms to help the boys aboard, his powerful legs twined around the rope rungs of the ladder.

As the shore boat bumped against the barque's hull, Jean looped the bow line to an iron eye near the waterline on the larger ship. "Captain Willem," Jean said, as he transferred his charges, "I never thought your ugly face would look so good."

Abelard and Marie shepherded the boys to the swinging ladder. Luz and Jean put Elisabeth between them for the climb up the side of the ship.

Once all of his passengers were safe on deck, Capt. Willem turned to Jean and dropped his voice. "The pressure in the glass is falling like a ball of lead to the bottom of the sea. A big blow is coming. We have to leave this harbor for open water as soon as possible."

Jean said, "I'll help as much as I can to get some canvas up to get us out of here. Francois can see to settling the rest of the passengers."

"Here they come," Willem said, pointing to the shore where Courbet and his men had seized a boat and were rowing toward them at a furious clip.

An angry bank of clouds already formed at the horizon in the direction they would have to make for open sea.

Jean gave a bitter laugh. "We have two choices – the devil on one side, the angry sea on the other." He motioned to Francois and Abelard. "Take everyone below – *Vite!* Francois already had scooped Elisabeth into his arms and was helping her to the captain's cabin.

For once, Luz voiced no complaints or arguments. She and Abelard herded the boys between them to the steps to the lower cabins.

The two remaining men raced to prepare for the storm. Jean took his place at the capstan to crank up the anchor chain from the depths while the captain stood at the wheel.

The first tendrils of short, gusting bursts of wind reached the barque just as she shot free, sails snapping like gunshots.

Marie lit the swinging oil lamp in Captain Willem's cabin while Francois settled Elisabeth on a bench at the chart table.

"I need clean cloths and spirits as soon as possible," Marie said. She knelt and steadied the younger woman, her heart beating in time with the prayers racing through her head. She could not allow infection to set in. Jean's sister had to survive this latest outrage.

Courbet must be stopped. If unchecked, he would destroy Jean and his entire family.

Francois opened trunk after trunk and ripped through the contents until he found a clean shirt. He handed Marie the cloth to tear into strips while he searched for a bottle of spirits.

Sweat dotted Elisabeth's forehead. Marie held back her hair and cradled her head while Francois soaked one of the cloth strips in a cup of the captain's fiery rum. One of the trunks had held a collection of bottles wrapped in blankets.

Jean's sister jerked her arm in a spasm of pain when Marie first touched the soaked cloth to her wound, but she didn't cry out.

"Gerard is safe?" she asked, her voice quavering. Francois held her in a firm grip while Marie cleaned her wound.

"He's below with Yancey," Marie said. "They think our escape is a great adventure. The boys will be fine." Marie used one of the fine linen shirt strips to pull back her own hair while Francois repositioned Elisabeth in his arms so that she could not see the wound.

"Has he asked any questions?" Pleading and fear fought with the pain in her eyes. "About Courbet's accusations?"

"Gerard is very young." Marie chose her words with care. "Today's events will not be as hard on him as they've been on you, but," she added, "you must talk to him as soon as you can. He needs to know the truth."

Elisabeth flinched again, and Marie shifted her position to allow Francois to block the view while she cleaned the path the ball shot took across her upper arm.

Marie winced as if feeling the young woman's pain and prayed she could soon find the plants she would need for a poultice to draw infection away. From the feeling of the ship heaving its way toward the open sea, she feared landfall would not come soon.

Elisabeth fell quiet for a long while, her eyes closing several times before she gripped Marie's arm hard.

"Where are my mother's letters?"

"They're safe. Jean has them."

"You must bring them down here. Please?"

Her plea made sense. The tin box inside Jean's shirt should be saved from the already building wind and sloshing waves above decks.

"I'll be right back," she mouthed to Francois and tied the last piece of cloth binding.

"You can't go up there now," he warned.

"I have to. There's no one else. We've come too far to lose what might be proof of Jean's innocence."

"Be careful. Wrap lines around your arms wherever possible. Never let go of the ship, or you'll be washed overboard." Francois gave her one last stern look before carrying Elisabeth to the captain's feather mattress on a wide bunk.

Marie turned to climb above decks, only to find Luz hovering behind her. "Did you settle the boys into Abelard's safekeeping?"

"Dey both asleep."

"So soon?"

"Dem boys bragged about going above to help before Abelard fed dem some watered rum he said all sailors have to drink in a storm."

"You gave them spirits?" Marie asked. She gave Luz a questioning look and then pulled on one of the captain's heavy wool coats hanging on a peg next to the cabin entry.

"How else we goin' calm dose boys down?" Her housekeeper threw up her arms.

"I'm sorry, Luz. Of course you did the right thing." Marie headed through the cabin entry and looked back at her old friend. "Please help Francois take care of Elisabeth. I promise I'll be right back."

At her old friend's puzzled look, Marie whispered, "I must go above and rescue Jean's mother's letters. I'm sure he's forgotten them in all he's done to help Captain Willem outrun the storm."

Luz did not argue, but stepped over to Marie and held her close.

On the climb to the deck, Marie had to keep a firm hold on the rope loops placed along the steps. The barque rolled sharply and banged down the sides of the huge waves spilling on board across the gunnels.

The sight above deck unnerved her. Sheets of rain fell so hard, she could barely distinguish storm water from waves.

How would she keep from being swept overboard, let alone find Jean?

She fell to her knees and felt her way to the spindles along the sides of the deck where the heavy sail sheets were attached. She grabbed the bitter ends of the lines swinging loose to the deck and crept forward, seeking a glimpse of Jean.

Someone gripped the back of the captain's coat she'd thrown over her dress, and she was hauled against another wet, soaked body.

"Get. Back. Down. Below," he bellowed. Jean's face pressed tight against hers, his hair spray-soaked and blown back by the keening wind.

"Give me the box," she shouted back.

A flash of recognition crossed his face, and he transferred the metal box from inside his shirt to the safety of Marie's bodice.

"You would be a rogue even if the end of the world were near," she said with a snarl and slapped at him as he paused a second too long at the warmth of her breast.

"If I could steal one last touch of your sweet body, I would go to my grave a happy man," Jean said. He bent forward against the force of the wind and pulled her back toward the companionway.

Marie shook her head at him before turning to descend to the relative safety below. "What are you going to do now?"

"Captain Willem needs a rest from the helm," Jean said, and gave her one last grim glance before he retraced his steps toward the wheel near the stern of the ship.

Her final view of Jean was as he disappeared into the foam of a huge wave crashing onto the deck.

Marie grabbed an extra blanket from the chest in the captain's cabin and spread it flat across the chart table.

She met with resistance when she tried to pull open the lid on the metal box. "Francois, find something to pry off this lid."

After a tender, backward glance at Elisabeth's sleeping form, he moved toward a locked chest stored near the cabin door. He retrieved the key from behind a navigation book on a nearby shelf.

Marie sucked in a sharp breath at the sight of a pile of weapons inside the trunk. Francois withdrew a dagger lashed inside the lid.

"Here. This should be sharp and thin enough to fit under the lid." He handed her the dagger, jewel-encrusted handle first.

"These gems must be worth a small fortune," Marie said, while she pried at the box lid. He shrugged and went back to his vigil next to Elisabeth.

"Luz, help me spread these sheets on the blanket. If I hold them to read while they're wet, they might crumble and we'll lose forever the clues they hold." She placed the open box at the edge of the table.

With the tips of her fingers, she pulled one sheet loose and asked Luz to do the same. "These were written on the backs of sheets ripped from one of Courbet's plantation ledgers. If she was his prisoner, she took a terrible risk to write these letters. They have to be important." She and Luz lifted the soaked, fragile sheets individually.

A loud crack followed by a sideways lurch of the ship sent them sprawling and scrabbling for handholds. Thank God she'd re-attached the oil lamp to the gimbaled holder on the ceiling.

The wet sheets and blanket didn't move, the lip around the edge of the table holding them snug.

Once the ship righted, Marie helped Luz back to standing. Francois still clung to Elisabeth's side, having kept her from being flung from the bunk.

She turned to her housekeeper. "Luz, please find some parchment, a quill, and ink in Captain Willem's desk. We have to record *Madame* Blanchard's last thoughts."

MADAME BLANCHARD'S LETTERS

My dearest Jean and Elisabeth,

He's gone to another plantation today, and forgot to bolt the door behind him. This is my only chance. I have to get a message out of this hell on earth before that monster returns.

Your father - I'm sorry, Jean – he is dead these three long weeks, ever since the night Monsieur Courbet lured us here to purchase Marigot Plantation.

When we sat down to dinner with him, he pulled a pistol from inside his waistcoat and shot your father in the chest. When I tried to help, his guard dragged me to this hidden room where I've been his prisoner ever since.
At first I thought he would try to ransom me, but I was naïve. Courbet is the devil incarnate. Torture is his pleasure.

I cannot write more now. The ledgers – I have to steal a page here and there and pray he doesn't discover what I've done.

Your loving mother,
Honore Blanchard

J&E – not much time, must scratch out a few more words before he returns. If these letters are ever found, you must promise on your dead father's honor – there will be justice.

Now that monster wants me to agree to live with him as his wife – pretend your father's death was an accident. He is mad.
— HB

Jean –
Before I lose my wits – this is how much he took from our family – every last bit of money we brought with us – 10,000 francs.

*He threatened the two of you to assure my
compliance in his wicked plan. If he is still alive
when you read my letters, you must kill him.*

Our family will never be safe as long as he—
— HB

This is the last —
Cannot go on —
PROTECT YOUR SISTER

"Luz, what do we tell Jean? We can't show him these letters." Marie buried her head in her arms and curled her legs around the chair to keep from being bucked off by the storm's constant pounding.

"Got to," Luz said. "He da only one can make dis right." Another rolling lurch of the ship forced Luz to reach over and cling to Marie's side.

At a touch on her shoulder, Marie raised her head. Francois squatted next to her.

"You can't hide the truth. He'll find out anyway."

"I can't let him kill your father." She swiped at a tear sliding down her cheek. "It's not fair."

"If anyone ever deserved killing, it's that man, but Jean doesn't have to be the one to take him down," Francois said.

"Surely you can't consider killing your own father." Marie's eyes widened. And then she turned away and gave the letters a light touch, testing them for dampness.

A huge boom, like thunder on Judgment Day, echoed through the ship. Water cascaded down the companionway and flooded into the cabin above their feet only to recede just as quickly.

When Elisabeth moaned and tried to sit up in the bunk, Francois returned to her side and calmed her with soothing words and a restraining hand on her forehead.

"She's feverish," Marie said. "The infection took hold faster than I thought."

Luz found more linen strips and dipped them into a china basin of water. She handed the soaked strips to Francois to cool Elisabeth's brow.

Marie handed Francois a teacup with more water. "See if you can get her to drink some of this. We have to keep the fever down until we can get back to land where I can gather supplies for a poultice. I've not had a chance to replenish my supplies since I treated Jean's crew."

Marie stood next to the bunk where Elisabeth tossed, muttering nonsensical words, her face flushed. Jean's sister sat up in an abrupt move and clutched at Francois's arm. "Where? Where are Jean and Gerard? Please, don't tell. Don't tell Jean. He mustn't know."

Jean kept watch at the wheel as morning light seeped through bands of heavy gray clouds hiding the sun. He'd sent Captain Willem below to rest for a few hours. They'd decided to make for a cove on the northwest coast of Martinique to wait out the battering winds.

The captain's last argument before leaving the deck still haunted him. Why sail into St. Pierre to take his chances with the French magistrate at the garrison when they could just as easily drop their passengers on Marie's island and then head on out to sea?

After searching his soul, Jean could find only one answer. He would have to face Marie soon, and he dreaded the moment.

Marie stood in the side cabin with Captain Willem, her emotions in tatters. What he suggested made so much sense, but her heart ached as if being ripped out of her chest. When she squeezed her eyes shut to prevent the flow of tears, all she could see was Jean's face.

"How soon can we make port on my island?" she asked.

"The worst of the storm seems to have passed. There's still heavy wind, but that should calm in a few hours," he said, sighing as he stripped off his sodden coat and sank to the bunk. "We're making for a small cove to ride out the wind. Should be there in a few hours. After that, maybe another four-hour sail to your island. You'll be home by morning."

"And then?" She couldn't bear to finish the rest of her question.

"It's better if you don't know where we're going." The big man rolled to his side and added, "Wake me when we make landfall."

Marie firmed her resolve. "You're right. I won't ask any more questions."

Although she knew she should rest, sleep was the last thing on Marie's mind. She had to see Jean, touch him, feel his arms around her before she could let him go.

She dragged herself past the main cabin where Elisabeth still lay under the care of Francois and Luz. She kept moving, without the strength to face anyone until she said her private farewells to Jean.

The wind had come down considerably since her last trip up to the deck at the height of the storm. She still had to hang on to lines, but now, she could walk upright without dropping to her knees to escape the `gusts.

Jean stood tall at the wheel, his long, dark hair tied back with a leather thong. A few long tendrils had escaped and whipped at his cheeks.

She was near to his side, but he still didn't acknowledge her presence. As she edged closer, he snatched at her waist without warning and squeezed her close.

"Don't you know it's dangerous to surprise a heavily armed man?" A warm smile belied his stern tone.

"I talked to the captain," Marie said, the rest of the words stuck in her throat.

"I know."

"It is for the best," she said, turning her head away.

"Do you want me to leave?" Jean pulled her chin back to face him.

"I want you to live. If that means you must leave…"

"Marie, I'm not leaving you. Ever. I would rather face a firing squad than travel the world without you."

"But you can't. What if the magistrate refuses to consider your proof?"

"We will see. But when I die, I want to be looking into your eyes." He wiped sea spray from his face with his shirtsleeve before continuing. "Whether that day comes next week at the garrison, or years hence in our bed, matters not. I will be with you."

"But you must think of yourself. I will take care of Elisabeth and Gerard."

"I am thinking of myself. You and that small island are my world from now until the end." He shifted his hold to enclose her between him and the wheel.

"Now, tell me what you found in my mother's letters."

CHAPTER TWENTY-FOUR

Marie's mind still reeled from Jean's declaration. She was stunned to think he would risk death to stay with her. He stood close behind her, his hands steady on the ship's helm.

She turned and placed her hands against his chest, considering her words carefully. She feared more than ever the words in his mother's letters would wound him.

"Honore's letters can set you free, but the truth in them will be hard on you and Elisabeth." Marie cringed a little at the thought of what his reaction would be to the evidence of his mother's suffering.

His dark eyes watched the waves, the silence stretching between them. She sensed his anger building.

He pulled her back around in his arms so that she faced toward the wheel and lowered his chin into the mop of wind-tossed curls on top of her head.

"I'm sorry," she said, and tried to wriggle free to face him.

"Quiet," he said and held her tighter. "Just be still and let me hold you."

When Captain Willem returned, Jean still held Marie.

"Did you tell her?"

"Yes," Jean said, "but I've decided to stay."

"Why? There's nothing for you in St. Pierre but a bullet at dawn."

"Captain," Marie said, wrenching out of Jean's grip. Anxiety ripped at her gut. "Please make him sail away with you."

"I'm no magistrate, *Madame* Galante, but I don't see what Jean can do. It will be his word against Courbet's, and that man is an influential, wealthy planter."

Jean appeared unmoved as he stood at the wheel, rejecting their entreaties.

"Please, listen to us," Marie pleaded. "Think of what you're giving up." He remained silent, continuing his stubborn perusal of the horizon.

"If only we had solid proof of Courbet's involvement in the murders of his parents..." The captain stooped so that Marie could hear above the still screaming wind. "Jean shared with me his suspicions."

She sucked in a sharp breath. "What if we did have proof?"

"Then, by God, let's get what you have to the court." The big man smacked a fist into his other hand. "Jean's a smuggler, but a damned fine man. He's never cheated me or any other traders. Never been anything but aboveboard with that devil, Courbet, come to that."

"Marie." Jean's shout silenced both her and the captain. "You will not expose my mother's letters in a public court."

"But it's all we have." Marie walked across the deck and grasped his arm. "Her words might save you. It's what she would want." Marie stood on tiptoe and gave him a tight squeeze. "Perhaps all we need to show is her first letter where she describes your father's murder. Please do not leave us now. Let your mother do this one last thing for you."

Jean stood in stoic silence, oblivious to the heaves of the ship. After a while, he said, "Her letters are for the magistrate's eyes only. I will not allow them to be read in open court. You must plead with your son-in-law. He's a good man. He will understand."

She leaned against him, her arms around his waist and hid her face, letting her tears soak into his shirt.

"That's enough." Captain Willem stomped across the deck and reached for the wheel. "You two go below and get some rest. You'll soon need your wits about you."

Marie turned her head toward the burly captain. "Do you trade with the tribes in Brazil? Would you possibly have any honey on board?"

"Beggin' your pardon?"

"Honey. As much as you can spare."

After Marie smeared a bit of Captain Willem's honey on Elisabeth's wound, she and Jean collapsed onto the bunk the man had vacated. Jean turned Marie so that her back snugged against his chest. He rubbed the coolness of the sea spray from her arms and neck until she glowed.

The steady thump of his heartbeat quickened and Marie's breath gave a little hitch when he grasped the hem of her dress.

The ship slowly swung back onto a southeast course, the barque heeling harder as she moved close to the wind and picked up speed for St. Pierre.

Once the ship had changed direction, Jean removed Marie's tattered dress and rolled her beneath him. The smell of ocean and wet woman filled his senses. He cupped one of her breasts and suckled the nipple, his tongue laving the sensitive tip. When Marie moaned, he covered her mouth with his.

He sensed when the ship had fully turned and pressed them against the bulkhead next to the bunk.

"Marie, open your eyes," he said, and slid his cock into her hot sheath.

St. Pierre harbor finally hove into view during Jean's turn at the helm.

Captain Willem still slept below, and Marie was at Elisabeth's side. Jean's sister's fever had subsided a few hours before and now Marie and Luz were trying to tempt her with broth and tea.

Although Marie had explained the contents of his mother's letters, he still could not bear to read them.

Francois appeared at his side, ready to help with bringing the barque into the harbor.

"Are you sure you can use your hands so soon after the burns?" Jean asked.

"A little pain, maybe, but my mother slathered on plenty of salve before winding the bandages. I want to do what I can to atone for past sins," he said.

"In that case, throw the lead line over and tell me when we're at thirty feet." Jean gave the orders to anchor as if nothing had changed since their old smuggling days together.

When Francois signaled good depth, Jean headed the barque into the wind, tied off the wheel, and struck the sails. His partner lowered the anchor over the side with a splash followed by the rattle of the chain sliding to the bottom.

"Where is Cecile?" Jean asked, when Francois returned.

"I'm not sure. My father complained she's gone."

"Why would she disappear?"

"I suppose my father's never-ending treachery might have something to do with her loss of interest." Francois lowered the shore boat suspended near the stern of the barque, and Jean followed close behind.

Marie and Abelard appeared on deck with Elisabeth supported between them. Luz followed with Gerard and Yancey.

"*Vite*," Jean said, and motioned for everyone to descend the rope ladder to the smaller boat.

Marie made sure Jean had his mother's precious, damning letters tucked securely in the metal box inside his shirt before she took her place behind him in the shore boat. She was happy to see him more optimistic about his chances of convincing the magistrate of Courbet's true motives.

The sound of gunfire exploded nearby, and Jean pitched forward into the bottom of the boat. Francois grabbed his oars and shouted to Abelard and Marie, "Pull. Everyone else — down."

At that moment, Courbet's men rowed closer in another boat. They must have been hiding behind the barque. Marie's mind reeled. They'd slipped into the harbor earlier and had waited to attack.

She pushed and pulled her weary arm at the oars, rowing as if they were being chased by the demons of hell.

The lighter boat pulled quickly alongside. When Courbet grabbed onto one of their oars, Francois pulled a pistol from his pocket and fired. The ball ripped into his father's thigh, blood spraying over the rower next to him. Francois reached across the gunnels and gave the other boat a firm push.

In the chaos following the shot, all rowing on the other boat stopped, allowing Francois and his small crew to put distance between them.

Marie did not falter. She kept rowing. A quick side glance revealed one of Courbet's men had ripped off his shirt and tied the cloth around his leader's bleeding thigh.

After they'd gained a decent distance away, Francois yelled over his shoulder to Marie to see to Jean's wound.

Although her heart battered against her chest, she turned him over. No blood flowed from a wound, but Jean's eyes were closed. She bent low over his body and nearly cried in relief when she felt his chest rising with his shallow breathing.

Jean's eyes flew open, and he tried to get up. Marie pushed him back down. When she pulled his shirt off in search of injuries, the metal box filled with his mother's letters tumbled out, a tiny round dent in the lid. Beneath the spot where the box had lain, a dark bruise swelled on his chest.

A single lead ball from the shot rolled in the bottom of the boat beneath where Jean fell.

"Your mother saved you." Marie's hands shook as she continued feeling his chest for injuries. "That settles the matter. You are going to live, you insufferable man."

Francois and Abelard still rowed like madmen, but Courbet's boat had disappeared.

Jean could not believe he was about to surrender of his own volition. Barely a month had passed since he first invaded Marie's island. He'd been a brash smuggler who took what he wanted when he seized the healer.

But now, all he wanted was Marie and the rag-tag family they'd formed. There was no turning back. He had to make up for past sins and hope he would not have to face the firing squad the following dawn.

That risk still did not outweigh his need to keep Marie close, to hear her sweet breathing in the night, to one day see her body swell with his child. He'd wanted many things in his lifetime, but nothing more than the simple family pleasures he'd shared with Marie.

At the end of the long cobblestone road leading to the garrison, she stopped and banged at the gate.

Jean clenched his fists when the sergeant at the gate let his gaze linger on Marie's battered bodice. He kept his counsel, however, and let her work her magic. The gate swung open and the small group entered.

Although Jean kept his head lowered, a flicker of recognition still swept over the man's face. He kept his hands tight to his sides, willing himself to remain calm. A sudden vision loomed in his mind of a large, dumb hog plodding in ignorance to the butcher.

"Thank you, Sergeant Larousse," Marie said. "You may accompany us to my daughter's house if you wish. And how is your leg today? Do you need something for that old wound?" Her hands fluttered like birds as she rustled through her bag of herbs and handed him a small bundle. "Here – mix this with a little warm water and keep your knee raised while the herbs do their work."

The quiet sergeant took the packet without comment, merely nodding in thanks while he continued leading them through the garrison. So far, Larousse had gone out of his way to ignore Jean and Abelard and Francois, who kept to the rear of the line. For once, Luz and the boys remained unnaturally quiet.

The door to the commandant's cottage flew open and Marie's daughter Rianne rushed into her arms. She squeezed her mother tight, but Jean did not miss the anger in the younger woman's eyes when she saw him.

"Mother — why are you here? What has happened? Did he...?"

"Nothing bad has happened," Marie said. She turned her daughter back toward the house, twining her arm around her waist. Marie gestured to the rest of them to follow.

⟨⟩

"Where is Henri?" Marie asked as soon as they crowded into Rianne's tiny parlor.

"He's inspecting the armory this morning," she said.

Marie's grandson Maurice had run to her as soon as she called his name, and now was nestled in her lap, his warm cheek against her neck. He raised his pudgy fist and socked his thumb into his mouth. She smiled in spite of the fear swirling through her.

"We sailed here through the storm last night from Marigot after finding evidence at Courbet's north shore plantation. We believe he murdered Jean's parents and stole their money after pretending to sell them the plantation eighteen years ago."

"Can you prove such an accusation?" Her daughter's eyes reflected disbelief. "He will deny everything. You know he will."

"Yes, we have proof, but of a very delicate nature. Unfortunately, all we have are letters written by Jean's mother while she was held captive by Courbet after her husband's murder."

"*Maman*, please. You must not make such dangerous statements. *Monsieur* Courbet is so powerful and vindictive. What if he decides to take revenge on you?"

"He's already tried to steal our family land by cheating your poor, gullible father. What more can he do?"

"You still have your *life*. You could return to France and live with your aunts. Surely they would welcome you?"

Jean rose and stood before Rianne. "I know you resent me, but I tell you I love your mother. Courbet will have to kill me first before he harms one hair on her head."

"You forget one thing, sir." Marie's daughter's voice crackled with indignation. "You are a thief. You've been a smuggler all these years. The magistrate cannot overlook such a long career of deception." She sucked in a breath and continued. "Courbet must pay for his offenses, but yours the court cannot forgive, either."

Gerard and Yancey played quietly in the corner with Maurice's collection of wooden blocks. The smaller child slid off Marie's lap and toddled over to join the older boys.

Marie bent her head to her daughter and spoke in a whisper. "Gerard thought Jean was his father until recently. He now knows Jean is his uncle, but these accusations are hard for him to hear."

Luz rose without a word and herded the children out into the enclosed, sunlit garden behind the cottage.

Although Sergeant Larousse had remained silent in the parlor, leaning against a wall, he came to attention when Commandant Henri Renaud charged through the entryway.

The commandant's boots dropped with two loud thumps as he moved toward the parlor. He stooped to enter the room without a glance at Jean or Abelard. After planting a kiss on both his wife and mother-in-law's cheeks, he turned toward the two ex-prisoners and acknowledged both of them with, "*Messieurs.*" The two men stood along with Francois.

"The garrison throbs with news of your presence. Now you must tell me what prompts you to risk certain death by venturing into my home." Henri remained standing, and his sergeant pulled his pistol from his belt with an ease belying the tension in the room.

"Commandant, we bring proof of Courbet's dark business which consists of letters my mother managed to scratch out on the back of his ledger sheets while she was his prisoner." Jean held out his hand. "You have my word I will go peacefully to the court to plead my case."

Francois stood so quickly, his foot inadvertently flipped over a delicate footstool. "And I will testify as well to my father's black dealings."

Elisabeth, next to him on a well-worn floral settee, seemed startled at his words.

"And what about you, old friend?" Henri inclined his head toward Abelard. "What part do you play in this little tableau?"

"I spent years in your jail for crimes against *Monsieur* Courbet I did not commit. But then mine is just the word of a slave against his master."

"Sit, rest your aged bones," Henri said.

The old man settled with a sigh onto the cushions next to Elisabeth. "Escaping to help Jean find his proof seemed like a good way to get some fresh air before returning to your prison." He patted her hand.

Henri paced the floor between his sergeant and Marie. "*Madame* Galante — please explain what any of this has to do with the charges against *Monsieur* Blanchard. Is there any reason we should not put him back where he belongs? Any reason we should not make him face the firing squad?"

"It's a story which began eighteen years ago. Some of the tale is simple, some complicated."

"Surely you can explain to my satisfaction before nightfall?"

"As you wish." Marie leaned back onto the settee and rubbed her daughter's arm. "Eighteen years ago, *Monsieur* Blanchard's parents sailed here from *Nouvelle Orleans* to start a new life with their children. Jean was twelve and Elisabeth, six.

"The Blanchards had a fortune in francs from their trading business, which they took to *Monsieur* Courbet to buy his plantation in Marigot.

"When they sat down to dinner before finalizing the sale, Courbet shot *Monsieur* Blanchard. He kept their mother captive for several weeks, according to her letters."

"Wait." Henri held up his hand. "How were these letters posted, and why are we only now seeing them?"

Marie hesitated, and glanced at Jean. He hung his head, his hands covering his face.

"When we went to his plantation seeking proof, we found a secret room where he held *Madame* Blanchard," Marie continued.

"How do you know he held her there?"

"Because he built a shrine of sorts to her: many candles, her jewelry, and rotted bits of an old dress she wore that night."

"But why would he kill *Monsieur* Blanchard and then hold his wife captive after he had the money? To what purpose?"

"Henri, her letters are very painful for Jean and Elisabeth to read. I read them in their stead."

"And?"

"She remained in fear for her life until she finally died, probably by his hand. According to her letters, he was trying to force her to marry him and go along with his lies about her husband's death. He believed he would be safer from detection than if both of the Blanchards disappeared."

"How did she get the letters out?"

"She ripped random sheets from his ledgers when he left her alone. Her letters covered the backs of the sheets. I believe his ledgers were the true records of his illegal dealings. They were hidden along with *Madame* Blanchard in the secret room."

"She enclosed them in a tin box which she tucked above the door to the secret passage out of the room." Marie leaned forward to accept a cup of water from her daughter.

"And how did they come to be in your hands?"

Jean stood. "The box fell onto the floor when I kicked the door off its hinges."

"And you did that because…?"

"I wanted the fire to consume all the pain in that room."

CHAPTER TWENTY-FIVE

Henri leaned toward Magistrate Emil Cabasson and handed him the metal box. He straightened quickly as if the container had burned his hands and stepped back.

"What is this?" He spread his black-cloaked arms across the wide table in his courtroom and reached for the battered rectangle. He pulled the container to him and turned questioning eyes toward the commandant and Marie, who stood quaking behind her son-in-law.

The hardest thing she'd ever done had been walking away from Jean in his temporary cell beneath the cannons overlooking the bay. The trust on Jean's face had nearly been her undoing. Now their only hope lay with the stern man in front of her about whom she knew precious little.

Cabasson had been the island's only arbiter of justice for as long as Marie could remember. His wife had died of a wasting fever the year before, and both his grown sons had long since returned to France.

His large hands with long fingers and blunt nails handled the letters and contracts with a gentleness she didn't expect. She had no idea, though, of the direction of his loyalties. Was he a tool of Courbet's? She hoped not.

He positioned spectacles on the end of his nose and tilted his head for a better view. Opening the box as if he expected snakes to slither out, he maneuvered the fragile papers onto the surface in front of him.

Long minutes passed, and Marie feared apoplexy would claim her. She waited for some sign from the man who would decide their fates. She envied Henri his military posture and bearing. How did he maintain that stance for hours on end?

She had difficulty stifling a smile when she pondered the bigger mystery. How could such a disciplined man manage to share a life with her will-o-the-wisp daughter? Love did seem to strike at odd moments and places.

She smiled at the direction of her thoughts, but guilt forced her to sneak another glance at the man in somber robes still sifting through *Madame* Blanchard's letter fragments.

The longer she waited, the more she settled into her surroundings. The tiny hearing room smelled of stale smoke, the source of which appeared to be a pipe leaning against a book on a shelf behind the magistrate. And something else — acrid and foul — like fear. She shuddered at the vision of doomed souls who had passed through this very room over the years.

The hard wooden bench began to bore into her backside as an hour passed, and the man still showed no sign of finishing his perusal of the fragile missives.

Only now, he seemed more interested in the ledger entries on the back of the letters.

Marie snapped out of her silent vigil when the large man cleared his throat and removed the spectacles pinching his nose. He pulled a muslin square from inside a robe pocket and wiped at the glass rounds for several minutes while staring into the distance.

She took in a belated breath just as he motioned for her to rise and approach.

Her son's scuffed boots peeping from beneath her skirt seemed detached from the rest of her, but she willed them to move. She gave up trying to keep her shoulders from quaking.

"*Madame* Galante." The judge's voice rumbled as if from the depths of judgment. "This court gave you a serious responsibility less than six weeks ago. And now you are before me again in blatant violation of the intent of my previous order.

"Instead of keeping a convicted criminal on your plantation for the sole purpose of helping with your harvest, you've allowed him to roam the islands in search of proof of his innocence.

"This so-called proof might explain why he chose to become a smuggler. However, the facts remain the same. He and his men have engaged in illegal activities in a French colony. In their favor, though, they have also helped the king's navy with many acts against our enemy, the English.

"However, not only must he and his men pay for what they've done, they must make reparation. More importantly, they must find honest work to sustain them without resorting to their former criminal endeavors."

When he paused and polished at a spot he'd missed on the spectacles, Marie breathed again.

"My brother, Father Cabasson, has been trying to get the French Navy to re-build his church for three years. Although the destruction occurred during a battle in the harbor between the English and the French, no one claims responsibility." He jammed the muslin back into his pocket and continued. "Since France is in the midst of a great war, I believe the crown would be happy to exchange the repair of Our Lady of the Safe Harbor for the freedom of Jean Blanchard and his men."

Marie wanted to sink to her knees and cry at the news, but was afraid to show any emotion in front of Cabasson.

"As soon as the smuggler and his crew help bring in your cane, they will report to Commandant Renaud for duty as stonemasons."

"Thank you, bless you, your honor." Tears streamed down Marie's face. When she steadied her shaking and backed toward her son-in-law, the magistrate extended his hand toward her.

"Not so quickly, *Madame* Galante." His voice deepened in censure. "You've spent the last month in outrageous behavior, scandalizing the small community on your island. I cannot let willful moral transgressions stand."

Marie's shoulders shook again.

"I'll send word to my brother to meet you at the home of your daughter and son-in-law where you will wed *Monsieur* Blanchard without delay."

A blush heated her entire body and flooded its way to her cheeks.

"Your honor…please. He is younger than I and would not want me as wife."

"*Madame*, your lover is a prisoner in a damp cave beneath this garrison. Any sane man would have kept on sailing to safer shores. I believe his actions speak for themselves. What further declaration of love you require I cannot imagine."

"But…"

"If you wish to challenge the power of my office, perhaps you would prefer to join *Monsieur* Blanchard and his crew in the cave to await their executions at dawn?"

"You would not…" Her face transformed from heated flush to clammy cold in seconds.

"Of course I would." He rapped on the table and dismissed them.

When Marie held out her hand for the metal box, he stared at her above his spectacles.

"I will return your smuggler's property once I've heard *Monsieur* Courbet's explanation for these damning letters and ledger entries."

Henri slipped close to Marie, and Magistrate Cabasson peered at him. "Commandant, you will inform the prisoners of my decision and carry out my wishes. This couple must be married by nightfall."

Her son-in-law saluted sharply before towing Marie toward the door.

"And, *Madame* Galante," he added.

Marie snapped her head back toward him as if shot.

"You should know you look a great deal like your beautiful mother, God rest her soul." With his parting words, he turned and retired to his rooms behind the court bench.

Once back in her daughter's parlor, Marie sat on a worn but comfortable settee and stared at the threadbare carpet. Henri had returned to the cell beneath the garrison after they'd both explained to Rianne the terms of the judge's decision.

When her daughter forced a small cup of strong, heavily creamed coffee on her, Marie lifted the cup to her lips and bolted down the contents. They were silent for a few minutes before Marie said, "I'm sorry to have brought all of this into your home."

After Marie described some of what was contained in Jean's letters, Rianne moved to her mother's side, knelt at her feet, and leaned her head on Marie's lap.

"*Maman*, I've always known you were not happy with Papa."

She rose and reached for her small son who had toddled into the room with his nurse. She pulled him close and kissed the top of his head. "Jean may be a smuggler, but I'm proud of you for helping him find justice for his parents."

"I've made his life worse now." Marie moaned and buried her head in her hands. "How can a man love a woman he's forced to marry?"

"With all his heart," Jean said. He stood next to Henri in the doorway.

Marie jumped up at the sound of his voice and said, "I swear I will never give you reason to regret this day, and if you ever want another…"

"Stop," he said, and reached his manacled wrists toward her. "You are all I've wanted ever since I first saw you emerge from the sea on your island that day." He rested his head on top of hers. "If only I could get you to believe me."

Marie's daughter shoved them apart. "You two need to walk along the shore and decide what you want before the priest arrives. He will be angry if he believes you are not taking seriously the sacrament of marriage."

They stared at her as if she'd sprouted wings, then turned and headed for the door.

"I will send two of my men to accompany you, at a distance of course," Henri said.

An angry look from his wife made him throw up his hands. "I cannot let a prisoner roam free or I'll be the next one in the cave beneath the garrison."

Henri beckoned through the open door to Abelard and Francois who still stood in ankle cuffs and chains outside the cottage. "Come in and wait while your leader faces his next gaoler." The men laughed, but Rianne did not smile.

"Go on with you then." Henri knelt and unlocked the cuffs on Jean's ankles but left the ones on his wrists. "Make your peace before the priest arrives."

After he waved them out, Marie and Jean picked their way down the fortified embankment toward the shore. True to Henri's promise, his guards hung back, allowing them privacy.

Marie reached down and pulled off her boots. She dropped them one by one at the bottom of the stone steps before they walked toward the crashing waves.

The smell of fishnets drying mingled with the clean odor of the sun leaching out of the rocks. Large shadows circled just beyond the reef, the big fish coming in to feed. A strange melancholy overtook her.

She felt more like something was ending rather than beginning before she realized with a start this would be her wedding day. And with this exchange of vows, unlike the first, she would be pledging herself to a man she could care for.

She shivered with fear of the unknown, but tried not to lean into Jean's shackled hands. Without warning, he sank onto the sand before her.

"Marie." He bowed his head like a penitent. "I'm begging you here in front of your son-in-law's guards." He raised his head then. "Will you be my wife?"

Marie shifted awkwardly. "Jean, please get up. You don't have to do this."

"Ah, but I do, as long as you are reluctant. Tell me you'll take me in spite of my past. I promise you will never regret your decision."

"Stop. You must. The guards are staring." Marie fumbled with the restraints on his wrists, trying to pull him to his feet.

"If you don't say the words, I'll kneel here all night."

Marie glared down at him and jammed her hands on her hips. "Yes, you stubborn man, I will marry you. Now get up," she insisted, with a low hiss.

A golden twilight had set in now that the sun had disappeared below the horizon. When the guards caught up with them, one said, "The priest will be at the house by now. You have to go back."

When they helped him stumble to his feet, Marie sighed and linked her arm through the crook at his elbow, his hands still chained together.

Marie attempted to cover her nervousness with fidgeting while her daughter helped with the wedding dress. It was the one Rianne had worn the day she married Henri. They'd been surprised to discover the frock fit her mother perfectly.

Of course, the stays chafed at Marie's flesh after weeks of wearing just her simple linen work dress. She'd nearly forgotten the feel of silk stockings rolled onto her legs and tied above her knees with ribbons. Her feet felt swollen from working barefoot in the fields when she jammed them into Rianne's dainty silk slippers. She'd even let her daughter talk her into layers of petticoats over a hoop.

Still shifting her posture to minimize the pain of the tight lacings on her stays when she walked into the parlor, she stopped at a sharp intake of breath from Jean.

A small smile curved at her lips at the thought he hadn't seen her dressed as a lady since the night of his beating at the hands of Courbet's guards. She particularly recalled the day he'd vowed never to be tempted to ravish a woman dressed in baggy sackcloth.

Her smile broadened. Henri had taken the cuffs and chains from Jean's wrists and ankles. Her daughter exchanged a stern look with her husband. Marie could guess whose idea the unlocked chains had been.

She glided toward the priest who stood with Jean at the windows overlooking the garden. A full moon threw its light into the parlor, adding to the soft glow of candles. When Luz and Abelard joined her, her housekeeper squeezed her shoulders tight and handed her a bouquet of lilies.

Elisabeth gave Francois a brilliant smile as they prepared to take their vows along with Jean and Marie. When Jean's first mate had pleaded for his blessing earlier that day, he'd relented only after vowing to kill him if he ever did anything to harm his sister.

The priest insisted on giving both couples communion before the service. The man's calloused hand brushed her lips as he placed the host on her tongue. The accompanying bittersweet wine dissolved the bland wafer.

Marie barely heard the priest's words but gave her responses in a clear voice. Her first marriage ceremony had been much grander, but these vows rang true. Luz stood behind her, arms full of heavily perfumed, deep pink flowers.

Rianne carried island lilies and stood next to Henri. The two would serve as their official witnesses. Her son-in-law wore full dress uniform, the polish on his high leather boots smelling of wax and ashes.

At the end of the ceremony, Jean pulled her close and touched her lips with his. When he deepened the kiss, a fire of claiming seared her mouth.

When at last he released her, Henri's men immediately put the cuffs and chains back on and led Jean, along with Francois and Abelard, back to the cave cell. From the look on Rianne's face, Marie assumed this was the compromise she'd negotiated with her husband.

Luz and Elisabeth moved to her side, and they held each other as the men were led away. The service had passed so quickly, Marie hadn't been able to absorb the full truth. He was hers, and she his.

She'd thrown her lot in with a man she didn't really know. She didn't know if she could trust him, she didn't know if he would live, and she didn't know if she could live without him.

CHAPTER TWENTY-SIX

St. Pierre Garrison, Magistrate's Courtroom

Jean stood as tall as possible in the courtroom even though weighed down by iron cuffs and chains. He prayed for the strength not to lunge for Courbet's worthless throat as the horrors of his mother's ordeal and his father's murder were revealed.

Both Francois and Abelard stood with him, ready to help reinforce his side of the story.

He and Marie had not had a chance to discuss Magistrate Cabasson's comments. All he knew was he would finally face his accuser in open court. He had no idea of the extent of Courbet's accusations. He could only hope each one would be rebutted with the truth contained in his mother's letters and the altered contracts.

Courbet entered the courtroom quietly, flanked by three of his guards.

The magistrate lifted his head and took a long look at Courbet's party. "Do you men have anything to contribute to this inquiry?" They gave him blank stares.

"Were you in *Monsieur* Courbet's service eighteen years ago?"

"No, but…," one said.

"Then you must leave the courtroom." He motioned to Henri to usher them outside. "You may wait for your employer until this inquiry is finished — but in the courtyard, if you please." He raised his head toward Jean and his cellmates. "You three — please sit until called upon."

After the guards left, the judge continued, his manner brisk. "*Monsieur* Courbet — I have in my possession letters written by *Madame* Blanchard while she claimed to be your prisoner. What is your explanation for such an atrocity?"

"She lied."

Jean struggled against his restraints and tried to rise from his seat. Henri placed firm, warning hands on his shoulders.

"What possible reason would she have to lie?" the magistrate asked.

"Her husband abandoned her and the children. She hoped to pull me into her web and became vindictive when I refused her."

"This is indeed curious," the magistrate said. "You have approached the court as a plaintiff alleging *Monsieur* Blanchard committed crimes against you. He has charged separately that you murdered his father and held his mother against her will. How do you answer these accusations?"

"I am innocent of all such preposterous claims."

"Then where is the elder *Monsieur* Blanchard?" The judge sighed and leaned back in his chair, folding his arms across his chest.

"I have no idea. Perhaps he sailed back to *Nouvelle Orléans*. Who knows what such a vagabond would do?" Courbet lifted his shoulders in an elegant shrug.

Jean pulled sharply against his restraints. Henri's grip tightened, causing him to wince in pain.

The magistrate sat in silence for many minutes, all the while boring a stare into Courbet. With a sudden relaxing of his arms, he leaned across the table and said, "*Monsieur* Abelard, how long were you in the employ of *Monsieur* Courbet?"

"Twenty years, your honor."

"So you were there when the alleged incident occurred?"

"Yes."

"Do you remember *Monsieur* and *Madame* Blanchard?"

"Yes."

"That was long ago. I'm sure *Monsieur* Courbet entertains many guests at his home. How can you be sure you remember this couple in particular?"

"One never forgets a woman like *Madame* Blanchard."

"And *Monsieur* Blanchard? You're sure he was there with his wife?"

"Yes. He was a very attentive, affectionate husband," Abelard added.

Courbet struggled to stand, but was pushed back down by Sergeant Larousse. When Cabasson motioned for him to be allowed to stay on his feet, the sergeant released him.

"Your honor," Courbet said, "This man is a slave testifying against a landowner in a court of law. You forget your duty. You cannot take his word against mine."

"Do not lecture *me* as to duty," the magistrate said, his voice rising. He nodded to Abelard who had just raised his hand. "Please continue."

"*Monsieur* Courbet is correct. A slave's voice has no veracity in this court. However, I do have proof." Abelard reached inside his shirt and withdrew a carefully folded cloth packet.

"Here," Abelard said, after unwinding the cloth and producing an old pocket watch. He handed the object to Sergeant Larousse who gave it to the magistrate. "You will find *Monsieur* Blanchard's initials on the back, along with an engraved endearment from his wife."

Jean was astounded.

The judge turned the polished gold watch over and adjusted his spectacles while he read the inscription on the back.

Courbet leapt to his feet. "These two men were jailed together. They could have conjured this scheme to incriminate me. Why, Blanchard could have brought the timepiece with him to jail to hand off to Abelard."

"You are right, *Monsieur* Courbet," the judge said, and nodded in assent. "Fortunately, there is a way to prove this part of the tale. Commandant Renaud – does not Sergeant Larousse also serve as your chief jailer?"

"Yes."

"And does he not search each of your prisoners and keep their belongings with him until they serve their sentences?"

"Of course, always," Henri said.

A fleeting grimace of uncertainty crossed Courbet's face only to be replaced by a hard glare focused on Jean.

Jean smiled at his enemy's discomfiture. If Abelard had such a watch with him in their cell, he would have known. The discovery was as much of a surprise to him as to Courbet.

"This court is adjourned," Magistrate Cabasson said. "We will untangle all these conflicting tales in the morning." He pointed at Sergeant Larousse. "And you will check your records to see what *Monsieur* Blanchard brought with him to jail."

"Commandant, you will see to the jailing of *Monsieur* Courbet for the night in our cell in the cave beneath the garrison."

"With what crime am I charged?" Courbet leapt to his feet, hands clenched in fists.

"I have not yet decided. We must hear more evidence and explanations for your actions."

"It is simply an abandoned woman's word against mine."

"*Monsieur* Courbet, do you know what paper *Madame* Blanchard used to write her letters?"

"No…" Courbet lost his composure and sputtered.

"The lady was very clever and resourceful." Cabasson pulled out his muslin square and polished his spectacles again. "She used the backs of pages ripped from the ledgers you stored in your hidden room."

"That cannot be," Courbet said.

"I found the entries from your ledgers every bit as interesting as that poor woman's letters. You have a great deal to explain."

Before Courbet could reply, the judge banged his fist on the table and rose to retire to his quarters.

Sergeant Larousse summoned two garrison guards to escort Courbet to his cell for the night.

CHAPTER TWENTY-SEVEN

St. Pierre Garrison

Sergeant Larousse shifted from one boot to the other outside the cave cell beneath the cannons, his nerves on edge. He cursed under his breath at his only prisoner. Courbet had not ceased bellowing since he'd locked him inside after the magistrate's last hearing.

Commandant Renaud had the others under house arrest with him at the officers' barracks in a far corner of the garrison.

Larousse would have liked just a few moments alone with that arrogant smuggler, Blanchard. For all the trouble he'd caused over the years. Truthfully, the real reason he hated the man was for his treatment of *Madame* Galante, Blanchard now.

Thank God Cabasson had forced him to make her a respectable woman again. He, Larousse, would have been happy to take care of the poor woman, but he would have waited a decent period for her mourning to end. If that devil did anything to harm her…

At that moment, a tall, turbaned beauty walked toward him and interrupted his thoughts. On her hip she balanced a large basket covered with a linen cloth. Incredible smells issued from beneath, causing his mouth to water and his stomach to growl.

"Dis be for de prisoner," she said, in a husky, sing-song voice. "And, Sergeant, if I be you, I'd not eat any." Her mesmerizing eyes held a hint of threat he took seriously.

"Who should I tell him brought the meal? *Madame, Mademoiselle?*"

"Jes tell him Cecile loves him still." With that she stuffed a handful of coins inside his cartridge belt. After handing the sergeant the food, she left him in thrall to the sensuous sway of her hips as she walked to the steps leading up the embankment. She moved slowly as if she knew he still watched.

Once she disappeared into the upper level of the garrison, he lifted the linen to be sure no weapons were hidden inside. Satisfied, he hesitated for a moment, wondering if the prisoner would miss a few bites. He leaned close to inhale the luscious smell and then thought better of the temptation. He had a long night ahead of him. Spicy, heavy food would make him sleepy.

Sergeant Larousse turned the key to Courbet's cell, and the rusty, salt-encrusted door swung open with a creak.

"What?" Courbet said. "Has the magistrate come to his senses?"

"*Non.* Your friend, Cecile, brought you an evening meal, much better than what we serve. You are a lucky man." He set the basket on a wood bench, the only flat surface in the crude enclosure.

"Yes, I am," Courbet said, and knelt down. He pulled back the cloth and tucked into the feast, sighing in pleasure. "I knew she would be back. That woman cannot stay away."

After the sergeant closed the cell door and turned the lock, he sat on the hard stone bench outside and pulled from his pocket a box filled with the simple fare of the regiment.

Marie enjoyed the morning sun outside Henri and Rianne's cottage, stretching like a satisfied cat while her grandson tugged at her skirts.

"Nana play?" Maurice begged.

"Yes, you can with Yancey." The other boy scooped up sticks and threw them into piles while chanting a ditty. Gerard concentrated on learning to juggle with three lemons he'd begged from the garrison kitchen's cook.

Cabasson had yet to resume court that morning to decide Jean and Courbet's cross claims. Elisabeth sat on a bench near the ramparts watching the boys.

Out of the corner of her eye, Marie caught sight of Cecile, gliding toward the barracks where Francois was held along with Jean and Abelard. Marie felt a vague sense of unease around Jean's former cook and so determined to follow her.

"Elisabeth, I'm going for a walk. Could you watch the boys?"

"Certainly," she said, with a smile for Gerard when he kept the lemons flying a few seconds longer than any of his previous attempts. Her shoulder wound from the pistol ball graze had nearly healed.

Marie hurried through her daughter's garden gate, Cecile fifty or sixty feet ahead of her. The cook turned her head toward Marie, their gazes locked for a second, and Marie knew. She had to stop her. Cecile, like Courbet, would not stop until she'd destroyed Jean and his family. Within seconds, however, the tall woman had slipped behind a lean-to and disappeared.

On instinct, Marie ignored the direction Cecile had taken. Francois's scheming mother would have come to the island under sail, probably in a small fishing boat. And since the only reason she would come to the garrison would be to see Courbet and Francois, Marie turned toward the ocean and sped down the uneven stone steps to the bottom of the cliff. Within a few minutes, she smiled at the sight of a boat bobbing in the outgoing tide, tied to a scrub tree near the shore.

She scrambled aboard and flattened herself to the bottom. Crawling under a cloth crumpled in the bow, she pulled the smelly cover over her.

Within a few minutes, a light step crunched on the rocks along the shore. Cecile took her time loosening the line and then pulled the skiff into deeper water before hopping aboard.

Once the other woman raised the single sail, Marie threw off the oilcloth and confronted her tormentor. "Why do you still plot against Jean and his sister? Haven't they suffered enough from your family?"

"What do you or they know of suffering?" Cecile said, and spit overboard, showing little surprise at Marie's sudden appearance.

"Let me see." Marie held up her hand and began ticking off Cecile's transgressions. "You helped destroy Jean's parents; you probably had a hand in my stupid, departed husband's loss of our plantation; and now, years later, you still try to undermine Jean and Elisabeth. "Why?" She finished her impassioned condemnation by spreading both hands wide.

Cecile had remained silent throughout Marie's tirade but reached forward quick as a snake and slapped Marie so hard, she reeled speechless, back onto her haunches.

Cecile tied off the tiller as they sped out to sea, grabbed a paddle from beneath one of the gunnels, and closed in on Marie.

"You have no idea de hatred I keep here," she said, poking a bony finger toward her heart. "I've waited and waited all these years for *Monsieur* Courbet to bring us together as a family. But does he? *Non*. Over and over again he denies us.

"He can't hurt us now. I am finally free and so is Francois." She gave a low, guttural laugh. "You should have seen the look on his face when I sneaked back to his cell and picked the lock to watch him eat his favorite feast. 'Cecile, my pretty girl. I knew you would never leave me,' he said, and just like dat, he finished the food and began to die. I stayed to make sure he suffered."

"You killed him?" Marie reeled from Cecile's confession. Her stomach lurched from the woman's cold-hearted description of how she destroyed her lover.

"But what about Sergeant Larousse?" Marie asked, edging as far away from Cecile as she could in the tiny skiff. The other woman's horrible confession made her stomach drop.

"That clumsy soldier was no match for me. He was easy to distract." Cecile rambled on, lost in her tale of hatred. "I tried to warn Antoine about that she-devil, Honore Blanchard. But did he listen? *Non*. She caused so much trouble, I had to give her a potion to make her sleep. When she hid the powder instead of taking it, I told him to have her watched. And den, when she killed herself with all of the powder at once, he blamed me. Me." Cecile clenched and unclenched her hands, her shoulders shaking.

"If he'd let me kill her at the beginning, she wouldn't have written all dose letters, now, would she? And yes, *Madame* Healer, your dead husband was worthless. You're better off without him. Now you have a young man to warm your bed."

Marie considered a denial before remembering she was married to the young man in question.

"But my man – Antoine – he never learned. He wanted to make her pay for leaving him. All dose years later he had to find the daughter and rape her. Dat was his idea. I had no part in his revenge."

Marie levered herself upright, bit by bit, mesmerized. She was in a daze, as if charmed by a snake, torn between the need to escape and an even greater desire to hear Cecile's story.

"He never knew the boy was his till just days ago, when he found him on the plantation. I hid in the cane fields to watch and finally saw what I refused to believe for years. He never cared for his first son, Francois. He never cared for me."

Cecile had admitted her crimes with glazed eyes staring out to sea. Marie's heart went out to the poor, tortured woman in spite of the twisted soul she'd revealed.

When Marie reached toward Cecile's hand, the other woman advanced on her without warning, wielding the paddle with madness in her eyes.

"And now I'm going to finish what I started on the cliff trail that night." Cecile slammed a glancing blow to Marie's head, flinging her over the gunnels into the water. She plummeted as far into the depths as possible and began a desperate underwater swim toward the shore.

When Marie finally pulled herself onto the rocks beneath the cell in the cliff, shouts already rang from above. Sergeant Larousse raced away from the cave and charged toward the embankment steps leading to the garrison before stopping short at the sight of her soaked, bedraggled form.

"*Madame?*" He hesitated in confusion before climbing down to help her up the slope.

"I just escaped from the murderer you seek." She smoothed at her soaked bodice and skirts and then gave up any attempt at modesty. "*Monsieur* Courbet's mistress, Cecile, confessed to killing him. I'm sure he's quite dead and beyond our help after the effects of her poison." She gulped in some deep breaths and pushed wet, tangled hair from her face.

"Tell Commandant Renaud she has escaped." Still exhausted from her long swim back to shore, Marie leaned against a boulder before continuing. With a vague sweep of her hand back toward the sea, she added, "She went that way."

The sergeant continued to stare at her, his mouth gaping like a large fish out of water. "*Madame*, I have survived many battles, but I've never seen anything so horrific as *Monsieur* Courbet. His face is blue and his tongue bloated. His dying expression is terrifying." Larousse shivered and made the sign of the cross.

"After you've told Commandant Renaud, have the guards bring large amounts of water and return to the body. Warn them not to touch anything with their hands. Poison can harm even through the skin. We'll sweep the remains over the cliff."

As she faced the glare of the morning sun across the sea, a tiny sail glided into the horizon. She did not shout a warning, but simply watched Cecile disappear around a headland. How, she wondered, could so deep a love could turn to such intense hatred?

"Thank God Jean was under guard when this happened," Marie said when the sergeant returned some time later with brooms and a tub full of water. "He would never survive a charge of murder."

"You're right. I would have killed him myself." Larousse dumped the tub, and then gave a vicious push of the broom, sending water cascading over the edge of the cell floor and down the side of the cliff to the crashing breakers below.

Jean, Francois, and Abelard were once more in Magistrate Cabasson's court. All restraints were now gone from their ankles and wrists. Jean could once again hope past the next twenty-four hours. The magistrate emerged from a door behind the bench and subjected them to a few minutes of silent scrutiny.

"You know I could still change my mind about what to do with you three scofflaws."

They hung their heads, and Jean's heart hammered inside his chest.

"However, I have decided the crown would not be served by three able-bodied men wasting in a cell, being fed out of our stores, when you could make yourselves useful to the colony.

"Blanchard and young Courbet — I'm confident the wives you've chosen will keep you from straying from the path of honest labor. You've two plantations full of cane to be harvested and readied for shipment to France. When the harvest is finished, a master stonemason will train you and your crew.

"Our Lady of the Safe Harbor should be ready for my brother's congregation within a year. The jail cell destroyed in *Monsieur* Blanchard's attempt to prove his innocence needs restoration also.

"You are not entirely free yet, but I release you to your labors. You will report back to me each month on your progress. My brother will hear your confessions each week, as well as that of your wives. Do not attempt to shirk any of the duties assigned by this court."

Sweat trickled down the inside of Jean's arms with each new warning issued. When the magistrate finally signaled the end of the hearing, he feared he might collapse from lack of oxygen. He'd been holding his breath without thinking during most of the lecture.

"Go and steal no more. Too much work awaits you to dally here." Magistrate Cabasson tipped back his chair and reached for his well-worn pipe on the bookshelf. Shaking tobacco into the bowl from a small bag, he smiled and waved them from his courtroom.

CHAPTER TWENTY-EIGHT

Marie's eyes burned from rivulets of sweat as she hefted cut cane between the wagon and the huge grinder rolled by two oxen. A leather thong held back her soaked, frizzy hair. Salty drops rolled into the corner of her mouth, stinging her weather-chapped lips.

The heady, sweet smell of boiling cane juice mingled with the earthy odor of the oxen. She handed an armload of stalks to Abelard, who shoved the prickly bundle to Jean. He stood at the rolling stone cylinder, stuffing cane in as quickly as he received the bundles.

The relentless sun was near its end-of-day drop to the horizon. So many stacks of cane left to crush and feed the steady stream of sticky sweet juice flowing toward the drying ovens.

At last, the man on the wagon held up his empty hands. They were done for the day. She whirled toward Jean, who also signaled he was finished.

She couldn't believe that in spite of the few workers, they hadn't fallen far short of the rhythm of harvest she'd come to know. The cane would be finished on time to load the ships waiting to set sail for the refineries in France.

As soon as they'd returned from St. Pierre, everyone had thrown themselves into catching up the cutting and boiling. Three days of unending labor had brought them to the end. She'd spent each night curled in Jean's arms, but they'd fallen into immediate slumber.

Now, with the cane harvest nearly finished, a familiar warmth curled from low in her belly. She would have a proper wedding night with that impossible man she'd married. A smile teased at her lips at the thought of his reaction when she demanded her rights. While Jean and the others unharnessed the oxen and moved downhill to check the boiling room, she ran up the path to Galante House. She had a lot to do.

As soon as she pushed open the front door, lemon and oil fragrances assaulted her senses. Hmmm. Luz had been busy.

Flickering candles sat on each of the steps leading to the second level of Galante House. Where was her scheming housekeeper? Sloshing sounds filtered down of water being poured from buckets into a copper tub.

Luz stood at the top of the stairs, hands on hips. "What you tink? One tub or two?"

"Mmmm, I think one large tub should do."

"You finally ready to share wit dat man?"

"Of course. He's earned his pleasure."

Luz folded her arms over her generous bosom and gave Marie a skeptical look. "And why you back so early today?"

"I, um, had things to do."

"We way ahead of you." Luz gave a soft order over her shoulder to the kitchen workers who had carried the buckets. "Dat man deserve a wedding night." She poked her finger at Marie.

"I haven't forgotten. We'll see if he remembers." She lifted her chin and stared back at Luz, defiant.

"A few more days like this and we'll be ready to load Captain Willem's ships," Jean said. Willem had invested in another ship with the money Jean had given him for rescuing them. He whipped off his straw hat and fanned his heat-flushed face. All that remained of the harvest was the final cooking and drying of the sugar.

Abelard rubbed a hand across his forehead and then stared out toward the sea. "Save us plenty of days him coming here instead of us having to sail the hogsheads across to Guadeloupe." After a few moments of shared silence, he turned back to Jean and slapped him on the back. "Has Marie decided what she'll do after the cane is sold?"

"Her sons come home this fall after the stormy season ends."

"Will she turn over the plantation to them?"

"With the way she feels about the slaves, I think she'll have to look at her father's legacy in another way."

Abelard raised his brows. "Go on."

"What we need on this island is a refinery. The planters could keep more of their profits, and Marie could steer her sons into a new family venture."

"And just who will build this refinery?"

Jean grinned and poked a dirty finger at his own bare, sweaty chest. "You are looking at the island's next stonemason.

"Once the cane from here and part of the cane from my family's plantation is safely aboard Willem's ships, my men and I leave for St. Pierre to repair the church and the jail. Magistrate Cabasson found a stonemason who has promised to teach us the trade."

"Only some of the cane from Elisabeth and Francois?" Abelard asked, a puzzled expression on his face.

"They want to keep a portion of her cane this season to distill a batch of rum.

"Grand plans for men who not so long ago were just smugglers and thieves." Abelard chuckled low, softening his stern words.

"I have to learn an honest trade before the child arrives."

"The lady says there is no baby." Abelard bent over laughing and slapping his knees.

"We'll see about that," Jean said, and pulled his shirt from a peg on the side of the wagon. He threw the cool muslin over his head and motioned for Abelard to follow him. "Let's find out what those women of ours are plotting."

"Ours?" Abelard opened his mouth, a protest forming.

"You think I haven't seen you and Luz lurking about the halls at night?"

Abelard waved away Jean's accusations. They gathered their tools and began the climb back up the path toward Galante House.

Marie lay flat on the bed, rolled into a cool sheet. The night breeze and the light cover gradually dried the moisture lingering from her bath. Jean stared out the window overlooking the ocean, the drying sheet wrapped loosely around his hips.

She rolled to her side, the better to enjoy the view. His shoulders and rope-muscled back, all the way down to his waist were dark even in the moonlight. The moon was a mere crescent, but the explosion of stars reflected off the ocean surface gave her all the illumination she needed.

In fact, she knew her husband so well, she could see him in her soul. She squeezed shut her eyes to test the theory, only to have them fly open again when his weight pushed down on the bed.

He lay above her, suspended on his forearms. "Look at me, Marie."

She closed her eyes again but couldn't keep the smile from her lips.

"I love you, Marie Blanchard."

Her eyes flew open in surprise. Would she ever get used to this man's devotion?

"I want you forever." He leaned down and planted a soft kiss on her forehead. "Don't you have something to tell me?"

"What?" She struggled to maintain a look of innocence.

"You know what I long to hear." He pulled back her sheet and drew his hand up the inside of her waist.

"I'm sure I have no idea, *Monsieur* Blanchard."

He captured her hands and kissed the palm of each one, sweeping his tongue across her palms. He suckled the sensitive skin inside each of her wrists.

Jean inhaled deeply the scent of lilies Luz had left floating in the bath water. The floral essence lingered on Marie's skin along with some other elusive smell he couldn't identify.

He moved both her hands above her head and slid his cheek along the sensitive skin inside her upper arms.

"*Monsieur* Blanchard, you are making it impossible for your wife to think." She giggled and swatted his hands away. "Your beard tickles."

"I don't want you to think. I want you to tell me you love me." Jean bent back to his leisurely attentions. He imprinted more kisses down her neck and onto her breasts. He lingered, thoroughly suckling each one.

"Stop." Marie shivered and backed away from his mouth.

"Why?"

"I can't collect my thoughts when you distract me."

"Tell me you return my love, Marie." He was back to the level of her lips.

"I..." He smothered her protests with a kiss.

When Jean paused to breathe, she sat up and whipped the sheet back around her.

Placing her hand flat against his chest, she studied his face. A deep breath drew his essence more fully into her body. Their scents mingled with the heat from their bodies.

The light through the window revealed one side of his face, leaving the other in shadow. At that moment, the two sides of the man came clearly into focus, his dark and light sides exposed equally. A chill swept her body, even though the night air lay heavy on her skin.

"What's wrong?" He smoothed a thumb across her lips.

"I'm afraid," she said and scooted away from the temptation of his body. "I don't know what the future will bring."

"No one knows the future, Marie." He abruptly left the bed and paced back toward the window. "Except Luz, of course, when she wears that turban on her head."

"You're laughing at me."

He strode back and crawled across the bed, cradling her in his arms. "You have nothing to fear from me, or the future. I will love you with everything I have for as long as we both have."

"Even when my hair is silver and my face is covered with wrinkles?"

"You are a difficult woman, Marie Blanchard." He shook his head, fell silent, and moved away. He retrieved his clothes from the floor where he'd tossed them earlier and pulled on his pants.

"Where are you going?" Alarm filled her voice.

He said nothing but headed for the door.

She waited, unbelieving, until the moment he walked into the hall and shoved the door closed behind him.

Marie sat motionless for a few moments, thinking he would return, but when his footsteps faded and the silence lengthened, she jumped from the bed and threw on her shift. She raced down the stairway and through the house to the kitchen garden where Abelard sat smoking a pipe on a chair in front of the outdoor oven.

"Where is he?" she asked.

"Haven't seen him tonight, but sometimes he goes down to the cove to think." The old man turned away and hid his face, leaning over when he tapped the ashes out of his pipe.

Marie ran along the same path she'd followed when she'd first encountered the smuggler and her life had been forever upended.

Marie moved by memory down the dark bluff. A sliver of moon glow and stars reflected back from the water gave enough illumination when she reached the sandy shore.

She shook her head at the thought of the dangers of a headlong rush down to the sea at night. In some ways, Jean had not changed from the arrogant smuggler she met that first day.

Humid night air lay heavy on her skin. Broken shells along the shore gave off the essence of the ocean, of fish and salt and birth and death.

She glanced toward Jean's ship swinging at anchor and caught sight of a small shore boat rowing for the larger ship. "Jean – where are you going?" she cried out. When there was no answer, she peeled off her shift, walked into the calm waters behind the reef and swam toward him.

When she finally reached the side of Jean's sloop, she called out again, but he still did not answer. Frustrated, she pulled herself around the hull until her fingers found the boarding ladder. Just as she climbed to the top rail of the ship, a hand shot out and gripped her wrist like an iron clamp, pulling her aboard.

Before she had a chance to protest, he pulled her close to his body, the seawater dripping from her skin soaked his pants.

When she tried to jerk away, he pressed her more tightly to him.

"You frightened me," she said. "Why did you leave our house?"

"*Madame*, you are mistaken. I own no house. You trespass onto my ship, and now you must leave or pay the consequences." He swept his eyes down her bare, dripping body. "I am nothing more than a heartless smuggler. I can't be responsible for what might happen to your virtue if you stay."

"Stop talking like you're a stranger. Come home now to our dry bed. Please?"

He suddenly abandoned his stern lecture and the expression on his face was so sad, she would say anything, promise anything, to make him smile again.

"Tonight I return to my island, Marie. I will remain your husband in name only. If you ever have need of me, I am a few hours' sail away. Send a message with one of the fisherman, and I will come."

"But you *are* my husband," she said. "You cannot leave."

"I will not live with a woman who refuses to say she loves me, who behaves like a siren from the sea, who will one day return to the deep and abandon me." He pushed her away and kept her there with a squeeze of his hands on her shoulders.

"But you know how I feel," she insisted.

"*Non* - I do not." He crossed his arms and stepped back, leaning against a barrel on the deck.

"I barely know who you are," Marie said. "How can I say I love you?"

"Look into your heart, Marie."

She closed her eyes and reached toward him. He stepped away. After a long silence, her eyes flew open to an empty deck. She was alone.

"Oh, that man." She shivered from the night air drying the salt droplets on her body. She yearned for a blanket, or Jean's warmth. Now her own body conspired against her.

She walked toward the companionway and then felt her way down into the belly of the ship one step at a time with her bare feet. The glow of a candle showed through an open door to

Jean's cabin in the stern. The light flickered with every sway of the vessel.

"Now I am angry, Jean Blanchard. You go too far," she said, and shivered.

Silence greeted her complaint. She took another tentative step before being pulled into the darkness against a warm chest. Hands cradled her shoulders and then inched down to her hips and back up to her breasts. When his mouth closed over one nipple, she forgot to breathe.

When she remembered a few minutes later, she moved her fingers to his face and traced the curve of his lips. "Tell me again why it is so important that I say 'I love you.'"

"Because I am the father of your child." He suckled one of her wandering fingers into his mouth.

She shoved him away and poked at his chest. "You have to stop hoping. There is no child. I'm well past child-bearing age."

He pulled her toward the open cabin door. "We will have to see about that, *Madame* Blanchard."

"But I haven't said the words yet." She dug in her toes to stop his forward momentum and pulled him back.

"That is no longer a concern, *ma petite sirene*. By morning you will have declared your love for me many times."

EPILOGUE

1762 – Guadeloupe Archipelago

Jean toed another pile of sand from his boot and repositioned the little body, a squirming mass of energy, to his shoulder. He struggled to stand and brush the excess from his breeches.

"Mmm-mm." Her chubby legs flailed, and she pointed toward the clear turquoise water.

"What do you see?"

"Mmm-mm," she repeated, louder. Exasperation etched the child's delicate features. A dark cloud of hair curled just above her shoulders, auburn glints catching in the morning sun.

Jean placed her firmly on a large table-like rock near the water's edge while he shaded his eyes for a moment to view the rolling waves. A dark head broke the surface beyond the headland, and he smiled. The babe hadn't begun to form full words yet, but she always knew when her mother returned from the sea.

His tiny daughter, momentarily distracted by a pretty shell that had just washed ashore, sat motionless for the first time since he'd retrieved her from her cot sometime before dawn.

The sun's rays licked across the waves from a sliver of a bright orange orb just showing above the horizon. He scooped her into his arms again and moved toward the water's edge where he waited for the sight of which he would never tire.

Marie knelt in the tidal pool inside the reef, long, dark strands of hair plastered to her breasts. A bit of seaweed still clung to her, making the woman framed by the glittering waves seem like one of the mermaids of sailors' legends. A siren who enchanted seamen and lured them into the depths.

Jean didn't care. He would follow this woman anywhere.

Thank you for reading *Secret Harbor*! Hopefully, you enjoyed the journey. If you did, please help other readers find this book:

1 – Write a review

2 – Sign up for my newsletter with upcoming releases, special goodies, links to bonus materials, and exclusive peeks at what's coming next by visiting my website at **www.andreakstein.com**.

3 – Come like my Facebook page at Author Andrea K. Stein

4 – Share my offbeat take on the writing life on Twitter @andreakstein

There's nothing I enjoy more than connecting with readers, so feel free to drop me a line at **andrea@andreakstein.com** with any comments or suggestions

AUTHOR BIO

Andrea K. Stein lives and writes at 9,800 feet in the Rocky Mountains, just fifteen minutes from the Continental Divide. A retired newspaper editor, she is a USCG certified sea captain who spent a number of years delivering yachts out of Charleston Harbor to destinations up and down the Caribbean. One of many cruises on which she crewed visited the sugar islands setting for *Secret Harbor*.

BONUS EXCERPT

Turn the page for the beginning chapter from
FORTUNE'S HORIZON

In another high seas romance featuring a working hero on the cover, a spoiled American heiress tangles with an arrogant British sea captain on a mission for the Confederacy.

NYT Bestselling Author Cheryl Bolen said of **FORTUNE'S HORIZON** ~
"This sparkling debut novel has it all: action, spies, the high seas — and a sigh-worthy romance."

FORTUNES'S HORIZON available from Amazon (http://amzn.to/1H4mjXG) and Barnes and Noble online (http://bit.ly/1FlmUJx) :

FORTUNE'S HORIZON

Wednesday, April 15, 1863
Faubourg Saint-Germain, Paris
48°51'48"N, 02°19'20"E

Lillie Coulbourne chewed on her thumbnail and peered out the window of her hired hack. Where was Sarah Devereaux? The hardest parts of this blasted assignment were the waiting and the uncertainty.

Expatriate American Southerners spilled from luxurious carriages on the Rue de Varenne onto the huge turnaround of the Devereaux mansion while footmen raced to quiet horses and move conveyances. Her friend had to be caught somewhere in the crush of guests eager for an evening of music.

Fueled by her mission, Lillie gave up on Sarah's help and ran across the courtyard. She would have to find Captain Bulloch on her own.

Rough cobblestones cut into her flimsy evening slippers and made her long for riding boots and breeches. The real reason men made better spies had to be the clothing. She gathered in her heavy silk skirts, clutched her book to her side, and edged past the throng waiting to greet the Devereaux family. Scooting down the hallway, she stopped at a salon on the first floor and slipped through the door.

The thought of the secret notes in a small cavity midway through the copy of *Jane Eyre* she carried made her fingers burn through all the pages and binding. However, that was nothing compared to the feel of the folded paper crammed into her petticoat pocket. Every time the packet brushed against her knee, fear and curiosity warred within her. Curiosity was winning, hands down. She had to complete the handoff and then find a quiet corner to interpret the message for her eyes only.

She forced her mind to focus on the task at hand and swept the room with a glance. Sarah's mother had gone a little over the top with the mirrors. Every bit of wall not covered in dark, crushed velvet had a full-length, gilt-framed mirror embellished with curlicues, angels and flowers. If Lillie were to drop over dead in there, she'd be sure to go straight to heaven.

Drat. No sign of the captain. Although the Confederate master spy was based in England, he made frequent trips to Paris. One night at a ball given at the Devereaux home, he'd asked her to dance and by the time the music ended, had snared her into an elaborate game of passing decoded messages. Instructions for his blockade-runner enterprise were embedded in dispatches from the South she translated for the French Finance Ministry.

The door swung open behind her, and she froze as the voices of two men floated in from the hallway. As soon as she ducked behind a heavy, hand-painted screen in the corner, she berated herself for hiding. What on earth was there to be afraid of? Besides —

Good God, her side profile was reflected in one of the damned mirrors, and then over and over in all the others across four walls.

With a silent prayer, she inched as far as possible behind the screen. Gathering in her full skirts, she crouched low and crossed her fingers. Thankfully, she had chosen her dark burgundy silk for the musicale that night. Maybe she would blend in with the wall coverings.

One of the men closed the door, and they moved to a sofa across from her.

She silently repeated her favorite calming phrase — "I'm as good as any man, and I can do this to help the Confederacy."

The two men spoke in low, guarded tones, and she strained to hear. One of them sounded like Captain Bulloch, but she couldn't be sure. The second man had a distinct, English accent.

Suddenly, their tones became more intense, and she began to pick up snippets of conversation.

"I know you're firmly behind the cause, but I tell you, sir, the South is in severe straits. I don't know how much longer they can hold out. They just don't have the resources." The unknown voice paused then continued. "The people behind the lines seem to be losing the will to continue to fight."

She leaned forward to grasp more of the thread of their exchange, and without warning, a hand seized her arm and dragged her into the center of the room. Her cheeks burned in mortification, and, for once in her life, speech deserted her.

The stranger was so tall he nearly lifted her off her feet as he plucked her from behind the screen. Angry, blazing blue eyes rudely assessed her, and she prayed Captain Bulloch would save her.

"Miss Lillie, whatever possessed you to crouch behind that screen?" Her friend tilted his head, and a forelock of dark hair dipped across his face. He peered around the obnoxious man who had her imprisoned like a child. "Captain Roberts, please release her."

Bullock paused for a moment when his companion refused to comply and raked his fingers through his hair. "She probably didn't expect anyone to be in this room." He stared at her, the question hanging between them. "Did you?"

"Then why did she hide?" the rude man interrupted. Instead of releasing her, he tightened his grip.

"Why, I...actually, I was searching for you, Captain Bulloch." Despite the pain of a growing headache, she gathered her wits and jerked out of his hold. "I wanted to return this. So sorry to have intruded." She thrust the book into Bulloch's hands and wheeled toward the door only to be stopped short.

"How do we know she isn't spying on us for information to take back to Yankee operatives?" Bulloch's companion demanded while detaining her again with a painful grasp on her arm. Lillie turned and tried to wrench her arm free while giving the oaf her most scathing look.

That was a mistake.

His unblinking gaze radiated irritation from a deeply tanned face. Long, silver-blond hair tied neatly at the nape of his neck with a narrow black ribbon accentuated his rugged good looks and formal black evening attire. Her chest tightened, and she couldn't breathe.

"Whoa. Let's start over." Bulloch stepped between them. "Miss Coulbourne, this is Captain Jack Roberts, a colleague of mine. And, Jack, this is Miss Lillie Coulbourne, the daughter of a friend. We've been exchanging books from our libraries for some time now."

"I'm pleased to make your acquaintance, Miss Coulbourne," Captain Roberts said, then released her arm and gave a curt nod of acknowledgement.

"I'm sorry if I gave you a false impression earlier," Lillie said, "but I couldn't help overhearing your comments on the situation in the South." She softened her murderous glare under a warning glance from Bulloch. "Surely you must be mistaken," she continued.

"Oh? So you're one of those Confederate zealots waiting out the war in comfort here in Paris," Roberts said.

"I can't believe you said that." Bulloch ground out.

"Trust me. If I were a man, I would be back in Dixie, teaching those Union bullies a Alesson," Lillie insisted.

"Pah!" Roberts shot back. "You would have to be a little more imposing than you are now to take on the Union Army."

"I assure you, I can shoot, fight, and ride as good as any man." Her chest pounded in irritation. She had to get away from this awful man. "Now, I'll leave you two gentlemen to your business."

"No need to hurry off." Bulloch motioned toward a large brocade settee. "Please join us."

"No, no — I've already intruded too long." She moved toward the door, fixing a wary eye on Roberts.

"Please stay, Miss Coulbourne. Don't let me frighten you off." Roberts ducked his head in contrition. "It's been a long time since I last wore formal clothes." He pulled at his tight collar and grunted in discomfort. "I apologize for my rudeness. I'm not accustomed to being confined. Makes me claustrophobic."

"And cantankerous," Bulloch added, with a wink at Lillie.

She flushed and fought a sudden urge to reach out and help the prickly captain undo his top button. "Um, I think I'm going to leave you two to your meeting. Miss Devereaux is waiting for me, and patience is not one of her virtues." She turned and fled the room as if the hounds of hell were on her tail.

Once she regained the coolness of the hallway, she leaned against the door and trembled. After a few moments, she straightened and moved toward the crowd in the front hall. She had to find Sarah.

Made in the USA
Charleston, SC
25 May 2015